I0618600

The
Word Collector

A NOVEL

Alexandria Nolan
Copyright © 2016 Nolan

All rights reserved.

ISBN: 0692646124
ISBN-13: 978-0692646120

for Terrence, as always.

She dealt her pretty words like Blades—
How glittering they shone—
And every One unbared a Nerve
Or wantoned with a Bone—

She never deemed—she hurt—
That—is not Steel's Affair—
A vulgar grimace in the Flesh—
How ill the Creatures bear—

To Ache is human—not polite—
The Film upon the eye
Mortality's old Custom—
Just locking up—to Die.

—Emily Dickinson

The Three Oddest Words
When I pronounce the word Future,
the first syllable already belongs to the past.

When I pronounce the word Silence,
I destroy it.

When I pronounce the word Nothing,
I make something no non-being can hold
—Wislawa Szymborska

"Be not afeard; the isle is full of noises,
Sounds, and sweet airs, that give delight and hurt not.
Sometimes a thousand twangling instruments
Will hum about mine ears; and sometime voices,
That, if I then had waked after long sleep,
Will make me sleep again: and then, in dreaming,
The clouds methought would open, and show riches
Ready to drop upon me; that, when I waked,
I cried to dream again."

— William Shakespeare, *The Tempest*

She was old now. The thought made her laugh. Now? She had decided in this moment that she was no longer new? She looked across the purple rivers that wound their way under her translucent flesh.

Old.

She was so old she forgot what it was to be old.

So old that she felt that time was like a stream that she could sit back on the banks of and stare into. And then, on a whim, she could bend forward and dip her hand into that stream of time, feeling the strong current of it flowing around her, but somehow, never carrying her away along with it. She sighed.

This body of hers was old, looked old. But her spirit, that twinkling invisible light of a million stars thing that thought and considered and remembered... it was even older.

But also, sometimes, it felt as though it had only arrived a moment ago. And with new eyes she would gaze into her looking glass and she would gasp. Who is this strange, ancient woman? And then it would come to her. It was her. She.

She supposed she could move on from this body and into the next place, wherever that was—but she didn't want to. Not really. Too much effort.

This was home. And this was her place. If she wasn't here, who would remember? Who would keep watch? Who would guide them all and heal the broken things inside of them? She gazed out onto the lake, her constant, and for a moment, was jealous. Why did the water never show its age at all, and it was more ancient than she? She silently laughed, her chest bouncing, creaking back and forth at the thought. Peculiar things came to her mind now and again, little jokes she had to keep to herself, lest folks think her crazy.

She licked her papery lips and reached again for the fine silver handled looking glass. Just a small thing. A love trinket, though not for her. She could almost not remember her beloved's face anymore, and he'd never given her any gifts. Not tangible ones anyway.

No, this was a love token from another couple. Their initials etched beautifully in script on the glass. She was glad to have it in her keeping. She could almost, if she squinted hard enough and pulled at the strings of her memory just so, see the reflection of the two lovers within it.

She liked to have the hand mirror nearby. It was pleasant to be near those one loved. Loves. Still loves.

No, she could never leave.
Can't ever leave.
It had been her choice, after all.
Her destiny.
Her curse.
Her home.

Forever.

1

BOULEVERSEMENT:

an inversion, especially a violent one; an upset or upheaval.

Petra stood in the kitchen, staring at the plate in her hands. The cheery pink roses in eternal bloom spoke of sweet spring time and the hopeful newlyweds, now long dead—she was certain, who had received this as part of a set on their wedding day. A now incomplete set. She had been pondering the dish for so long that the angry impulse to grab hold of it in the first place melted into annoyance. The movies were all wrong. One never could trust the cinema to portray life as it happened. Nor books, now that she thought of it.

When a woman is irrational, venomous, exploding with bitterness, cross, enraged, choleric or any other synonym for furious—she is supposed to find the nearest plate and smash it in a glorious fit of rage all over the kitchen.

But, Petra had taken hold of the little plate and then…thought about having to pick up the pieces, and the feeling of her bare feet being pricked with shards for weeks afterwards. And suddenly Evan's words came back to her and she was embarrassed rather than angry. He had been right. She did overthink everything. Her mind lived in the past and within the weathered tomes she pored through for research. He had said those words so easily one of the last times they were together; he hadn't made a scene or seemed upset. As if her flaws and she as a person weren't worth the extra effort a passionate argument would have demanded. She lived in the past and he wanted a future. He'd cast a critical eye over her stacks of books, sniffed at the dust and familiar scent of old pages, vanilla and decay making him wrinkle his nose in a way Petra realized she hated. And then he was gone. It was over a year ago, but in some parts of her heart it was yesterday.

It was past, after all, and that's where Petra dwelt.

Looking at the plate, she couldn't even remember what had made her so angry in the first place, but she grew still more furious that she couldn't remember. The plate was a mirror of her own life. She was shattered and broken, and she was going to be spending the next while continuing to pick *herself* up, and then stepping on sharp remnants of memories of Evan. And of her father. And Toby. Always Toby. Those same shards pricking her when she was vulnerable. Did she really need to add a broken plate to that as well? The cheerful roses were silent, and Petra replaced the plate into the cupboard and sighed. She was prone to these momentary fits, brief and fleeting shades of madness. And she was weary of them. Petra reached up, gently, and skimmed her fingers over the scar on her jawline. She could barely feel it, but she knew it was there. Her reminder to stay sane.

So, to clear her mind, she placed both hands on the edge of the counter and screamed until her throat hurt, poured herself a glass of wine and walked mechanically to her desk. She had work to do.

Evan had been right, she *did* live in the past. She was a linguist, so words were her domain. Especially rare ones. Phonology and vowel shifts, Indo-European morphing gracefully into Latin and Germanic languages, all tied up, back, back, back, to the same language lost to history. Words, gorgeous, meaningful words. Words that described the people that used them, and spoke of their history, their priorities, their lives.

Finding the precise synonym to express oneself was the true mark of a native speaker. The verbs and states of being that most closely suited one's current mood or lifestyle. What lovely things, words. What powerful weapons.

She preferred Wordsmith to Linguist herself. Word Wayfarer? Adjective Adventurer? Verb Voyager? Noun Nomad? No, none of those suited. Laughing at her own foolish fancies, and pulling a strand of unruly wavy hair behind her ear, she chewed on her pen and thought again, of Evan.

Evan said she was more of a hoarder, searching out words, unearthing ancient terms that expressed something in a different way. Words that were lost. Obsolete. He said she wasn't an explorer or a liberator of these words, but instead a dragon sleeping on her treasure of them. A word collector. Part of that was true—if everyone knew the words that she found, would they be as special? Or, if she was being honest, perhaps the reason she hadn't published a new work of her findings for so long was because she worried people wouldn't care. Apathy. Boredom. Indifference.

And so, she read and she kept her careful notes with annotations and references to other books that only she understood, because she was one of the few to have acquired a copy of the obscure texts in the first place. Like her namesake, Petra seemed to petrify. She became harder and denser with each day, weighted to her chair, anchored to her notes. She was a paperweight holding back the words she rediscovered from flying back out into the world on the winds.

And when Evan left, and her world was shattered and her father died leaving her this quiet, out of the way little cottage in a small village, she thought she would slowly turn to stone in her chair. But the sudden emergence of a wayward and unsocial tabby-cat padded her way into Petra's life. The cat forced Petra to roll out of herself, out of her desk chair, like a pebble rolling down a hill and down to the store she went to purchase cat food whenever it ran out. And she was out. Again. Jinks was picky, and so Petra would have to go to the specialty store across the lake —the one near the dock that happened to face the antique store. An antique store that she had heard sometimes had old, arcane books. The exact type of store that Petra couldn't resist.

It wasn't a terribly long walk, only two miles or so from her little cottage in the woods, around the lake and into the family run grocery. But, she had known even before she arrived that she wouldn't be able to resist a peek into Love's Antiques and Curiosities. A woman she'd met at the library had called it a "Curio Shop" while her eyebrows strained upward toward her forehead in a meaningful way that Petra hadn't understood. But, the word *curiosity* attached to anything has a way of piquing the feeling in those hearing it, and most certainly had resonated with Petra. Old books were often purchased by these types of shop-owners. Leftovers from estate sales, texts that most people didn't recognize and weren't interested in. She knew her father had visited this same shop a few times, to pick her up a book as a gift. Periodically throughout the year she would receive yellow padded envelopes with a curt note tucked inside one of these purchases. Her father didn't have the words himself, she knew, never knew what to say or how to say it, so he sent books to say it for him. Never the right type of book, of course. Too mainstream or not quite obscure enough to be part of her collection. She had understood though, it was his way of connecting, even though there had been nothing about them that linked anymore. And now it was too late.

But today would be Petra's first day inside. She ignored some of the stares, or imagined stares, she received from some of the children playing in their yards as she walked into town. She could have sworn one of them had pointed to her jawline, urging his mates to see the red scar that began under her ear. It seemed to grow brighter when she was conscious of it. Sometimes she forgot all about it; when it was hidden under her heavy hair she could pretend it didn't exist at all.

As the shop came into view, all thoughts of the jagged line on her chin and Jinks' incessant, hungry mewling left her mind. Smiling and shaking her head of ugly thoughts, she stepped forward and her hand grasped the knob on the door. Before she had even opened it she could smell the musty, earth-tinged with something like cinnamon scent from the shop. It was another of her favorite smells, the odor of relics. Of days gone by and memories lived. Gently she pulled the door toward her and softly stepped inside.

Petra loved the sound of the bell on the door ringing, thought of all the times it had rung, the other lives that had passed through and heard its music. An old record player could be heard after the bells on the door fell silent. It popped and hummed, the sound of Edith Piaf's impassioned, "Padam, Padam, Padam" playing powerfully. Petra translated the French in her mind, realizing that this too was a song about remembering the past, and being tormented by it. A tune, a voice, a memory that follows behind you, footsteps like the beat of your heart. Exhaling she almost turned around and walked right back out the door. Perhaps this had been a bad idea. Maybe she *should* change—maybe Evan had been right, the past wasn't a safe place to decorate and settle into, but instead a dangerous place that smothered her future possibilities.

No, Evan was gone and for the thousandth time, she assured herself that she was better off. Certainly. He may have been right about some things, but it was clear he wasn't correct about everything. Besides, she'd come here hopeful, excited to pore over some crumbling, forgotten pages, to perhaps add some new words to her collection. Shaking off the memory of Evan, she looked around.

The place appeared empty. Somewhere there was probably a little old woman watching a game show or a soap opera on a boxy television set, who would putter and mutter and creak over to the cash register when Petra was ready to make a purchase. Good. She liked the solitude. Not that she was unfriendly—was she? When she had worked for the university she had been outgoing, gregarious, convivial, genial... garrulous in fact.

But then the first two books had been a success and she'd started working from home. Then Evan had moved in, and then...he had left. She'd been in the hospital for some time—she put her hand to her jaw, briefly, just a touch, she couldn't think about that now.

And then her father had fallen ill, and then too soon afterward, he'd died. The cottage, oddly, unexpectedly, was hers, and she'd left any friends she might have had back in her old life. She'd moved here, and although she'd been in town a few months, Petra had gone out of her way to go out as little as possible. To avoid people and conversation and stray glances and....questions. Perhaps she *wasn't* friendly anymore. Maybe it was like a muscle that she hadn't flexed in so long, it had atrophied. She'd grown irritable, reclusive. Making conversation, once such a delightful way to make connections, had become draining, zapping her energy. As if other people had become vampires of her vigor. She sighed again. Today had become much too emotional, and it was only four in the afternoon.

Petra walked through rooms stuffed with old vinyl, antique baby prams and Hull and McCoy vases. Mismatched silverware and chipped tea sets. A case full of jewelry that had once been given and received in love, and now was the final physical proof of the exchange of affection between different sets of bones in the ground. Another right after that, and she found it.

The room was smaller than she would have liked it to be. But there was a elementary-school-library-style low stool in the corner to sit upon and books packed floor to ceiling with no apparent organization. Petra allowed herself a smile. Perfect. She preferred this. When a shop owner attempted to catalogue the books, they often muddled it all up. This way, it truly was like finding treasure; one never knew what gem might be waiting beneath the next book in a stack or behind a pile of haphazardly placed tomes.

A particularly promising red leather book with a cracked spine called out to her. Settling herself on the small metal stool, she gingerly opened the cover and saw something magic. The title.

"*Ancient Indefinable Peculiarities*, published 1803" she read aloud to herself. She smiled again, and allowed her mind to drift along with the soft melodies of Edith Piaf in a faraway room, and the specific song of the turning pages of the rare book in her hands.

Seconds, moments, minutes later, a hollow cough interrupted the rhythm of her reading. Petra glanced up, irritably, annoyed to have been so burst in upon when she was occupied. Some other obnoxious customer, no doubt, bumbling into the room searching for something interesting to put on his reproduction coffee table. She took no trouble to hide the scowl on her face when she looked up at the intruder.

Tawny brown hair that was cut precise and short, atop a face that was all blue eyes, strong cheekbones and faint freckles like angel's kisses. He wasn't overly tall, perhaps only Petra's height, and he was dressed in pressed chinos and a polo-style collared shirt. The shirt wasn't quite indecently tight, but it showed the muscled chest and arms to advantage. Probably a businessman or lawyer just come from the office. She gave him a pointed look that only scowled more deeply. Somehow his boyish handsomeness irked Petra even more. There was something familiar about his face, and Petra decided it was because all men of decided attractiveness look blandly similar. Blue eyes? Honestly, how *predictable*.

Those same eyes seemed to be laughing at her, and he grit his teeth mischievously before he spoke. "You going to buy that then?"

Instinctively she tightened her grip on the frail pages. "Haven't decided yet." Her voice was quiet, and she spoke dismissively. The nerve!

"Well, you'd better buy it, or I'll be forced to bring you a blanket and a proper chair."

Petra sputtered so hard that she laughed. "I beg your pardon?"

"I'm sorry, but I close at five and its now gone 7. You'll either have to allow yourself to be locked in, or you'll have to buy the book and continue reading it at home."

He was smiling, and Petra had pinked at the realization of her error, sputtering into a cough as she fully grasped what he'd said.

"7? But I've been here since, well, since half four! I've only just sat down. I thought at least."

He laughed again, not at her but in a warm way that suggested he'd seen it happen before.

"You're the owner then?" Petra asked incredulously.

"Guilty." His blue eyes were making her uncomfortable. Too intense.

"But...you don't look like the owner..." She

blurted, clapping a must-smudged hand to her mouth. "I mean…that is…"

His smile grew wider, displaying a row of white teeth, the top left chipped just the tiniest bit, so small that she shouldn't have noticed. Just the smallest nick of a china teapot, giving his face a little more character, more mystery. She was suddenly seized with the idea that it had been chipped in the climbing of a large tree. She shook her head, *insanity*. She truly was alone too often, inventing histories for those she didn't know and hadn't properly met.

"Don't worry about it. I'm sure that's a kind of compliment. I'm a software developer, freelance. This shop was my mother's. It's a labor of love, I suppose. Every room seems to have a little of her in it and all that."

"Ah, that would explain the sentimental name then." Her voice had come out a little sarcastic, which had not been her intention. What was wrong with her? Evan had been on to something—she wasn't properly equipped to deal with the present, let alone the future.

"Yes and no" He answered. "Love was her name —her nickname. Olive was my mother's name, but my father called her Love."

He spoke quietly, as if he were surprising himself. The moment had become suddenly intimate. Petra cleared her throat, a trifle overloud, and said the first thing that came to her mind. Which was, as usual, the wrong thing.

"Eke-name."

He narrowed his eyes uncertainly. "Excuse me?"

"Eke-name. Nickname is a corruption of Ekename, which literally translates to, "additional name" from the Old English *eaca*, 'an increase'."

"Oh, of course. How interesting…"

Silence settled over the room again, and the man coughed. Petra got to her feet and stretched.

"Yes, well, I'll, um, I'll take the book then. I'm sorry about your mother—and for my own clumsy words. I'm a linguist and so, well, words are my solace in every situation. I…I just can't seem to string them together properly."

They were walking toward the front of the shop, the sounds of Edith Piaf growing louder. Now it was "Je ne regrette rien" which Petra knew was "I regret nothing" when translated. As if that were possible.

He rang her up with a small card reader attached to his iPhone, neither of them speaking. She mused on the strangeness of something so old being purchased with a technology so new. He wrapped up her book, taping the brown paper around it with care.

Shit. Her hand flew to her forehead, creating a loud *smack* to break the calm quiet of the store.

"Excuse me?"

"Oh, I apologize. I realized that the grocer next door will be closed now, and I was supposed to grab some kibble for my cat."

"Is it called kibble if it is for a cat? I thought it was only kibble if it referred to dog food."

Petra wrinkled her forehead. Was he making fun of her? In spite of her misgivings, her mind was already scanning through definitions.

"No, as a noun, *kibble* is any kind of ground meal that has been shaped into pellets. Any pet food."

He looked up at her, wide-eyed, and gave her another warm, lazy smile. It didn't irk her as much as it had a few minutes before.

"You and your words..." He rolled his eyes teasingly. "Well, if your cat is a connoisseur, like the shop cat, then I have a few tins you can have for a very low price. They're human grade cat food—organic" He added the last word with a raise of his eyebrows.

Petra laughed. "Shop cat?"

"Yes, it was Nelson's day off today, and by that I mean he refused to come in. So he is back at the house, impatiently awaiting his own dinner, no doubt."

She reached for the book, and making up her mind, met his eyes straight on. "Ok, what's your price?"

"A drink."

She cleared her throat, startled. "Well, I don't...I don't know you. And, I'm not too sure about the idea of a drink."

Suddenly the plate from earlier in the day flashed into her mind. The china so thin, so fragile. Was she too much like that plate? So ready to break and scatter when life handled her a little roughly. Not ready for new experiences outside of her safe china cupboard?

"Oh, no pressure intended. Truly. I actually—honestly—have a book at home I'd like you to take a look at."

"Oh?" Petra wasn't certain if this was a come-on or if he was in earnest. The musty shop and the soft French coming from the record player twisted her thoughts and her tongue.

"Yes, it's a kind of diary. Very old..." He reached under the counter producing four cans of cat food that looked better than some of the meals she'd had lately herself.

"A diary?" Petra asked, excitement creeping stealthily into her voice.

"Yes, though, almost unreadable. But, perhaps not for you. Especially if you are any kind of decoder or word sleuth. My mother bought it when the chest surfaced."

She had eagerly followed his every word until the the last sentence, which made no sense to her.

"I'm sorry? Chest? Surfaced?"

His face had a shadow of something that looked like hurt, but a moment later she reckoned she had imagined it. "Ah, that's right, you haven't been in Traverston long."

Petra shook her head, "My father had a cottage here. I moved in…after he passed." He gave her a knowing look, and she realized that they had that in common. Taking a step backward into their past lives, lives that belonged to their parents.

He put the tins in a bag and placed it on the counter with the parcel that contained the book and then extended a hand.

"Dane. Dane Fintan. Does Thursday evening work for you? Across the street—the wine bar attached to the Traverston Inn?"

"I…I think that will be all right. I'm Petra, by the way." Petra took a hard swallow, Evan entered her mind, the wound still mending, though she knew it would always be a scar. As if he'd really left her a long time ago, and never really left, and also was only gone yesterday.

Squaring her shoulders, she shook his hand firmly. It wasn't a date, after all. More like a consultation. Networking. She smiled brightly and shook his hand a little more enthusiastically.

"Yes, it would be a pleasure. Absolutely. But, can you tell me a little about this chest? Was it found in the lake? Dropped from a ship or something?"

His smile grew large again, as he walked her toward the door, the little bells jingling in the evening air. "You'll have to wait and wonder. Put it this way, another book—with these words—exists nowhere else in the world. But, you'll have it in those curious little hands on Thursday!" He winked and shut the door, the bells jostling once again.

Petra was practically salivating. It was Tuesday, so she would use the next days for research on this chest, there had to be some resources available online. The excitement for this mysterious book with its promised strange words, burned like a fire in her chest. She hardly noticed the lake, glittering in the last rays of the Indian Summer sunlight, nor the cool breeze through the northern pines, that grew colder as sunset turned to gloaming.

The top step on her porch creaked and groaned as if complaining about how long she'd been out. The door opened at her touch, and she cast her eyes skyward. She had forgotten to lock it again. Within seconds Jinks was yowling, threading figure eights through her legs.

She opened a tin and kicked off her flats, pouring herself a glass of too-sweet cherry wine. She stepped into the bathroom to wash the old book smell from her hands. Looking in the mirror, she saw sallow olive-toned skin that wanted sunlight, murky hazel eyes and long ash blonde hair that wasn't straight or wavy, but instead, disheveled.

Her fingers were ink-stained and she'd only put blush on one cheek for some reason. Well, it *had* been a long day, and gratefully the room had been dark when she'd spoken with Dane. Mr. Fintan.

Petra shook her head in the mirror, and rolled her eyes at herself. No. It didn't matter how she had looked. He was interested in her skills as a linguist. That was all. Professional. Besides, who said she was interested in him? His over-familiarity was grating and he was, well, annoyingly handsome. Networking. Colleagues.

She sat with her wine on the tufted couch that had been her father's favorite "thinking sofa" and listlessly turned the pages of the book that had so fully engrossed her just a little while earlier.

Her mind was stuck in her Irish etymology codex, which she realized was rather rusty. *Dane* was English, but *Fintan* was Gaelic, meaning 'white fire'. Something about the name tugged on her brain, and on the edges of her lips. White fire, the hottest part of a burning flame. Petra realized that Evan had been right about a lot of things, but he was wrong about words being safe. When you really knew what they meant, and where they came from, words were very often your first sign of danger.

2
ADUMBRATION:
to foreshadow vaguely

Whether it was the memory of his freckles or the lazy September sunshine calling to her, Petra worked at the rickety bistro table on the back porch the next two days. At first it had felt strange to leave the semi-darkness of her study, the steady hum of Debussy serenading her research. Instead, only the song of her air-conditioner kicking on, the twittering of a number of birds she couldn't identify, and the random discomfiting mewl of Jinks. Once in a while this symphony was punctuated by the passing woosh of a far-off car, the nearest road being half a mile away.

The book she had purchased at Love's was beautifully written and charmingly confusing, but had yielded no unknown words as of yet. English was her favorite language to read in, for it seemed to her the youngest descendant of the grand line of the Indo-European languages. It hadn't yet solidified, and so in its fluidity it seemed a language that bent and folded, somersaulted and promenaded. Borrowing words wherever it could from other languages and using them in every which way to express and communicate over time. English changed the words it stole, anglicizing them, combining them with other borrowed terms until it produced something new and exciting. Or, in her case, hundreds of years ago a word might pop up, dance among the diarists of the day, shine brightly in its ability to convert an idea that was all important in that moment, and then, inexplicably, burn out. Not to be seen or used again. Petra found these words, she dug them out from between the lines they were kept in, and she breathed life into them. And they into her.

But this book hadn't added any words to her ever-growing lists. She hadn't published in four years now, but that wasn't her concern. Instead she fretted sometimes that she would find them all—had found them all. She worried that she had tracked down every archaic, rare, bygone, old-fangled, anachronistic, atypical word that there was. After all, the amount was not like numbering the stars—her search was finite. There would come a time when there was nothing left to find.

Sitting in the sunshine and working, however fruitless from the point of view of her research, had been pleasant. It had also stolen away the sallow tinge from her skin, giving Petra back the glow she had always waited all winter long to find. But that had been before. The old Petra. And even now when she looked in her mirror and saw a glowing, bronzier version of herself, ashy blonde hair now touched with sunbeams, she did recognize that old version of herself. But, she knew it was no longer her. It couldn't be. Too much had happened.

All the same, she was pleased to observe that she appeared a little more human, more polished and coiffed. If for nothing else because *he* had seemed so put together. Dane. Dane Fintan was most assuredly the type of man who woke up and went to bed with the same breezy, nonchalant style. A careless attractiveness that Petra found irritating. Everyone should look like hell once in a while, and she was certain that he never did.

Her cheeks fluttered with heat when she realized she had been thinking of how he looked when he went to bed. Professional. Networking.

When Thursday night came, it didn't occur to her to take her little Fiat into town until she'd already walked part way. She was wearing a black shirt dress and some kitten heels, and had thought, when she left, she looked the right mix of smart and business appropriate. Petra was above average height for a woman, and Evan had been her same height—much like Mr. Fintan. Evan was uncomfortable with the idea of her ever looking taller than he, so she'd stuck with flats or small heels. But, even with the lack of lift they were uncomfortable on uneven, mostly unpaved roads. Not to mention, she now realized she would now be dusty at the meeting. It was too late now though. With a shrug, she continued on, focusing her mind on the one thing that made her forget the tightness of her pumps.

The book.

Petra had tried not to wonder about it too much, especially since she knew so little about it from his description, and hadn't been able to turn up much of anything online. She'd begun to wonder if the whole thing was some kind of strange joke. There was no mention in any of the newspapers from the past ten years of anything relating to a chest—or a mysterious shipwreck unearthed. About the only interesting thing she'd found was that Traverston was a town built on an older city called Travers Town. Traverston had been re-founded in the 1850s by a woman, one Coralie Delacroix-Rast, who was somewhat of an early female Indian Jones type. There were more articles online about her and her physician husband, their dealings with local tribes and other discoveries and community building projects they had undertaken, but nothing more of Traverston. Why it had been abandoned or when. It seemed that at some point everyone had left, picked up and began somewhere new, leaving the lakeside village without explanation or backward glance. A *real* mystery, then? Perhaps.

Petra thought it had something to do with those same tribes in the area, or perhaps disease, but could find no proof either way. She was still searching her memory of the articles and beating down her imagination as to the contents of the strange book when she arrived at the Traverston Inn.

It was a lovely old place, built in the 19th century with turrets and balconies, giving it a fairytale castle appearance, which seemed at once at odds and at harmony with the pine-studded and beach cottage filled town. It was run by a local family, the same local family that had built it all those years ago, who now owned a nearby winery. Petra smiled, she liked the idea of the continuation. The son following the father's trade was an old fashioned idea, but when it worked out, it seemed singularly fulfilling to her. Perhaps because the inn had been passed within the family, it had retained a charm and elegance of days gone by that Petra had rarely seen equalled.

She walked through the candlelit restaurant and into the wine bar. All swooping, swirling chaises and padded leather club chairs. Dane was sitting near the fireplace, though, thank goodness, there was no fire lit this evening. She sat down in the chair facing him, her eyes scanning for the book, and the waiter zipped to her side with a cocktail menu.

Petra waved it away, ordering red wine, and then turned toward Dane Fintan, unsure why blood rushed so quickly to her cheeks. Excitement for the book, most certainly.

He cocked an eyebrow playfully and said, "Red? I had you pegged as a white wine and pink-lipstick type."

Petra bristled at the comment and the overly familiar tone he had used. "I'm afraid I'm more of a red and red kind of woman. I hope, personal preferences notwithstanding, that I still fulfill the conditions to have a look at the diary."

She put a hand out, imperiously, ready to take the book, put off by his manner, and suddenly on edge.

His hair was untidy, but in the same effortless way she predicted. He was wearing a white linen shirt, wrinkled in all the right spots to suggest he'd worn it all day instead of changing for their drink. His khaki pants were tightly tailored—almost Italian in style, and suddenly her smart outfit seemed blowsy.

She curled her lip and half-rolled her eyes, almost violently snatching the wine glass newly arrived on the proffered tray.

"I'm sorry, I really do know better, I promise." he began, "My mother did say to never make a comment about a lady's cosmetic or her drinking habits— and somehow I've done both. Allow me to explain…" He cleared his throat, ignoring her outstretched hand, which she awkwardly let fall back to her lap.

"Listen, Mr. Fintan, there is no need for apologies or explanations. We aren't here for a date or a friendly drink. We are here because you have a book and I have a skill."

His eyes went wide, and he pressed his shoulders into the chair as if needing the support.

"I'm not around people much." Petra muttered, almost voicelessly, realizing how abrupt everything that came out of her mouth sounded. When had she become this person? Her fingertips lightly traced the line of scarred flesh under her jawline, a self-conscious habit she'd developed. Her fingers just began to brush over the skin a second time when she, again, let them drop clumsily to her lap.

She was surprised to see the cool, affable man across from her appeared hurt by *her* manner, but shaking it off, he smiled and spoke.

"No matter, I'm sure you're right. But I'm afraid I *do* have to explain a few things or else it will be difficult to understand what you are reading."

Petra took a sip of her wine and knitted her brows. She could almost *feel* the strange words in the book he had brought. They clawed at her, and her hands began creeping down her legs toward wherever he was keeping the book. Quickly, she grabbed the wine glass off the table again, disturbing a few drops of the contents, and then took a gulp to pull herself together.

"All right, go on then."

Dane Fintan exhaled, winning a battle he hadn't expected to fight. He sat back more completely into his chair and leaned over to his briefcase, pulling out a small book. He hugged the book to his chest, like a talisman or beloved teddy bear. The action made Petra oddly jealous, and the thought crossed her mind that she wasn't sure what she was jealous of—the man holding the precious book? Or the book being held by the man? She pushed both thoughts out of her mind as being unworthy of her, straightened the skirt of her dress, and gave him her full attention.

He swirled his wine glass, the thick dark wine like fresh blood. The sight was unnerving and somehow sensual. Both of their eyes were trained on the spinning liquid as he began to speak.

"What you must understand about this diary is that it was owned by an islander. Before the lake covered it up, before the waves swallowed the people."

She tilted her head to the side and she could feel her eyebrows knot, utterly confused. But his eyes were seeing a past or a story that was not visible to hers. His voice had changed too, and it coaxed her further in.

"Long ago, when Michigan wasn't even an idea, and America had barely been dreamt, there was an island, not far from where we are now. I've heard many names for it, but I most often think of it as

Traversint. It was an island that was very different than the rest of the areas being settled or traded with in this place. The French trappers who found it—stayed. The English that made their way here, remained. Not all, you understand. Only wily, adventurous types. Europeans with education and a lust for something that could only be found on this strange island. Word spread, but always hushed. A wondrous isle. Crystal blue waters filled with the most tender and delicious of fish, and game to hunt on the mainland. Fresh pine forests, and maple trees easily tapped for the sweetest sugar. What's more...there was culture here. Brilliant minds came and found solace. Writers, poets, artists, freethinkers, any man with advanced ideas—or woman—would find rest here. A place of fairies and mermaids and magic."

Petra by this time, had drained another glass and hastily refilled it from the decanted bottle Dane had ordered. One eyebrow was seemingly permanently cocked. She wore doubt as easily as she would a fresh layer of face powder.

"Bullshit." she said simply.

His eyes came back into focus, briefly, and he took a sip. "Truly, this is part of the legend."

"I don't have time for legends. Give me facts."

He grinned, sheepishly, "It's a grand tale, isn't it? My mother used to tell it before I went to sleep. A northern utopia or something like. You don't remember hearing it before?"

"Why would I have heard it? I'm new here. And I don't remember much about my mother, but I hardly think she was one for stories."

He cleared his throat, and nodded. "Right, yeah. I forgot. Now, then, that might be mostly fancy, but there are grains of truth in the legend, believe it or not. There *was* as island here, just 600 or so hundred yards out into the water at the closest point. And it *did* mysteriously disappear in the late 1700s after having thrived as a community for a few hundred years. It *was* a strange place, distinct from the rest of Michigan. A community that was oddly closed off, and regarded as somehow…off… by the mainlanders. Didn't interact with them much. The few, scanty local records we have say nearly 120 people lived on the island at its peak, with an average population between 75-100. Men often came to Traverston, Travers Town as it was called in those days, or other nearby towns to find a bride, not wanting to mix blood on the island too much. Though, I'm sure that was no easy task. Not a lot of women would be willing to leave their families behind, for people that went to live on the island seldom came back. Some say it was because it was so beautiful and the people so welcoming that few wanted to."

He took another sip, his eyes far away again. "Strange folks, the records say. Unusual accents, and when they spoke to one another, the locals in Travers Town could only understand three words in five."

"How do you mean?" Petra interrupted, this part especially intrigued her. They were drifting into the realm of languages—her world.

"Well…" he brought a thumb up to his front teeth and bit on it lightly, an unusual thinking habit that seemed weirdly familiar. "…the sentence structure seems the same, but they've changed words. Made new up, combined different languages. Latin roots and tribal endings, and all things in between. To be honest, I'm not really sure, it's not my area, and I'm obviously over my head."

Petra felt feverish. This might be her Holy Grail,

her Ark of the Covenant, her Hope diamond all held between two leather covers.

He smiled quizzically at her expression, and rubbed his hands together, placing the book on his legs for a moment to do so. "The book then, is a diary by a young woman named Nerissa Swifte, and it is an account of the final year before The Great Vanishing."

"The Great Vanishing?" Petra felt overwhelmed, and wanted very much to call bullshit again, but felt that his words rang true.

"Yeah, it's what they call the day the island disappeared." He spoke low, and with a sense of reverence.

"What do you mean the day it disappeared?" She asked, incredulous. "You mean the last day that it could be observed before the waters rose?"

"No." His face was utter seriousness. "No, you see, the island *vanished*. One morning the town here awoke to find only lake. No island, no people, no houses. Nothing has ever been found. Nothing, excepting the chest, which contained this book."

Eyes locked on hers, Dane extended a cautious hand toward Petra, gripping the book as though her touch might break a spell that kept the little diary safe, and it would burst into flames. Or perhaps all the strange words would translate themselves and he wouldn't need her assistance after all. Or, maybe there was something else in his gaze. Something that felt dangerous and mysterious, something...painful. Petra rolled her eyes and snatched it from him like a runner grabbing a baton for the next leg of a race. She wasn't good at reading people, so she should stop trying. Books, words...those she could read and give meaning to, even when others couldn't. She'd stick with those.

The cover was an unusual shade of royal purple leather. She guessed that water and time had changed it. It had probably been a striking shade of deep blue at one time. She marveled for a moment, holding it, imagining the type of woman who was fortunate enough to have such a fine book to put her thoughts into. It would have been quite unusual for a common person to own a book so fine—especially one intended only to put ones own scribbles into. Why, Petra only allowed herself the plastic covered five-subject variety for her notes and journal entries.

Dane cleared his throat and widened his eyes. "Are you going to open it, then?"

Petra exhaled, irritated. "Yes. In a moment. I am *attempting* to get a sense of the young woman who would have written in such a book. It will help in translating." Rolling her eyes again, she reached to her handbag and brought out a pair of gossamer thin cotton gloves. She hadn't pressed them, so they were wrinkled, but no matter, they would work all the same.

"Ah, you come prepared." Dane said, approvingly, his lazy smile crinkling his eyes. There was nothing antagonistic about him, but the heat that smile brought to her own cheeks irked her. So she responded in a more clipped tone than she might have otherwise.

"Always, Mr. Fintan. I am a professional."

"Oh, no doubt." He replied, his voice good-natured, but she didn't see the look on his face as he said it. Her eyes were too thoroughly captivated by the little book in her hands. She'd held many rare and ancient texts. Original documents and writings, with little pictures, personal drawings, on the sides. Sparks of people on the pages she was reading. But she'd never held something that felt this personal and rare and special. Although it was old and a little worse for wear, it seemed somehow as though the author of it wasn't far off, and would be dropping by the room at any moment to retrieve her diary.

She lifted the cover. On the front leaf, in a bold confident hand she read:

This booke belongs to:
Nerissa Arcadia Swifte
Isle of Traversint
1798

She liked her immediately. There was something about the bite of the ink on the page, something powerful and intelligent. A person's handwriting was a defining aspect of their character, Petra had always thought. It announced if you were a planner or impulsive. Was the penmanship careful and neat—or did ideas and thoughts float so quickly from brain to pen that the ink could hardly keep pace? Yes, Petra fell in love with this woman, separated from her by hundreds of years, and yet—they had both touched this same page. Petra would read her thoughts, no matter how well Nerissa Swifte concealed them in whatever strange language spoken on this island that had sunken into the lakebed, folded back into the earth.

She looked back up at Dane, tearing her eyes from the page with some effort. She was pleased to see he had pulled out a book of his own, novel it looked like, and was sipping wine with a creased brow, focused on his reading. When he wasn't trying to charm her, he was even more handsome. Oh damn, Petra thought. No time for that nonsense now.

Gently moving her hand to the corners of the page, she decided he was giving her time for a glance through. She wouldn't try to translate or attempt to collect any words now, she only wanted an idea of the difficulty. Her stomach filled with butterflies and her hands were hot inside the gloves. The writing, though obviously the same author, was erratic. All of the letters were formed the same way, but sometimes they were larger, sometimes neat and organized— and in some pages, the writing was almost like a floating stream of consciousness. Words shot from the nib hundreds of years ago like arrows flying. This was a very personal account then. It was the only type of writing she'd seen that way. Not the calculated accounting of tasks accomplished and dry lists of happenings in town. No, this was a soul on the page. As her eyes scanned the strange words, stringing meaningless letters together, she had the idea that it was a bit like a conjurer's spell and each word read would produce an ectoplasm, a hovering ghost of the woman who had written them. Petra shook her head, nonsense, flights of fancy. Dane and his damned legends had scrambled her logic and her brains.

On some pages were strange symbols, almost like runes, and on one page she saw that Nerissa had written her name alongside a man's name several times. A beau? A child? A relative? She'd have to decode to find out.

The writing ended a few pages shy of the back cover, and she felt a sudden surge of loss at the abruptness of it. The creeping possibility of something having *happened* that prevented the book being finished to the end. A kind of hollow sadness settled briefly in her chest, like a stone slab piled on top of her. The feeling passed as quickly as it had come, and the air in the room seemed to have lost some of its charge. Shaking her head again, she carefully closed the book and softly ran a finger over the purple spine. So many words for her to collect.

But there was more good news.

Dane sensed her closing of the book and had shut his own, and looked to her expectantly.

"Any joy?"

She nodded, one corner of her mouth creeping upward. "I think so. It will take some time to take down all the words and translate them into something everyone can understand." She began, keeping her answer vague on purpose.

"Ah! You think you can wade through the gobbledygook made-up language, then?"

Petra bit her bottom lip and looked at him sidelong. "Yes, because that gobbledegook, as you so eloquently put it, is English."

"Can't be."

"I'm afraid it can, and it is. Only, it is in a very lazy code. Fortunately, I think there are many new words hiding in there too. If I had to guess, I would say the islanders had their own names for things, words that evolved or that were coined based on their unique experience of island life. Quite common."

"But...it's English? Are you certain?"

Petra smiled and ran her tongue along the bottom of her top teeth, an old tick she'd had since childhood when she was annoyed. "The foundation, absolutely..." She almost wished she had glasses to peer down at him from. How many more times would he doubt her answer? Infuriating man.

He sat back into the chair and brought his thumbnail back up to his teeth and looked upward, his face twisted in confusion.

Petra cleared her throat, drawing his attention. "There is the matter of how the financials will work on this project..."

He waved his hand. "Name your price—within reason. And any expenses you might encounter of course."

Petra wrinkled her nose. "I am a scholar of some reputation, Mr. Fintan. I do not want your...money."

Now she really had his attention. "You don't? But, then, I'm sorry? What? You just now asked about the financials..."

Exhaling, Petra leaned forward. "In exchange for my services, I require only that I possess all the words I gather so that I might publish them in an obscure words text with annotations and examples. You will receive nothing from any and all resulting public notice or profit from such a work. In exchange, however, you *will* receive the manuscript, translated into modern English, so that you may publish it or do what you will with it, as you see fit."

Dane stared at her in bewilderment. Petra sipped her wine, and tried not to look at the book in her lap. He wasn't going to agree. She needed those words. The anxiety built up into cacophonous noise, and she had to fight the urge to take the book and bolt with it. She *needed* those words.

"No dice."

"Mr. Fintan, it is a very good deal. If I can't have the words then I'm out. You'll have to…"

He raised a hand, cutting her off. "Let me finish, woman. You can have all the damn words. But, if I do publish the diary after you finish, and I haven't made my mind up either way, mind you, I would insist on your name being on it. And, you would have to split the royalties."

He put his hand down and leaned forward, pouring more wine into his not empty glass. Now it was her turn to stare at him in befuddlement."That's my offer, take it or leave it."

Without thinking, without needing to, Petra whispered her reply. "I'll take it."

"Wonderful. Let's drink to that." He raised his glass and refilled hers quickly. "To forgotten stories. To uncovering the past. To remembering. To bringing it into the future."

She felt a catch in her throat that made her eyes glaze. So simple, but so powerful. She wondered, just for a millisecond if his words were only about the book, or if he, like her, had something in his past that he kept close.

She raised her glass, clinked it against his, and whether it was the wine or the strangeness of the day

—or both—she could almost imagine ghostly devilish eyes of Nerissa Swifte watching her.

She stretched her neck from side to side, trying to clear the kinks and pops of her thoughts that were caught in her bones. Fanciful. There was no telling if Nerissa Swifte had devilish eyes or not. But, a voice inside Petra whispered—*they probably were.*

3

SLURG:
to laze around; lie sleepily or sluggishly

It was late, and somehow her zeal for decoding the book had burned off in her journey home. He'd insisted on driving her, opening her door and then asking her interested questions about her writing, her travel, her self. Dane was a handsome man, an elegant man, who moved with the litheness of someone whose body had been honed by athletics. But there was an insecurity there too, which made him endearing. A man who treasured books, and the words within them. A man who felt comfortable treading the path of the past, but was not so lost in its labyrinthine turns that he did not see the present.

He was a man that Petra could fall in love with. A man that maybe she was already a little in love with. Except that she had no heart to love with. Evan had taken that with him when he left.

She had walked in the door, her head full of moonlight and the stories of Traversint that had dripped from Dane's lips like wildflower honey, each facet of the tale sweeter and more golden, capturing her imagination and excitement until she buzzed. But, she had watched the headlights disappear from the drive, two beams of possibility leaving her in the blackness of isolation. A self-created prison she didn't remember shutting herself into.

The book sat before her, beckoning like a lover. Her notebook, brand new, naked white lines ready to be lovingly caressed and filled with the magic words of her pen. Magic because when she wrote them, the story would spring from the page, what was hidden would be revealed. Abracadabra, a whole world would pour from the ink.

But for now, she sat. The peppermint and lavender tea steaming on a tile she'd brought back from the Mediterranean. The bright painted colors on it seeming too cheerful for her midnight blue, reflective mood.

Sadness, like love or anger, is thought to be intangible. An emotion that passes through your soul in times of woe, softer and more silent than wind. Petra knew this was a lie. Sadness, sorrow, despondency, misery—these were weights that bound themselves to you. Sometimes sticking in your throat like dry bread, sometimes clinging to your chest like a wailing child. Sometimes despair seemed to sit behind her eyelids, a persistent presence that pushed out tears without warning. Tonight the grief had settled into her shoulders, stooping her like an old woman, and it sat like a stone in her stomach. When her father died, people had said, "I'm sorry for your loss" and it had made her smile. If only it were that simple. A loss. But he wasn't lost, he was dead. She hadn't left him at the movie theater or forgotten him on a bench in the park, he had died. But people do not understand loss unless they are experiencing it along with you. A hole ripped into your life—you stranded on one side, and the rest of your life sitting on the other with no transportation to traverse the distance between.

And then...Evan. The thought of his leaving released a keening. An inhuman sound that scared her. Frightened the cat too, who jumped off her lap and ran into the bedroom. How could he have done it? How could he hurt her so?

Sometimes Petra wanted to crawl back into the snug comfort of childhood. Back, back, to the pale glow of flashlights or muted bedside lamps. Back to the words in the books that had been her companions. Words that her brother Toby would whisper beside her, and his voice gave them an enchantment that was new to Petra. Words like: Enthusiasm. Ravenous. Jubilation. Marvelous. Exhibition. Tremulous. Raconteur. Words that smudged like syrup onto her greedy fingers, all of the words, now hers, now theirs, waiting in her mind and on her tongue to be given life.

But then, then...life. Life happened. No more Toby beside her, no more whispered magic words in the dark. Toby was gone, and she grew up and things became complicated. Convoluted. Befuddled. It wasn't Petra and her words anymore, it was everything else nudging, pushing, jostling her away from that which was most essential and simple. Words had to make her money, words had to be put to work. And though the unrestrained glee at uncovering those treasured words remained the same, there was a burden there. A duty that hadn't existed in that long ago blanket covered childhood.

Her hand was shaking, but she forced herself to grab the cup and take a sip of her still-too-hot tea. Which reminded her of her earlier thoughts. Picking up the thread of them, Petra regarded the tea in her hand. Love was this. A tangible thing too. Love was warmth and comfort. Love was what steadied you when melancholy sent you reeling. Though sometimes it flamed too hot, burning your lips, blistering your tongue, time turned that heat into coziness. And memories to give you strength.

She inhaled deeply and exhaled slowly as the grief counselor had taught her. She looked back at the purple-blue miracle before her, and felt suddenly that Nerissa Swifte's diary was going to save her. And that perhaps it was her duty to rescue Nerissa's story. She had no idea then how deeply she and Nerissa Swifte were linked—and how important the connection between past and present would prove.

Diary Of Nerissa Swifte

A new book to fill with new thoughts—though I heartily wish that Phineas could have been more careful in the canoe. Or that he had the sense to jump in after it, as he is a swimmer born. My last book of days was 'lost at sea' as Da says, though it would be more apt to say 'lost at lake', though less romantic. Phin was daydreaming, he says, and I was writing—and between the two of us we hadn't seen the other, larger ship until we'd hit. The both of us falling overboard, taking Phin's paints and my diary to the bottom of the damned lake. A fact that was not remedied because he did not notice their loss until we had made it back to shore, and then, we had no notion of where precisely the tipping over point had been. At any rate, I am hopeful that the creatures in the lake cannot read, for I would be sore ashamed for them to see some of the nonsense that does fall from my pen.

Da says we are too old for daydreaming, and was fairly disappointed in us for our inattention. For Phin is now 18 and I, 23. But, he replaced the paints and the diary all the same, without accepting a word of thanks. Da is strange that way. He'd rather we thought the items had appeared out of thin air than admit he rowed to the mainland to procure them.

He's a good Da. Even though there have been a fair number of suitors, he will not give them permission to wed me unless I agree, a decision that most on Traversint think preposterous. But t'isn't, because the Swifte's aren't like other folk. I've got a bite of the nymph in me, Da says, like my mother before me. It's why I'm favored, he says. But the islanders, they ask my advice and they ask for my healing spells, and their sons want to share my bed to take my magic for their own, mayhap. But, I know what they say about me. I hear their voices as I have always heard whispers crawling to me like spiders. Witch. Sorceress. They believe me to be a witch, and they are not half wrong.

When I was young, I used to find it strange that my fingers weren't webbed like Phin's or Fisher's, my brothers. I would weep to see my weirdly naked fingers, spreading separate from one another. I thought I was an abomination. A freak. Once, Fisher had tried to cut his with shears, but Da caught him and slapped him so hard my own cheek stung. For Fisher is my twin brother, and we share all joys and pains half and half. The webbing, Da says, is the gift of the Swifte's. Da says our family came from the water. That we lived there, man-fish, beneath the waves for thousands of years. When I asked him why I did not have the gift, he said it was because the other part of our family is fairy. That a sprite and a man from the water fell in love. But he could not live in the air, and she could could not live in the lake, so the fairy enchanted this island so that they might have a place to live together.

I will admit that it is a pretty story, but with Da, there is no telling how much is truth and how much is legend, for he himself does not know the difference.

In either case, I am gifted with skills I do not completely understand, though I wield them all the same, as well as I am able. I cure illness, and babies do not cry when in my arms. Whispers from around the island fly to me like dragonflies, and I can look at two people and see if they will marry. When I weep you can be sure that rain is coming to the island and there isn't a body that can lie to me, the truth slips from their lips. I can look at a man and see the children he will father, but I have not yet seen the man who will father mine, and this is why Da has not made me wed. He knows that it is madness to try and bend the will of a Swifte, for he is one too.

I am writing from my little cabin that sits on the edge of the lake, deep within the forest. If I squint just the right way in the sunshine, I fancy I can see the houses of Travers Town across the gold-tipped waves. The cabin is newly built and smells of fresh split pine. Da did not like me to leave him and Phineas in the big house, but when Fisher did get married it no longer felt as home. I see Da and Phin every day, so his heart cannot be over-sore, and Fisher is only on the other side of the island. But his new wife, Annette, though she be pretty and full of smiles, she has cleaved Fisher and me. Cleaved me in half. Fisher, my other eye, my other hand, one half of myself. But if he is now a man, then I too must be my own woman. And so I sit in my cabin, scribbling my thoughts, waiting for islanders and mainlanders alike to seek me out. For seek me out they will, they always do.

If my appearance is strange to them, they do not say it; truth be told, they probably expect it. Hair so pale that it looks like a ribbon of moonlight. I keep the long braid of it plaited down my back, so long that it touches my hips. My skin is fresh milk, my eyes the same grey as the pebbles on the beach front. A child once whispered to his mother that I looked as though I might disappear into shadow or float up into a night full of stars. Perhaps he was right. I just may.

Da, Fisher, and Phin are all black-haired and black-eyed, bodies sinuous as fish with their webbed hands and toes. It is said any woman married to a Swifte man will never fear drowning and none shall ever lose anything precious in the lake. It is a good luck charm to be loved by a Swifte.

Unless you are loved by me. That is a gamble. Having a Swifte woman means she will always read your lies in your throat, she will see your thoughts and know your fears. A Swifte woman is powerful, but weak men are afraid of a woman with power, for power is frightening. Most of all, for me.

Today I am to collect a few herbs for my stores. There are quite a few young brides who will come knocking on my cabin door for charms come spring. They will want their wombs to be fruitful, and others will wish an unction to keep a man from straying. It is difficult now that it is fully winter. The herbs will be few and the wind off the water will be cruel, though the cold has never had much hold on me, it does make passage more difficult across the waters. Soon the lake will freeze and it will be dangerous to cross. I must see Phin—or Fisher—about making a last trip to the mainland for my supplies.

Ah, a rap on the door.

4

DESIDERATA:
things wanted or needed

Petra came out of her transcription completely spooked. There was a rapping on her own cottage door. For a moment she had to breathe in and out, slowly, reminding herself that it was merely coincidence. Telling herself that Nerissa Swifte had left off writing because of the knock on her door hundreds of years ago, not pausing so that Petra might attend to the rap upon hers.

The rapping continued, softly, and Petra stood up, trembling slightly, her mind still part-way stuck in the strange and fantastical world of the Swifte's. Petra stretched, and stopped to peer into the little mirror in the hall on the way to the cottage door. Dark circles under her eyes, and her dark blonde hair unravelling messily from the braids she'd put it in while working, but she looked passable, almost human. Or so she thought.

"Coming…coming…" Petra muttered, opening

the heavy oak door to reveal a crisp and tailored Dane Fintan.

"Hello, sorry, I'm afraid I woke you." He winced at his own error. "I would have called, but I never got your number…"

"Shit." She mumbled, checking her watch, "It's gone 7"

"Yes, I know, like I said, I'm really sorry. I just couldn't wait though, I tossed and turned all night wondering if you'd figured anything out." He paused to exhale, "*Have* you figured anything out?"

Without another word, she spun on her heel and walked back to her couch where she had been doing the transcribing, gesturing for him to follow her.

Shamelessly, she plopped back down on the cushions, crossing her legs beneath her and lifting her notebook back up to the pillow that served as a desk. Petra didn't look up, but still saw his form in the doorway."

"Ah, not early then. Late." His voice was sheepish and she found it oddly endearing. She knew if she met his eyes she'd find a blush on his cheeks, but she couldn't bring herself to do so, as though the sight would push her over some kind of edge. Instead she answered his statement.

"Guilty. I never made it to bed. Didn't even realize that time for sleep had come and gone." She yawned absently, and tucked some escaped hairs back behind her ear.

"Coffee." He said, not a question, but a decision. He turned right back around to her kitchen where she heard him rummaging around. Her first instinct was to be angry, or at least peeved. Petra didn't care for guests, especially nosy ones. And she didn't know what he was playing at, he'd never find all of her coffee things.

But when she crossed the hall to the kitchen, she found the French press on the counter, the coffee grounds out of the freezer, waiting expectantly at the bottom of the press. The creamer and raw sugar were likewise on the counter, and he was busily washing the floral china cups as if he'd done this same thing in the same kitchen every day of his life.

"How did you...?" Petra looked at Dane with an eyebrow cocked.

"Oh, that. It's nothing. A quirk."

"Knowing your way around a woman's kitchen?"

He laughed, and the sound warmed her. "No, I always seem to know where everything is. Or, where it should be. My mother was the same way." Petra noticed his eyes take on a faraway shine. "She could walk around the antique shop and lay her hands on any item. She just had to picture what she wanted, and voilà, there it was. And for me, it has been the same. I think "coffee" and all the things I need light up in my mind. My hands reach for them before I even realize I know where they are." He smiled the same sheepish grin, drying the cups.

"Must be nice. I'd like to know exactly where I belong sometimes." Petra offered up a lazy half-laugh and changed the subject when she imagined she saw his shoulders stiffen in response. "Any other latent talents?" She asked, changing the subject, just the tiniest hint of sarcasm in her voice.

He turned around and started the kettle, considering. "Well, I make a great cup of coffee, I'm a mediocre pianist and a fair plumber. Need any of those services?"

His voice was good-natured, his expression mischievous. He was flirting with her. The realization put an odd lightness in her belly. She sat down at the kitchen table, rubbing her temples. Petra considered telling him what she had read, thinking that in the light of the mysterious things she'd found in the diary so far, not only did his own claim of skills seem probable, the chances he would believe the diary seemed likely too.

Petra watched him roll up the starched sleeves of his pinstriped shirt, admired the way the early light of day reflected off of his glossy brown hair. On an impulse, just for the morning, she would let him in.

"To answer your question, yes. I have figured it out."

"You're kidding? Already?" He turned around and poured the boiling water into the carafe, his hands steady but his expression incredulous.

"No, I'm not kidding. And yes, already."

"How?" He was almost breathless with immediate excitement.

Before she answered, Petra had a question of her own. "How many other experts have tried to crack the diary?"

He cleared his throat, and turned around, his back to her once again. The only sound for some seconds was the tinkling of the teaspoon in the cups.

"Loads." He said quietly.

"Really?" She heard the disbelief in her voice and knew he did as well. "Define 'loads'."

"Well, that is to say…"

"Oh, Dane, come off it. None."

He exhaled, blowing the hair off of his forehead with the force of his breath. "How'd you know?" He asked, finally facing her and bringing the cups to the table.

"Because a child could decipher it." At the look of hurt on his face, she amended her statement. "Ok, ok, not a child. But certainly a linguist or languages expert. An historian or anyone with a degree in the arts would have easily caught on." Seeing the questions on his face, she explained. "Ok, each word was simply written backward. They simply needed to be re-written to make it make sense. Not even overly jumbled. Very primitive code."

He looked a little deflated. "Ah, so no good for your research."

Taking a sip of the now milky white coffee she shook her head as she swallowed. "Not at all. It's wonderful. Just because I could easily turn it back into the original language doesn't mean all of the words I translated were known to me. The first entry alone is full of words I'd never seen before."

He put his cup down, and at the same moment she jumped up, causing him to spill a little on the table. "Oops, sorry." Her eyes were level with his, and he bit his lip, a strange expression on his face. Hastily, she turned, backing out of the room. "Here, let me fetch my notes really quick. I'll show you what I mean."

She stepped into the study and grabbed the notes, pinching her cheeks and smoothing her braids with her fingers. Absently her hand pressed against the scar, which burned a little warmer than the rest of her neck. Stupid, she thought. Stupid, stupid. Idiotic, imbecilic, dolt, dunce. She needed to remain professional. Networking. Colleagues, she reminded herself.

Notebook in hand, Petra stepped back into the kitchen, and had to damper the smile that lit her face. Something in the scene, his cuffs rolled up, drinking coffee at the breakfast table, it felt so much like home that she had to swallow down the joy of it before it came bursting from her like a sneeze.

"Yes?" Dane looked up, all expectation.

Pulling the notebook to her chest, she glanced at the clock on the stove. "Are you in a hurry? I didn't think…"

"No! I barged in on you! No apologies. I have a meeting, but it starts when I get there. So don't think of it. I'm fairly exploding to know what the devil you've turned up."

Petra smiled and sat back down at the table, spreading her notes and translations out. She was usually very guarded and secretive about her work, but there was an excitement, a sense of needing to share what she'd found with another. A story too big to be hoarded by one person.

"Well, perhaps you should read it yourself." Petra extended the transcribed entry toward him, gently, carefully, feeling very foolish. It was only her writing after all. But it felt…more. For although they were the thoughts of Nerissa Swifte, a diary is an intimate thing. And Petra was sharing that with Dane. Mr. Fintan. A secret that would only live in the minds of the two of them. He took hold of the notebook, reverently, and letting go of it into his care didn't twist her stomach like she had thought it would. He was beaming like a new father, and he bent his head, reading over the text she'd labored to translate without another word spoken.

She absently stood up, and walked to the sink to do the dishes, a nervous habit she remembered dimly that her mother had. Scrubbing dishes that didn't need scrubbing until her fingers were raw and puckered from the water. Alas, the only dish in the kitchen was her cup of coffee, still sitting on the table, near him. Shrugging, she walked back over quietly, taking a seat so as not to disturb his reading, and tentatively reached for the coffee as though it were part of a spell and it would vanish if she grabbed too quickly.

She watched him read. His attention was fully absorbed in the words on the pages, and so she was free to study him at leisure. She told herself it wasn't ladylike to stare, but she couldn't stop. Something in his expression looked so much like Toby, her older and…younger brother, that for a moment she had to close her eyes to hold back the tears. She brought her hand to her chest, as if in not having it there her heart would be forced out of her body and would stand naked, exposed, showing all the rents and tears and damage to the man who sat quietly with her at the table.

But Toby was dead. And so were her father and her mother. And so was Nerissa Swifte. Lives snatched away from her, but not quite. Maybe it was why she wanted to share Nerissa with Dane. The diary was an opportunity to bring someone back from the dead. To reclaim something lost, to pull back shadows from the grave in a way which she couldn't with her father, mother or Toby. Toby, who'd been too young to even think of having a diary. Who was too new to life to feel the need to record his days.

Surely, that's what it was in Dane's face that reminded her of her brother. The expectation of excitement. Something like innocence, that wasn't quite. An uninhibited sense of adventure coming—as though he'd never been kicked by life before.

Damn. He'd caught her staring.

"Wow, a whole entry, and it proves no less mysterious! A witch's diary, no less. But all the words look normal to me, did I miss something?"

She was smiling, his excitement was contagious. "Well, I don't know if she was, in fact, a witch—or if her father and brothers were the descendants of magical lake people. She might have simply been eccentric, or a touch mad…or highly imaginative. And the new words are not in the translation. Instead, I translated them to the best of my ability and simply wrote it all in modern-ish English."

"Ahh, I see. But you don't believe that do you? You know she was a witch, same as I do. 'The Island Enchantress', as it were."

She bit her lip and shrugged. " I don't know about all that, Mr. Fintan. It is only one entry, after all."

He narrowed his eyes and looked at her silently, trying to read her inner thoughts. The way he studied her made her feel exposed, and for a moment she did worry he could see inside her mind. But then he looked away, and shrugged himself, pulling his hand lazily through his hair.

He cleared his throat and changed the subject.

"Ok, I'll bite. What were the strange words, and how did you know what they meant?"

Suddenly, he had stepped on something raw, and she wanted him to leave. The words were hers. Are hers. She alone is their keeper. She will not give them up. She will share anything else with this man—and she knew it. The realization scared her. She'd tell him about her mother, and about Toby. She'd tell him about Evan, if he asked. The real story, not the one she told herself to make the pain less, not the one they wrote in the newspaper. She'd share this coffee, this kitchen, her bed...but she couldn't share the words. They were hers. She needed them as they needed her. The words had become her armor. You could lose yourself in the tumbling of words, bury yourself deep in the ink blue of them—just like the buried Isle of Traversint. And she wasn't ready to come out of hiding yet.

"No!" She blurted, much too forcefully. Out, out, she willed him, before his eyes and his exuberance broke through the chinks in her chain mail.

Words buzzed through her mind, shielding her from an imagined threat. Astony- to astonish. Fluey meaning dusty. Rantipole; to behave in a rude manner. There, she had calmed herself. The lines in his forehead as he looked at her said what his voice did not, and she knew she had to give a normal answer.

"That is, no. Not quite yet. I would like to...um, wait. Wait until I have a more comprehensive list."

The clouds on his face cleared as if the sun had broken through. "Oh, perfect. I'll just wait until then."

He stood up from the table and smoothed the legs of his trousers. He had that kind of natural aesthetic that made all clothes flattering. She had to stop her mind from conjuring him in various outfits. Including a sheet. Stupid. Imbecilic. Inappropriate, Petra chided herself.

"Well, I'd better leave you to some rest. Will you finish another entry tonight, do you think?" His voice was bright, hopeful. And as much as she wanted him gone, she found herself almost asking him to stay. She bit the words back, they were not worthy of her.

A scratching on the kitchen door produced Jinks, mewling to put a newborn to shame.

"Ah, I'd almost forgotten." Dane said, reaching into his briefcase and producing a few cans of cat food. "It's not kibble, but I bet he prefers it." The cat was now very aggressively kneading Dane's legs with his paws.

"Thanks." Petra said, simply, her mind worrying at one of his words. "How did you know it was a boy?"

Dane laughed, "Your tabby is legend. Can't remember a time it didn't haunt around this house. Or, perhaps it's a family of cats that lives around here. But I daresay everyone in town knows this cat. I'd say you're pretty lucky he picked you."

Petra looked at Jinks sidelong, unconvinced and a little surprised. The cat met her eyes with a resounding yowl. Sure, 'lucky' was just the word she'd choose. With one more long look and a shake of her head, she shooed the nuisance cat out of the kitchen. They stood awkwardly for a moment.

"Yes, I think I'll have a nap and do a few more entries later on." Silence as he nodded his head.

"Right, well, I'll walk you out." Petra yawned and gave her braids a little tug. Her scalp was aching in a way that told her she needed to lie down.

At the door, they shook hands, a bizarrely formal leave-taking after sitting companionably in the kitchen with her in her pajamas. She thought for a moment he was going to kiss her cheek, but then he'd blushed and continued to shake her hand.

"I will ring you and let you know what I find." Petra muttered vaguely, not meeting his eyes.

"Right, thanks. Uh, good morning then." Dane

turned and walked down the steps, and then suddenly spun back around. "Listen would it be all right, possibly, I mean…" He looked so flustered that she was tempted to laugh. But he wore the discomfort so strangely that it was again, endearing. She had thought when they first met that he wasn't capable of being ruffled. It must be me, Petra thought. I make everyone uncomfortable.

Finishing his thought for him she called out to him, "Yes. Tonight after 7." And she shut the door. She wasn't sure if he was smiling or not at her answer, and at the thought of seeing her again that day. But she was.

Sitting back down at her make-shift desk made from cushions on the couch, she thought back to her anxiety that morning about the words. How could she explain? It was her own strange magic. She didn't like to use that word to describe her skill, but with all the words in her arsenal, she couldn't think of a better one. Expertise wasn't strong enough, neither was prowess, skill, ability. Enchantment was too fanciful as was sorcery, charm and supernatural talent. Dane couldn't understand and she couldn't explain. Words simply…revealed themselves to her. She would come across an archaic word, an undocumented, rare term, and she didn't have to wonder its meaning. Instead its synonyms and definitions would pop into her head as though she had known the word all along. As if there were no words that were strangers to her. And because of that, because the words were so immediately familiar, she wanted to keep them close to her like children. Or to twine them about herself like a lover.

So when she'd seen, **Grakan** written, the letters written in Nerissa Swifte's primitive code, the word had jumped out in its correct form. She had gotten an image of a man, part fish, a kind of lake mer-man who breathed in water like she breathed in air. She had written it as "fish man" in the translation, but knew that Nerissa's word was more correct. That it captured something that no clumsy synonym could. It fit the picture in Petra's mind more snugly. And then the beautiful, **faradie,** not quite woman, not quite fairy, and too lustful to be an angel. It was a word that sounded like music, a chiming trill that fit the image of a being that fell in love with a man who lived in the water. And so she had collected the words. **Grakan** and **Faradie,** writing them both on her list and etching them in blood beneath her skin with her memory.

A rebel part of her wanted to show Dane. To see his eyes widen with enthusiasm at her discovery. She wondered if collecting the joy of the moment would bring her more solace than the words. She dismissed the thought. Too much Dane Fintan. Appearing as suddenly in her life as the damned island had vanished.

*   *   *

Petra opened the notebook and reached for the purplish, forget-me-not blue of Nerissa's diary, her fingers tingling as they touched the leather. A short nap and a shower had refreshed her, and now she poised her pen over the notebook, slipping a glove on her other hand to turn the fragile diary pages. She was traveling back in time to a place she'd never been, a place she could never go.

But as she drank in Nerissa Swifte's words, she felt, strangely, for the second time that day, as though she were coming home.

Diary Of Nerissa Swifte

I have been to and fro like a madwoman since yesterday's visitor. The people from the mainland, they always are timid to step foot on the island. I know not what stories they are told from childhood about the place, but they are raised with some unnatural fear of it. A man on the island sometimes must travel many days to find a village whose daughters will agree to marry him and then return to this shore as his bride.

I cannot believe it is the isolation—though that is what Da tells Fisher and Phin. It is probably tales of dark magic and unexplained events. The same magic that the mainlanders eagerly seek from me. Hypocrites, the lot of them.

And 'tis silly too, I think, for most on the island are regular folk, with usual, albeit difficult, lives of toil, same as anywhere I'd warrant. There are not many women born with the gift any longer, and only a few families have sons with even the finest gossamer thin webbing between their fingers and toes.

The magic is fading, certain sure, though legends die hard—some say. And as long as there is one cunning woman, one holder of the magic on these shores, the stories will still be told. And the people will still come in hope of taking a little of the power of the place for themselves.

I receive less visitors in the colder months, as the temperatures make the lake difficult to traverse, even when it ices solid. Some men have been trapped, their arms frozen mid-row, while their eyes dart back and forth, frantically searching for rescue. These same men, too afraid to open their mouths to yell for that much needed help, lest they swallow too much of the icy air, and freeze from the inside out.

But yesterday's guest was too warm with worry to think of these things. It seems that the man has a relation—a brother in law, I believe. This relation has come to visit him from the eastern states, a rich man who has come to visit his sister, who is the wife of the man who did come to rap on my door.

Straight away I knew what it was that heated this visitor. And it was not concern for his wife's ailing brother. No, it was guilt that put roses on his cheeks and dots of perspiration on his forehead. A dark and hidden part inside of the rumpled and exhausted man before me desired the brother dead. And his own words told me why. Money. But he had come all the same, for his wife had coaxed him into it. All this I knew, and yet he said little.

It is a luxury I have that money is not something I think about. I am the "witch of Traversint," am I not? This house, my clothing, my herbs and tonics and all of my furniture, if they are not given me by Da, then

I am supplied by those who darken my doorstep. Enchantments, elixirs and answers all have a price.

But though this man did have this dark desire, he at least had the grace to be ashamed of his base thoughts. He had rowed over as quickly as arms could carry him, trying to beat the pace of his unworthy, deadly desires.

The man at my door, his name was Samuel Proper, his ailing brother, Alarence Attwater. Symptoms including: shakes, spasms, sweats, and delirium. Most interesting, indeed. Mr. Proper wished me to accompany him at that moment, but I told him that Mr. Attwater will keep until tomorrow. And I know he shall.

It seems to me that people are uncommonly frightened of death. How does one explain that death is like smoke in the eyes? Blinding, perhaps painful and then...clear. A change that gives one new eyes to see the world. It is life we should all quiver over. Daily life is a terrifying thing, indeed.

At any rate, after telling him I would delay, the lanky mustachioed man had not hidden his delight—and I let him know I saw his secret. This turned his rosy cheeks an even more alarming shade of red.

Even so, he had promised me my pick of whatever herbs and roots I find on his property and a credit at his store, for the abominable man is a merchant and his is the outpost in Travers Town. I could tell this was knowledge he had hoped I would not know (as it is Da or Fisher who most often rows across for any supplies that can't be gotten here), and that it brought him a great degree of pain to grant me any boon from himself. And though many think I have the power to read a man's thoughts—this is not one of my skills. Instead, those who would keep secrets or think dark thoughts, too often wear them plainly on their countenance. These speak louder than a man's voice.

So, it is agreed. I had wandered over to ask Da to row me over this morning, knowing he would not allow Phineas after our recent capsize in the lake. But it was Fisher I met on my way. He was headed to my cottage, trouble as plain on his features as a broken nose. And although I *can* read the faces of others, Fisher is impenetrable to me. Like pieces of my own destiny, I cannot see the depths of him.

As if my twin knew already my errand, he offered to row me to the mainland and assist me with gathering herbs. There are few besides him I would trust to choose the plants I need, but Fisher is someone who knows the medicine of nature almost as well as myself. Although we parted with understanding, his sadness has haunted me all night. Annette, I'll wager. Any sorrow he has was brought on by her. Though it is probably partially my own grief at being replaced as the most important woman in my brother's life that makes me think such things.

I hear him coming now. The soft sound that only his tread makes on the path. I must fix my mind to Mr. Attwater and away from my own thoughts. I am the witch of Traversint, and it is my duty to do so.

5

ANTHYPOPHORA:
to ask a question and immediately answer it oneself.

Petra exhaled as though she'd been holding her breath under water. The woman's diary was dark and mysterious. At some points she sounded reasonable and ordinary, the kind of person Petra would grab a glass of wine or a cup of tea with. And at other times she seemed like a heroine straight from a Gothic novel, something shadowy and strange hovering just above the action all the while. Nerissa Swifte spoke so oddly of death, it was as if it were a land she had ventured to on holiday and had formed no real opinion of the experience. At some points in her reading, Petra fancied she could hear the woman's clear voice speaking in her mind. Not musically high, but instead low and with a soporific effect. A seductive voice. But that was too many novels on Petra's end, she supposed. Though her description of herself had eerily matched the image Petra had in her mind when she'd first touched the book, and it was a strange and rare appearance to be sure.

There had been more unusual words in this entry, words that her mind, as usual, gave meaning to without hesitation. But besides the discovery of new words, she also found that she was jealous of Nerissa Swifte. Envious that she could live alone in her cottage, people coming to her door for her skills. The fact that people knew she was an oddity and still sought her out. The idea that Nerissa didn't care what they thought of her, and instead was proud of her place in her wild, far-off distance from society.

This acceptance of self, of talent, of confidence, it eluded Petra. Her initial success had not been enough; the academic community moved quickly. If she had wanted to stay relevant, marketable, she needed to keep pace.

Which was the problem. Her work wasn't about swimming with the current. It was about swimming back to shore and picking through all the detritus that had been left in the sand. She didn't *want* to be relevant, damnit. She wanted words. And the history, and the voices that had uttered and felt them. She was always attempting to bottle memories and then was surprised when the jar was empty, Evan would have said. But the bottle remained and the memory of filling it. Didn't anyone understand?

Perhaps Dane Fintan. Damn. Damn. Professional. Colleagues. Networking. She told herself for the hundredth time.

Petra looked down at the diary entry she'd translated and realized that she would like to be like Nerissa Swifte someday, when she grew up. Though, the woman writing the journal was almost a decade younger than Petra, and the woman herself long dead.

She sighed, and read back over the words she had added to her collection.

Propcurant, which she had translated as merchant. Though it seemed to be something more like an importer with a general store to sell his wares. Also, **Amfusious**, which meant something like delirium. A state of being so ill that the man did not know where, who or what was happening to him. Petra chuckled dryly to herself, thinking that sometimes that exact malady was all too real for most people.

Petra got up and changed into a pair of slim-fitting jeans and white t-shirt, pausing to brush on a dusting of blush—she must remember to work in the open air again tomorrow—and ran a hairbrush through her wavy hair. Her eyes darted to the little travel timex alarm clock on the bedside table, the same clock she'd brought when she first came to stay here, when she thought she'd be selling the cottage and going back to the city directly— and saw that it was only 4 o'clock. Still time to do another entry before Dane returned. Feeling foolish over her unnecessary beauty prep, she sauntered over to the kitchen for a snack, but the little rose plates caused her to lose her appetite. She was seized with the impulse to break it again, watching it snap into shards like her heart. But, caution and common sense won the day. How could one man shatter her heart—and another man still ignite the pieces?

She tumbled back onto the couch, pulled on her cotton glove and lovingly continued transcribing the story, until she was so lost in its depths that the clock on the wall ceased to exist, and the little rose plates called out to her no longer.

Diary Of Nerissa Swifte

A strange case. When I arrived home I could barely
speak of it nor write the words necessary to describe
it. It was not the sickness itself that perplexed me,
for it was not unknown to my experience. Common
ailments strike different bodies in varying fashions,
and it always seems that those who are rarely ill prove
the most worrisome when they do succumb to
sickness. Such was the case with Mr. Attwater. A large
man, robust and muscled as though he were a
blacksmith. Lying in his sickbed he was a giant, almost
to the point of being comical in the small bed, though
it was not the bed that was unusually small, only that
the man was uncommon large. I could not tell
whether it was the illness or the unpleasantness of
being cosseted that was more troublesome for the
man to bear.

But this was not what made the meeting a strange
one. Indeed, it was instead that it happened that I
have finally found the man who will be my future.

Beyond his sweating, sickness-infested body, I studied him. I found a good reason to send out the infernal Samuel Proper, asking him to fetch fresh water from the lake so that I might have Mr. Attwater to myself.

His eyes would not meet mine at first, and I knew it was because he thought himself weak and did feel shame. But when I did not stir, instead remaining as I was, looming over him, watching, taking in his every detail, he finally brought his gaze to meet my own.

I would like to write that there was a spark, a flame, a bolt of lightning between us. But the only heat in the room came from the unimpressive fire in the grate and the fever that held fast to him. Sighing, I bent over him further and began my ministrations.

I could wonder if he thought me beautiful, or if there was a charge in the air when he first beheld me, but I do not. Most on the island find me beautiful, if strange, and I have made peace that it is easier to be comely than homely, but other than that I think not of my looks. Love is so little invested in looks, as is destiny And for myself, I cannot separate the two enough for it to matter if they differ at all. If it was not ardor, or an instant flicker, it was something more mundane. In the first look at him, as pitiful as he was, I simply knew. Like I knew my own name. Like I knew the scar on my knuckle or the golden lights in Fisher's eyes. Like I had been holding my breath my whole life and I could finally exhale. As I applied unctions and bade him roll over so that I might look at his neck and peer in his ears, I studied him still more.

I have seen men more handsome, but his features were even and appealing. He was large, as I mentioned before, but not given to pudginess or awkwardness, or at least from what I could tell from his recumbent form. His eyes were an unremarkable hazel, but were quick and intelligent. His hair, though wet with sweat, was short and wavy without given to curls. His cheekbones were high and his arms almost burly, but his hands…his hands were beautiful. No blacksmith, nor laborer. This was a scholar or an artist. For they were not exactly the soft, feminine hands of an idle gentleman, but instead they were skilled, alive. Hands that desired movement and occupation, that existed to create, though I know not what.

This brawny bear of a man, this man that I knew to be my destiny—and the piece of him I loved first was his hands.

After a time, I saw that he was looking at me as well. His eyes followed my every movement, as though he were memorizing me. On any other day, I would have scolded a body for eyeing me thus, but on this day, it was not unwelcome. Neither of us did speak, but as I worked to cure him I could feel the illness leaving him, peeled from him like a snake's skin by my own magic and healing hands.

As I moved to stand, I placed a hand on his brow to confirm that which I already knew. Nodding in my approval of his broken fever, I was startled by one of his hands, coming close to my face. I was startled, but I did not move. His fingers touched my cheek as lightly as moth's wings. So tenderly, that it was almost a ghost of his touch.

Replacing his hand underneath his blanket, a small voice, so faint and cobwebby that I could barely hear it, asked me, "Are you a faerie?"

And I suppose now that I was a touch dramatic, but I stood up and swirled my skirts as I headed to the door. Before I stepped out I smiled and told him the truth.

"Only half."

So, it was a strange meeting. But I know that I no longer have cause to wonder what sort of man the world would find me for a husband. I have seen him, and though it is naught but a beginning—well, that is how all commences after all.

Just outside the sickroom I found Samuel Proper and his wife, Margaret, called Meg. Meg Proper looked nothing like her brother, and after a few moments of conversation I came to understand why. They were siblings only by marriage, and she'd sent for me to heal him out of duty rather than affection. Still, I gave the remaining tonics over to her able hands, and instructed her on how to administer to the recovering Mr. Attwater.

I confess it was on my tongue to ask from whence and for what purpose Mr. Attwater had arrived in our corner of the world, but I swallowed my curiosity and stuck my hand out to accept the credit to Mr. Proper's shop instead.

Outside the Proper's fine house, I found Fisher, who was waiting like a collie dog. We nodded at one another, and he brought up the large basket from the ground for my approval. Fisher knew the plants as well as I, and knew where to find them—and what stores I was low on without my having to tell him. Silently, we walked to the merchant's shop, though the silence was not one of companionability. There was something else. It was a shadow I could not quite grasp that grew like nightfall between us. Words unsaid, secrets that spread thin between us. But, I knew I could not force the words from him. I knew better than that and always had. Whispers could not stay muffled betwixt us for long. It was always thus for Fisher and I, and always will be.

It had to wait though, for once inside the shop, the two of us headed in separate directions, snatching up items here and there, foodstuffs and fabric, tobacco and spirits. I personally prefer my own blackberry wine or Da's cider to the rum and hard liquors Mr. Proper sells in his shop, but Fisher and Phin like it for their night swims. Fisher says it keeps his blood up after his laps about the lake when it chills. Da says that the water is often so frigid between his webbed toes that it could stop his heart, but such a fact would ne'er deter my men. They return to the water, night after night, as it calls to their blood, calling the Swifte men back to the water, at least for a few hours, back to the foamy waves. It seems that though the cold could stop a heart, refraining from the water would stop their heart entirely. Or rather, they would have no use for their heart, because it beats in time with the lap of the waves.

I worry though, that some of the spirits are for Annette. Not because I begrudge my brother's wife some of the reward that was given me for my arts, but instead because of how she does behave when she has imbibed. She frets and mutters when Fisher ever does leave her side, and then nags him when he returns. She screams and stomps and throws his things about. Which is how I knew that any ruffle in Fisher's calm was due to his harpy of a wife. Though,

I will admit that I could not have guessed the exact nature of why. I confess, I still can scarce believe it.

We had gathered our items, and taken them to the lanky, pimpled clerk who looked at the two of us out of hooded eyes, as though to open them fully and behold us would somehow curse him. We handed over the credit that Mr. Proper had written up, and the surly youth turned it over and over in the light, and sniffed. I thought the man might well taste it before he grudgingly decided it was authentic, but to my relief he did not. Instead he grunted, and then packed up our purchases.

We were silent again as we carried our bounty to the boat, and did not speak as we packed it in carefully. It was not until Fisher had taken a few long pulls of the oars that he fixed his gaze on mine, and spoke, his voice thick with worry.

Is it unusual to find your brother handsome? I think I always have because he is my foil, his beauty is the opposite in all ways to my own. Where he is dark, I am light. Where he is tall, I am slight of limb and features. For him not to be handsome, I would not be beautiful, and every surface I see myself reflected in tells me that I am. Strange looking, yes. But I revel in my oddities, and do not dislike my looks. How could I? My mother and father gave them to me.

But, lines of distraction marred his face and his fury of black hair looked limp. This was not the cocksure Fisher I knew. This man was almost a stranger.

"Nissa" He'd said, "I must tell you something." and I knew from the way his fingers grasped the oar a little tighter, his knuckled turning a shade paler, that it was bad news indeed.

I will transcribe the confession as closely as I can remember it, though I cannot believe I have forgotten anything, so strange his words rang in my ears.

"Annette was pregnant."

"Oh." I'd said, my ears still sounding with the clang of the word *was*.

"Yes, and she lost it. The beginnings of a child seeped from her womb and turned our bed into a scene of horror and sorrow."

I told him I was sorry, and started to tell him that there would be others.

"No, Nissa." He'd said, cutting me off. "I was relieved. I was glad. Is that not demonic? Terrible? A man who is happy that his wife loses his child?"

I asked him why, but gently, and his response was unexpected.

"When I married her, I thought nothing of children. I thought only of...the act that creates them. Do you understand?"

I nodded, a small smile tugging my lip, but he did not notice, instead his eyes were far away and his front teeth chewed his lips awkwardly for a moment, considering.

"I should have known... I should have looked more closely..." He said finally, his voice almost lost in the wind on the lake.

For a moment, I was elated to think he finally saw that she was unsuitable to be a mother to his children and a wife to him. He should have chosen one of the fisherman's daughters, plump and bonny and sweet as cream. Not a tiny, demanding little waif of a woman…and then I realized I was wrong.

Fisher did not find her unsuitable because she was a nagging, bitter, self-important shrew—but because he was afraid for her. He finished his thought just as I came to the realization.

"She is too small. Labor would kill her. I believe a baby would split her in two. Especially if the babe be a boy, a boy like me…"

I nodded, but did not speak. What he said perchance was true, but it is also true that many small women give birth uneventfully. But a Swifte, or a boy with Swifte blood, they are generally born overlarge, and sometimes in strange directions. The waters in the womb tend to invite…swimming. I understood his fears, but did not know how right he was to be worried. Birth is a hard thing on any woman. At any rate, there was nothing I could say. In my experience as a midwifery—though midwife I am not, only an occasional helper when a birth goes very hard—he mayhap spoke true.

The rhythm of the oars in the water and the silence that swelled after his last words had put me into a dreamy state. So much so, that his next words almost choked me, and I found myself so startled that my movements rocked our little boat.

"Annette does blame you" was all that he said. And then he turned his face as though something fascinating held his attention on the water.

"Fisher" I began calmly, "what can you mean?"

It was a few moments before he responded,

moments that made me tense. But finally he shrugged, as though surrendering.

"What I mean is exactly as I have said. She blamed you for the miscarriage. Says you perhaps put a curse on her." He shrugged again and continued rowing, but the rhythm was no longer soothing, but instead I felt jostled by every dip of the waves.

"But that's ridiculous! Preposterous!" I began, but he silenced me with a look and a little spray of lake water.

"Hush, Niss. Of course it is nonsense. But Annette is unhinged. You must remember, she lost a child. She told a few of the other women…"

"A few of the other women!" I had yelled. I was seething with anger at this stupid virago who would sully my name with her own disappointments.

"Peace, sister. She did make a scene of herself. But the women in the village knew better. You've delivered enough healthy children and nursed a fair number of people from death's door. And I spoke for you, didn't I?"

I had given him a small smile then, but still grumbled. "Once a thing's said, it's given life, Fisher. The women will not forget that they have heard such said of me. Remember, it is distrust like this that lost us our mother."

Fisher did not reply. I knew we felt very differently about mother, a woman we hardly remembered and had chosen to believe different things of. In fact, I doubt he was listening to me at all, so lost was he in his own torment. "Sure, sure, Nissa, but I must have you hear me." His countenance was twisted in fear, so much so, that I grew as cold as though I had been plunged into the lake.

"What is it, Fisher?"

He had all but stopped rowing. The boat floated in the water and the silence was so loud that I almost laughed to break it.

"Oh, Niss. I...was thinking of her dying you see. And the baby too. I prepared some evening primrose and pennyroyal to release the baby from her womb. I knew, you see, I knew that it would kill her if she tried to birth it. I was sore afraid, Nissa..."

His face had not been so since our mother had left. So full of agony that it broke shards of glassy tears from my eyes.

"But you didn't do it, Fisher. I know you didn't." I'd said.

"How do you know?" he'd demanded, his voice soft.

"Because you're too good." I'd answered.

"You're right. I didn't. But, I thought about it. And what if some of the oil from the herbs were still on my hands...?"

I assured him it would take much more than oil to have worked and he was relieved. We were both silent for the rest of the journey back, and even after, when we carried off our new stores and provisions from the little boat. It was not until he turned to leave that he turned back around to grasp my hands tightly, and left me with the farewell of our childhood.

"I'll be looking at the sky." he said

"I'll be watching in the waves." I replied.

That was nearly a week ago. I've spent my time

since then wandering the woods, canning the last fruits and vegetables from the garden, preparing mixtures of herbs and elixirs for the ailments I know I shall face in the coming winter months.

But this problem with Annette troubles me. I shall have to speak with Da and Phineas, gather their thoughts with my own.

And, Mr. Alarence Attwater. Do not think my mind has strayed far from him. Instead, I find myself wondering about him as I tramp through the woods, or when I sit companionably with Tabby at night. I wonder what his hands—his glorious hands—would feel like holding my own, or if the slopes and bracken of the island would give him as much happiness as they do me. I wonder what sort of man he is, and when the world will decide it is time for us to truly find one another.

When will he come for me? When will we fall in love? Has it already happened? How will I know?

6

NIBBLE-NABBLE
to do something haphazardly, or bit by bit

She was peering over her wine glass watching him read. Dane was chewing on his lower lip, and alternately squinting his eyes and then widening them —and smiling. Again, she held back the new words from the pages she'd given him, but she was certain that the words were the farthest thing from his mind at the moment.

She wished that the thoughts she was having about the bitten lip and those blue eyes would flee far from her mind as well.

Suddenly, his eyes met hers and she could have sworn they twinkled. She felt the heat in her cheeks, embarrassed to have been caught staring, but she did not take her eyes away. But whatever was about to be said or communicated in that glance was lost when Jinks yowled an undignified and unholy cat sound that scared them both—and the moment was over.

She stood up to drop a few pieces of newly purchased kibble into the cat's bowl, and Dane's voice followed behind her.

"Wow. Just…wow. This is page-turning stuff. A real historical mystery, right here in Traverston."

"I know." she replied, her voice somehow distant in the clatter of cat food hitting the porcelain. Petra straightened and tucked an escaped tendril behind her ear. She looked down and assessed herself. Black jeans, white T-shirt and her crazy long hair hanging in waves with no real polish or organization. She'd spent the whole day writing and translating, stopping only for a bottle of root beer, a few spoonfuls of hummus and a soft apple. She assessed the now rumpled outfit she was wearing, only applying an extra dusting of face powder and a smear of lipstick before his confident knock had sounded on the door. And now she saw the burgundy bloom of a wine stain on her shirt and her shoulders sagged. *What was she doing?*

Still, there was a part of her that was proud. Or that was glad that all this was happening. Something to get her to care a little bit. Not in the way that she had used to care about her appearance, or the way she'd obsessed about the colors and makeup that were used for her book-jacket portraits. But a step away from forgetting to shower and 3 day old tee-shirts and dirty hair. She didn't know what she was doing, but like the therapist said, that was ok. She was ok, and she looked ok, and none of it mattered anyway because how she felt was more important than how she looked.

But, even with the wine stain, she knew she looked pretty good.

For his part, Dane did not seem to have noticed the stain or her hair or any of the things she was worried about. He continued talking excitedly, turning the pages over in his hands as though there were stray words he might have missed somewhere.

"…and so, there ought to be records. Because, as I said, you wrote here that the gentleman came from…" He shuffled the papers back a few pages and squinted. "Ah, yes. He came from 'The East' wherever exactly that is. There's a lot east from Traverston, even just the more eastern parts of Michigan…but I really don't think…"

"I'm sorry?" Petra sat back down, shaking her head. "I'm sorry, but I haven't heard a word. What records? What are you talking about?"

Dane rolled his eyes and exhaled, blowing his breath upward so that it disturbed the hair over his forehead. "The mysterious Alarence Attwater, our witch's soulmate…"

"Our witch? I never said she was a witch…"

Dane waved away her words. "Nerissa the Good Witch's true love, Alarence Attwater. She says he comes from the east. As you translate, she might reveal more about where he came from, and we could probably find records for him, back in the place he was born. A lot of the eastern United States kept better records, better than out here in the forest, anyway."

Dane was so excited, his smile so wide, that Petra had to grin as well.

"That is, if she wasn't making him up." Petra wished that she could call the words back as soon as they had fled her lips, so immediate was Dane's frown.

"Why would she invent him? It's a diary, not a work of fiction." He was still frowning, but his face had grown a little pinker with conviction.

"I don't know" she shrugged, "It's all a bit...mad. Loony. Crazy-cooky stuff, isn't it? I mean the woman has a lively voice, but everything is a bit far-fetched, no? Love at first sight, magical connections, healing powers, fairytale islands and mer-people?"

He was staring back at the pages, his equanimity restored. "You think too much, Pet. It's a whomping good story, real or imagined. And I happen to believe it. Doubt on your own time, thank you very much."

Petra laughed at his tone, and sat down again at the table. She wondered, not for the first time, why the diary being real was important. Why Nerissa's story was so vital to him. And so she asked him.

Swirling his wine glass, he looked at the wall opposite him, an odd expression playing upon his features. She thought for a moment that he would not answer, and then realized that he often took longer to compile his thoughts. She was beginning to identify his habits and quirks—a dangerous thing, getting close to someone—but still she blushed, and waited. He tilted his head to the side, finally, and cleared his throat to answer.

"My mother was an incredible woman. You see... my father died diving in Travers' Bay. He was looking for proof of the legend—-and everyone thought he was, how did you so succinctly put it? Loony. But my mother was just as crazy. 'Island Fever' she called it" Dane recalled with a smile. "But I was like you. Especially after...after a time when all magic seemed to disappear in my life. A...tragedy. But anyway, I thought it was all hogwash. And so after high school, I went to university out of state, and traveled the world, trying to leave the past in the past, letting sleeping legends lie."

"So why the change of heart?" Petra was leaning so far over the little kitchen bistro table she was practically on Dane's lap. Straightening her spine, she looked down at her hands, trying to find something worth studying there, instead of holding the intensity of his eyes, and the rising color in his face.

"I wish I could say I changed when my old man drowned, but I didn't. I came back for the funeral and hoped we were burying all of his barking ideas with him. But, instead the change began right before I took off for Tokyo, just after the funeral, when the chest surfaced."

Petra sat forward again, transfixed. She brought the glass to her mouth but did not drink, and Dane continued, his mind no longer in the room, but instead in the past, in a moment that played before his eyes.

"Mom was certain that Dad had shaken it loose, and then had run out of air before he could make it back to the surface. His last message to her—his final proof."

He paused and topped off his glass, and then settled back into his recollection.

"When they auctioned the items from inside the chest, every piece that went to another collector seemed to give my mother physical pain. But she knew she could only pick one item to bid on, and she wanted the book, was sure it had the answers. And then…she won it. In the end, I'd given her some of my own money to secure it, but, a funny thing happened."

"What?" Petra asked, her voice breathy, her body hinged hungrily forward again.

"Well, she didn't read it. I mean, she didn't even try. Said the book was for me. My mom, Love, said my Dad had died without any proofs. He had died with only his faith in the legend, and she was happy to do the same. She passed the book to me, and when she died last year, she was pleased to see that I had fully caught 'Island Fever' by then. But all of the source materials are obscure. Hearsay and reports from other towns in the area, or visitors that passed through Travers Town, now Traverston—nothing exists that is a first hand account by an Islander…"

"Except this Swifte journal." Petra finished. "So, because nothing contradicts the legends—especially nothing from her diary, you consider it a kind of proof."

"It's good enough for me." He replied, the twinkle returned to his lake-blue eyes, the familiar grin pulling his mouth in the corners.

"I can see that. Were there any other telling items in the chest that surfaced? Anything that might have been hers or might add to the evidence?"

Dane thought a moment, and actually scratched his chin, his eyes looking upward as though the answer was written somewhere above him.

"I don't remember exactly. We could chase down the items. I'm sure you already know the whole auction was very hushed, the historical society needed the money and didn't want the state government sniffing around too much. I think there was a glass bottle, and a garment of some kind that was in very poor shape. There might have been a piece of jewelry? Silver or something. We could look into it."

Petra sighed, and impulsively raised her glass for an impromptu toast.

"Well, then I will put all of my reservations aside for now, and believe utterly all that Ms. Swifte writes in her journal. So, here's to impossible legends and impracticable dreams. To the infeasible, inconceivable, preposterous, fairy-tale past that we will be pleased to inhabit while I translate these pages."

Dane winked, gave a "hear, hear" and clinked his glass to hers, adding, "To Nerissa and Alarence, who were in love from the first moment."

And long after Dane left, practically begging to be allowed to come back earlier the next day as the antique shop wasn't open Mondays, Petra wondered.

She wondered as she wiped the lipstick from the top of her wine glass if perhaps he had read her thoughts when he raised his glass. If maybe when he'd said the names "Nerissa and Alarence", that he'd known she was thinking, "Petra and Dane". She swallowed, hard, thinking about Evan and how close was too close, how much hope for something was dangerous.

And then the glass slipped from her fingers. But strangely, when it hit the tile, it did not break.

7
NATTER:
to talk incessantly

Again, she couldn't sleep. Her mind was buzzing over the possibilities to come. Some hinted at in the diary, but also by Dane's ideas on sleuthing about to locate the real Alarence Attwater. They needed to give authenticity for the events written of in the diary. Dane didn't need further evidence, but if this was to be a scholarly endeavor, others certainly would.

Added to that was the memory of Dane's eyes, all blue sky and opportunity, and she couldn't have slept if she'd tried. He made her feel warm all over, like a memory of a time that never existed, a comforting blanket that tucked her in right to her chin and made the rest of the world disappear. Safe, but the child's version of safe where all is quiet and calm and good and there are no terrors or worries lurking under beds or in the future. She could still see the seams where she had broken herself into pieces with tragedy, but when she was with him the stitches between those pieces was less visible. But, as kind and interested as he was about their shared project—he'd given no signs of feeling anything more. He was friendly without being overly flirtatious. Solicitous without being demonstrative. A perfect gentleman. And even if her feelings were different than his, she was glad of the blooming friendship. It filled her up, somehow.

Her tragedies. Her mind swam back to the beginning and found only the murky white fog that had been there as long as she could remember. Toby. But only shards of him. Toby's smile, and the sound of his voice, memories of books under blankets and thunderstorms where she crept into his bed and slept all night, and he didn't even mention it the next day. She remembered him tying her shoelaces and a splinter he had gotten in his foot that he had very bravely pulled out with Dad's tweezers and didn't cry once. But there were holes everywhere else. The memories were only patchy vignettes. And of her mother, she remembered nothing. Just severe brown hair and the sound of a glass on the counter. That's all. 'Selective' her childhood grief counselor had said to her father when he didn't know Petra was listening. Petra had selected the memories to keep, he had said. And she had discarded the others, unhooked the weaker chains from her suit of armor. She had almost heard the counselor shrug his shoulders. She'd never be fully over the tragedy until she accepted what happened he'd said. But, Toby and Mom were dead, squealing breaks, the cacophony of a crash and crunch, all gone. What more did she need to dig up?

Maybe it was because her own past was so shadowy and murky that she threw herself so headlong into the parts of her past that she *did* remember. She tortured herself with the things that had gone wrong, or ran a constant picture show in her mind of nights she didn't want to forget. Anything to blot out the fog of that long ago part of herself. Anything to block the unknown shadowy future.

The future. She thought again of Dane, without meaning to. It had been a long time since she really considered possibilities. Not since Evan. But she wasn't sure that Evan counted. Not after what had happened. Not after all those plans had gone so terribly awry. She shuddered, she wouldn't put words to those memories, even in her mind. The images, dear God, the images of that day were too much. She pressed her eyelids together, hard, and prayed that she might find something within her that was even a little bit tired. Sleep suddenly seemed like the safest idea.

Petra shook her head, sleep wouldn't come. She gave her cheek a little smack. Enough. Focus, she told herself. Looking over her notes, the ones she'd kept back from Dane, Petra traced the letters from the new words she'd captured like fireflies in a jar. The movement and the whorls of the letters calmed her, her own private meditation and prayer. She enjoyed the mystery of a new word. Where did it come from? Why did it leave the language? What meaning did it have that was more essential, more fitting, than any number of synonyms one might have used?

The first of the new words from today's entry was **Evening Penny,** which, was not truly a new word, but instead a combination of English words. But, Petra hadn't seen them ever combined thus, and so she inked them into her notes with alacrity. Evening Penny was the abortifacient mixture of Evening Primrose and Pennyroyal. Such a combination would not only be potent, but correct amounts would be difficult to determine. Secondly, the word **Gelteez**, which was the way Nerissa described Alarence's eyes. The only succinct English word Petra could think of had been hazel, but it didn't do them justice. The color that had flashed into Petra's mind as she read the word was a glorious mixture of emerald and gold, with hints of earth—like a forest at daybreak—but hazel would have to do.

She sighed and pulled her mind away from the experience of now, and opened the cover of the purple and blue hued book, slowly taking up residence in the mind and life of Nerissa Swifte.

Diary Of Nerissa Swifte

It is fully winter now, and I must admit it crept in on tip-toe, slinking so silently in that I hardly knew it had taken over the island until it was all about me. One day it was crisp fall with the crunch of leaves underfoot and the smell of the first golden death of the year. The scent of wilted flowers and overripe apples fallen to the ground. It seemed that just the next morning, I awoke in my snug cottage to frosted glass drooping from tree branches and a coating of pure white sugar on the ground. But I knew that the appearance of the snow was all that was sweet. I could feel already that it would be a hard winter. Not only for the island, but for Travers Town as well. And I was not wrong.

For the past fortnight I have barely had occasion to rest at my own hearth, much less the leisure to write in my book of days, or to read for pleasure. Da had sent Phineas over with a new stack of books he had ordered all the way from a bookseller in Boston. Many of the tomes are rare and I pale to even imagine their great expense. And to think I have not so much as lifted the covers! Milton, Sidney, Marlowe and Johnson, all of which, will soon become my friends and my teachers, if ever my bustling about should allow me some repose. The greatest surprise came strangely. It arrived by delivery whilst I was away tending to a family with two dying children. The lambs always seem to be taken first. I believe it grows too cold too rapidly for little hearts and tiny lungs. How I hate to see them suffer. But, I suppose it is better that I am there to ease it, than to guard myself from the black truth of Death. He walks always among us. I, more than most, recognize his steps as they draw near, though his footfalls have never filled me with trepidation.

But, the surprise! The lake seemed to freeze solid in but a moment, quickly followed by the first sled to attempt the crossing between mainland and island. The mainlanders have little use for us after the winter steals into the branches and ices the lake like a glaze on a cake. That is, unless they need me, or my Da, or my brothers for their skills in shipbuilding and woodwork, though, that is less often, More of the time it is those on the island that desire supplies or news—or more importantly confirmation that they are not trapped through the cold, harsh northern winter.

After this first ice run from Travers Town—what would you suppose I came home to find? None other than a first edition of *The Life and Surprizing Adventures of Robinson Crusoe of York, Mariner* by Mr. Daniel Defoe. As if Mr. Attwater knew that I had coveted a

copy for my own, though he could not have known—
for we barely spoke to one another, at least not in
words. Inscribed on the flyleaf was the message:

*To my very own Friday, who deliver'd me most
expediently from my own Isle of Despair, and then
promptly disappeared, back across the waves, intent on
other adventures.*

Yours, faithfully, and with much gratitude,
— A. Attwater

A pretty note. Most charming and on the very
border of presumptuous. Which is no bother to me,
as I adore presumption and flirtation in a man. I
would have been more impressed to find Mr.
Attwater awaiting me in my cottage in lieu of the
book—as precious as it is—but I suppose that is
because I am an incorrigible scandal.

I did pause in my writing some few minutes, just
now, to read back over the inscription and to ponder
on the heart and hand that wrote it. It must be a
romance between souls to begin with a story, I think.
Even if it is the story of Robinson Crusoe. Which,
though adventurous and engrossing, could only really
be described as thoroughly unromantic.

Unromantic. A word that reminds me of the
dreadful Annette, my brother's wife. One face that I
had not set eyes on in this recent flurry of activity
that has caught me in a whirlwind was that of Fisher.
It was not since we were children, and we were both
ill with pneumonia that I had gone so long without

his presence. And even then, we had been kept in separate rooms as we ailed, but only began recovering when we were reunited. Fisher is a forthright and impulsive man, but I feel sometimes that Annette has a spell on him—and somehow she is more witch than I. He seems hunted. As though he keeps himself wary, speaking to me in whispers and keeping Annette and I apart.

This is not his way.

Fisher's heart is an open one, his tongue always too quick for his thoughts, his speech running on ahead on foolhardy legs. But, no longer. He is not the same wild brother I knew.

When Phineas and Da last came to the cottage, Da shooed away my misgivings, chasing them under the table and into hiding under my bed. But, before they took their final leave, Phineas found a moment to take me aside and add his concerns to my own.

I will admit that as heartbroken as I was to find Fisher a different man, and to hear that my younger brother shared these worries, these were nothing to the wretchedness that lay in wait for me.

Yesterday, I had been fetched to bide with Horace Rollingbrook at his sickbed. It was clear from the early morning when they came for me that there was naught I could do. Horace was not over old, but he had always been a weak man, a sickly man. He'd had a full life, with a wife and children and a business crafting oars and poles so straight and even that they slice through the water like knives. I knew that Death, my oftentimes companion—or perhaps I am sometimes his—was coming.

So when Phineas showed up at the Rollingbrook's door, I knew that his own concerns must be grave indeed. Phineas shies from death. He does not understand it, fears the darkness of beyond. For him to come to the door of one who waits for death was serious indeed.

He came to me and bade me leave the dying man's side for a moment so that we might speak. At first, I had been surprised to see him, and then annoyed to be taken from my work. But something in the fear of my brother's expression pulled me away. I will not recount the reaction of Mrs. Rollingbrook, who was angry that I should leave—to say the least.

I followed him outside, where he looked over both shoulders, anxiously, before grabbing me by the collar of my coat.

"Nissa, Fisher is missing."

His voice was urgent, but it held no cause for me to be frightened. Instead, I found myself intrigued.

"Missing?" I confirmed, and Phineas swallowed, looked around again and leaned in closer, his voice a whisper.

"He is not to be found at home, nor at work near the docks, nor at the neighbors. He is not in the pub, nor has he been seen in any of the island shops."

Phineas' eyes looked into mine, and I smiled. Phin is slighter and more slender than Da or Fisher, but he is a Swifte through and through. His black eyes have the same endless depth and hold the same secrets. Secrets that I was meant to read by looking into them. A Swifte cannot break a confidence, and I could see that was what Phineas was avoiding. He had been told not to tell anyone where Fisher was, and so instead, he was telling me where Fisher wasn't.

"Has there been trouble then?" I whispered, already knowing the answer.

"I can't begin." He replied. I had nodded, understanding that this was also part of the secret he wasn't to repeat, but also understanding what he wanted of me.

"I will go. Mr. Rollingbrooke will be dead within the hour. I will tell them I have sent you for Father Lemorale at St. Augustine's. When you return, we will go together."

Phineas nodded and walked toward the church. Some on the island would find it strange that I should encourage the visit of a Catholic Priest. The Swifte's do not practice the religion of the One God, after all, but we have always taken care to be on good terms with the priest at St. Augustine's. The priest is a man of learning, even if the truths he learns are not the same as our own. Da says bodies don't have to hold the same beliefs to learn from one another, and so I have ever showed respect to whomever serves the Christian God on the island.

In a quarter of an hour, Phin returned and Father Lemorale was in time to make sure Mr. Rollingbrooke was shriven. Though the good father respects my Da, I know in my heart he thinks me unnatural. A godless creature that sees Death, who too easily walks side by side with him, and ushers the dying down their final path with nimble fingers. And he is right. I would not cheat Death, but not because I am wicked. At least not murderously so. No, I partner with Death as I do with life—one cannot shirk destiny.

We left as the man breathed his last, and I followed Phineas to the wood, taking no notice of the path. Our island is not a large one, but the trees that border my cottage are thick and dark, and most do not attempt to wander them because there is no real path. When we were small, Fisher was wont to refer to them as The Kingdom of Darkness, where we were of course, the King and Queen. Unlike most things that become less impressive as one grows older, the forest still fills me with awe and wonder. As isolated as the island already is, the cottage in the wood is another thing entirely. It is a secret world, and though many follow the one true path—to my cottage—it is never a task for the light of heart or endured for the sake of vanity or frivolity. I am no gypsy witch with scrying glass and love potions and hexes for sale. I am the Swifte of Traversint, with the power of the island. If it is spells you want, better to track down Magda, The Lady of the Trees. She has many names, one of which she gave herself, but she is old, and powerful, and if they pay, she cares not what silly things people want her magic for.

The woods are mine now. That is how I think of them, though in truth, they belong to no one. It was here then, deep, deep, into the darkest part of the forest that I followed Phin. Past fragrant pine and sharp cedar, the crunch of fallen leaves and the whisper of wind walking in step alongside of us. I might have walked behind Phin, but I knew from the moment we stepped into the dark precisely where we were headed.

At the base of a large Apple Birch, much larger than an Apple Birch should be, we stopped and I spoke.

"How long have you been missing?" I asked, and the tree answered.

Or, rather a voice from some ways up the tree answered, "Two days."

"Does Annette know?" Though I did not look up to see his expression I could hear the frown in his reply.

"No, I told her nothing."

"Why are we here then?" I looked to Phineas, whose eyes were trained to the forest floor. A second later a thud sounded next to me and my eyes found the quiet glow of the forest, just enough to see Fisher's features, masking something I could not penetrate.

"I know not what else to do, Nissa. I went first to your cabin straightaway, but finding you gone, I could only think to come here."

I knew why he had done so, though for anyone whose eyes might trespass this book, it would not be so clear. If I'd heard either of my brothers had gone missing I would come first to this very spot to find them, or if I wanted to vanish myself this is the place I would come to.

The tree is ours. When we were very small, and Phineas hardly weaned, our mother had given us three seedlings. Three, rare Apple Birch trees that we planted in one spot. The seedlings fused, growing into a thick, twisted, braided rope of a white tree. She said the Apple Birch tree was white so that a man's story might be written on it. And so the trees became our stories, our lives, and they would be connected, twisted and sealed together by fate and time. As children we would bring ink and write on the white bark—wishes and secrets and memories. And so it grew, as did we along with it. But those stories we wrote on the tree, those secrets we shared, they seemed a magic tonic, and the tree grew rapidly, more rapidly than even an Apple Birch should. And grew hearty and strong, covered in our memories, but it has never borne fruit.

Standing beneath the white tree, its branches frosted with ice and weighed down slightly by a dusting of snow, I had looked at one brother and then the other. One, avoiding my eyes entirely, the other so locked onto my expression that I felt as I was being hunted.

"Why am I here, Fish? Why have you been hiding? Why did you swear Phineas to secrecy? I have no time for games."

Fisher nodded, and cleared his throat, and then violently grabbed my shoulders.

"Nissa, you must understand. Annette...remains unhinged. I...I will not lie with her. For the reason we spoke of...before." He looked sidelong at Phineas who did not smile or speak any words in jest as he normally would with such information.

"She has gone wild. She claims you have bewitched me from her bed. She...has kept a tally of which children you have saved in town, and those whom you were not able. She has told mothers not to call on you and young wives not to trust you if they become unwell."

"Why? What would I do?" I had asked, naïvely. My voice sounded high, even shrill to my ears. Fisher's eyes left mine, just as Phin's had.

"She says you will take their lives and bewitch their men to yourself. As you did with Searc."

"Do not speak his name." I had said quietly. I took

Searc from no one, as he belonged to no one, and I have not the heart to relive the memories of him. Of us. Another time, little book, another time.

Fisher shrugged, regret written in the lines of his forehead. "I am sorry, I said it only because others are saying it. Remembering it."

I ignored him. "Ravings, no one would believe such blather."

Phineas spoke, his voice quiet. "Mina Attbridge does. Her youngest died yesterday."

"Well, that is proof! I'd never seen the child. I had not known that they had illness at their house."

Phin and Fish exchanged a look and I understood. It would be blamed on me, regardless. If I had treated the child, and he died, it was a curse. If I had never been called to the child, and the child died, it was still my doing. I am a witch, after all. Folks do not care how magic works, as long as it works in their favor.

I felt my breathing grow quicker, my eyebrows rise on my head, and I stuck a finger right in Fisher's face. "I told you, Fisher! I warned you that her words would fester and rot in the minds of the women…"

Fisher grabbed my shoulders tighter and squeezed.

"You were right, and I am sorry, but I know not what to do. I…I never imagined she would say such things…Annette is…"

I didn't let him finish. I snapped my fingers in his face and cut his speech short. I am tired of hearing about Annette, I can hardly bear to hear of virtues that he imagines her to possess, especially as she drags me and my healing through the mud.

Phin stepped toward us. "Not all on the island or

on the mainland care about such lies. I have watched, Niss, as you scurry from house to house. Many here are glad of your skills, have seen firsthand your selflessness, and know better than to listen to a Sandling."

Annette had been a Sandling. A distant member of a prosperous farming family in a village some 20 miles down the coast of Travers Town. The family was not known for their kindness, but instead for their ruthlessness and cruelty to the tenants on their land. Fisher had seen her creamy skin and delicate bones, and believed her to be different.

For once, Fisher did not defend Annette's family. Instead, he hung his head. My darling, fool brother, loved her deeply. Still. Even though he was livid at her implications of incest and blatant claims of my nefarious deeds. I have never known the bitter taste of hate, not once, though I have been maligned before. But my disgust of her and her lies sat heavy on my tongue and gagged me as it slid down my throat and into my soul, where the hatred blackened.

He shrugged again. "I had to get away. I needed to think and had thought to do so alone." He gave Phineas a dirty look. "I knew not...I still know not what to do."

"He told me naught, Fisher. I don't need Phin's words to tell me where to find you." I reached out for him, but he shrank back from my touch, an action that surprised and pained me.

I then did something I never thought I would or could do. I lied to my heart. To my other half. To my twin. For like Fisher, I knew not what to do.

I said to him, "Go home. Be a proper husband to

your wife. I see healthy sons in your future with glossy black hair and midnight eyes."

"Truly?" He'd asked, his own black eyes suddenly shining.

"Yes, truly." And then I left them both, offering only the farewell of our childhood.

"I'll be looking to the sky, I'll be watching in the waves."

And then it was all I could do not to run like a madwoman back to this cottage and to this book.

Again like Fisher, I knew not what else to do except to quiet my mind and commit to this little blue book all the chaos that spins in my head and burns in my chest.

As I wrote before, I knew it would be a difficult winter—but I did not expect one such as this. My mind is full of Fisher and Annette and the continued goodwill of the people on Traversint—something I did not think to ever lose.

And my heart—it pulls strangely to the mainland and Mr. Attwater.

Though I do not like to do it, I will seek out Magda, the Lady of the Trees, and confer with her. Her magic is older than mine and she knows much, even if she will not share it.

But first, the Shallows family has sick children and Mrs. Waverly is ill in town. I must continue on, even if Annette would ruin me. I have a duty that I must fulfill, a skill that must be used and shared.

8

FARDEL:
a burden

Petra yawned and flexed her fingers, knuckles popping in a succession of loud snaps that rang discordantly in the pre-dawn lit study. She didn't need to look at the clock, she knew she'd been up for too long, the pinky grey light in the windows and the crick in her neck told her so.

She needed sleep. While not difficult, decoding the diary was time consuming. More so for Petra, because she not only decoded the words as they were written, but also strove to present the message so that it would flow in a more modern sounding rhythm. Many times she caught herself, pen poised, but not writing. Instead, reading and re-reading a line or an exchange of conversation. The code had become native to her, and she could read the words without having to think of the translation. Nerissa Swifte seemed so… vibrantly alive. So present and real, as though Petra could reach her fingers through the ink on the page and hold onto her hand on the other side, hundreds of years ago. She ran a gloved hand over the writing in the journal, almost looking for a crack to slip her fingers through, and then over her own, precise handwriting and wondered if she could possibly do the diary justice. Would others, upon reading the transcription, be as transported as Petra was? Would the vividness of Nerissa's life flash and sear itself into their minds? It was part of the reason she remained aloof when faced with Dane's excitement. It felt so real for her, and so she feared she really was living in the past, that a piece of her hovered on the frayed edges of the memories written in the purple book. That it was not only words she was collecting, but pieces of Nerissa's soul, then using them to fill the blank spaces of her own with them.

She ran her fingers through her oily hair and stretched. Standing up, she bent over to organize her notes and the diary on the table, and took off her cotton glove. With an audible sigh, she shut the door of the library, both to shut herself off from the story that lingered in the air of the room, and to dissuade Jinks from swatting at the papers on the table. Delirious, she thought to herself. Petra thought she must be going a little soft in the noggin. Bewildered, irrational, and imbalanced. Unhinged—as Fisher described his wife. She shook her head again. Great, now she was quoting long-dead brothers. Hopefully anything wrong with her mind would be healed by a nice, long rest. She smiled. Yes, a good sleep and then she'd make some soup for when Dane came over. She ignored the catch in her chest when she thought of him back in her cottage, filling it with the warmth and freshness of his simply being there. He'd read over the new pages and then...go home. Her smile faltered, but she checked her disappointment. Yes, he could come and discuss books and words and the past, and then leave, just as he should. Just as she needed him to. She wasn't ready for anything further. Business, networking. Professional.

She drifted off, curled up, half under the blanket, half out, the early morning sunshine pouring in the windows, and Jinks on the pillow beside her.

But, it wasn't to be.

One eye opened, and then the other. She lifted her head groggily, wondering what had awoken her. Her head felt heavy, and buzzed with not enough rest. A knock, not overloud, but not timid either, sounded from the front door. Pulling on a robe and tying the sash lazily, she yawned all the way to the foyer and brusquely opened the door.

If Petra had been more awake, she would have probably paused to check herself in the mirror. As it was, it wouldn't have mattered anyway. The woman on the other side of the door was bizarre enough in appearance that Petra's bed-mussed hair and the pillow indentations on her face looked normal.

"Ah, it's Pebble." An oddly young voice spoke from an ancient face. Petra's eyes opened a little wider, and took in the woman before her, and for once in her life, did not have the right words to describe her. Or any words at all.

She was old. Very old. So old that she was almost child-like. A thick rope of smooth white hair was plaited expertly and fell almost to her knees. Her back had no stoop, and instead stood straight as a reed.

Her face was lined, alarmingly so, but did not disappear in folds and wrinkles. Instead it was fissured like broken glass. Her body was small and almost elven, and her ears looked as though they had a small point to the tips, just to complete the impression. She was not shriveled or puckered, but instead—weathered. Like a photograph of a striking, petite woman that had been crumpled and stuffed into a pocket and then flattened out again.

Except her eyes. They were ageless; a brilliant quicksilver as bright as a polished spoon. Those eyes looked at Petra, looked through Petra, beyond Petra, and then her head tilted to the side.

"All right, dear?"

Petra came back to herself. "Yes, quite. That is, I was sleeping. I'm sorry."

Alarm crossed the strange woman's features. "Oh, dear me! I'm so embarrassed. It's gone 11, so I didn't think I'd disturb you. I should have phoned. Yes, I am certain, I should have called. But I don't have one, you understand. And I knew Gianni didn't have one either. So I just popped on by. As one does, you understand."

She was smiling, but Petra was more confused than ever. Gianni was her father, and this woman obviously knew him, and yet, Petra had moved into this house a year ago, and her father had died just before that. And she'd never seen this woman before. Indeed, she would be difficult to miss.

"I'm sorry, but you are...?" Petra knew she should invite the little old woman in, but there was something...off. It wasn't only her unnerving appearance, it was something in her demeanor. She felt oddly familiar and yet utterly foreign.

The woman laughed, a sound like wind through dry leaves. "Yes, yes, my mistake. Margaret Garzing, but you've always called me Maggie. I'm your nearest neighbor." She pointed toward a grove of trees to the right, no house evident. "About a half mile deeper into the wood."

Not able to think of another reason to keep her from coming in, and truthfully, very curious to know more about her, Petra bade her come inside.

"Again, I must apologize for barging in. Not much of a barger, I promise you. I was taking my daily constitutional and I saw Rock Cottage and thought, 'Oh, heavens! I must look in on the little Pebble. So here I am."

Petra was grateful to be occupied with tea cups, else she would have given the strange woman a very odd look.

"I see. I didn't know Daddy had named the place." The sentence fell lamely from her lips, but it was all she could think of to say.

"Oh, he didn't dear. Roccia, Italian for 'rock' as you well know. Everyone calls it Rock Cottage, since your grandmother was a girl. Since before she was a girl, I imagine. Not sure if the family named the cottage or the cottage named the family, now that I think of it."

Petra turned around slowly, the furrows in her brow deep and immovable.

"You are mistaken. My father only moved here after I graduated high school."

Mrs. Garzing sipped the tea and pursed her lips. "Pebble, be a lamb and pass me some sugar. When you get to my age you'll understand that everything could do with a little extra sweetening." She added a few heaping spoonfuls, and then poured some straight from the sugar bowl. "Much better. Now, what was it you asked? Oh, yes. Yes, he moved back here after you graduated. The Roccia's have been here a long time, though. One of the 'original families', you understand. Of course you do. You always do."

She sipped again, contentedly, nodding her head, and repeating, "you always do" with an emphasis on a different word each time she spoke the phrase.

Petra took a seat at the table and tried to gather her thoughts, prioritizing the unusual comments and the questions they had elicited in her own mind. "Original families?" She finally asked. "Pebble? Why are you calling me that? How did you know my daddy? Why weren't you at his funeral? What'd you mean, 'move back'?" By the time she spit it all out she was almost breathless, a hundred other variations of these questions swarming, unasked on the tip of her tongue, but she bit them back and the effort was not unlike swallowing bees.

The little woman sipped, and smiled, her eyes twinkling, but made no move to answer beyond adding another spoonful of sugar to the tea, so that now it had an almost slush-like consistency. She hummed a little and her eyes looked dreamily into the little cup, as though Petra wasn't in the room at all. Finally, she cleared her throat, meeting Petra's wild eyes.

"Tut-tut. What am I thinking? You're awfully in the dark, aren't you? Well, first, *You* are Pebble. A small rock, as you know. That's you. Your father called you that in his letters. And, he was a great one for letters, and I was a great admirer of your father's—

and his work." Petra's eyes panicked, and Maggie noticed.

"Oh, that's right. You don't know about that either. Ah, Gianni was too private for his own good. Not a warm man, but a kind one, you know? Of course you know. Of course. Anyway, I wasn't at the funeral because I don't like funerals. Not the place for Maggie, you understand. If you've been to one, you've been to them all. You understand, Pebble? Of course you do. Of course you do. I *can* call you Pebble, can't I?"

Her eyes had filled with such a sudden odd pleading that Petra shrugged and nodded without even considering. Whatever.

"Another thing you'll understand when you're my age, Pebble. Funerals are for the living, and when you're as old as me, you don't need a funeral for remembering. That's all you'll do! Remember in the morning and remember in the afternoon and reminisce in the evening and then memories will send you off to sleep…"

She shivered, and suddenly, fleetingly, her ageless eyes were ancient. But, a blink later, and the impression was gone, and they shone clear once again.

Petra leaned back, taking a moment to observe. A linguist is the scientist of the literary world, after all, and she needed a moment to consider this unusual encounter. Mrs. Garzing was sitting back in her own seat, which appeared overly large with her tiny frame resting in it. It was odd. She was the size of a child, but at the same time, her personality took over the room. Indeed, Petra was taken aback to see how easily the room and all of her father's bric-a-brac seemed to gravitate around the woman, as though everything in the house was used to her presence. Everything excepting Petra.

Gnarled fingers like the twists of a vine spooned out the sugary tea mixture and she smacked her lips in delight.

"Is there…a reason you've called on me? Or just neighborly?" Petra hoped she didn't sound rude, but she truly had begun to wonder if Mrs. Garzing remembered where she was. A sharp turn of her snow-white head, and Petra perceived her mistake. Her eyes were alert and lucid. She might seem silly or confused but behind the cotton-candy words was an active and piercing mind.

"Oh, the house called me, my dear. Reminded me to mind my manners and visit the darling Pebble. So, yes to neighborly. But, also more than neighborly. We are relations, after all. My niece's cousin married a Roccia, you know. Of course you know, somewhere in that pretty head of yours, you know. Of course you do. But, we have much, I think, to discuss this autumn. Yes, indeed. Much." Her mouth smiled, but her eyes held a challenge. Petra sat up straighter and met her appraising glance.

"Yes, such as those 'Original Families' you spoke of."

Mrs. Garzing's eyes sparkled. "Yes, well, next time, Pebble. Haven't the time at the moment, I've got to make the rounds. Yes, indeed. Places to go, people to visit."

She stood up, and walked more briskly than Petra would have believed possible for such tiny bird-like legs. In a moment, she was back at the door, and Petra found that she had followed her, although she felt herself panic at the thought that she'd had none of her questions answered, none of the darkness and mystery of the woman's claims dispelled. Mrs. Garzing, Maggie, took one of Petra's hands in her own. Translucent skin showing veins like lines on a map, but the hands themselves held a kind of grace and boldness that startled Petra.

"Take yourself up to bed, child. You need rest if you're to have any fireside chats, hm?" When Petra sputtered, trying to think of something to say, some words to make the woman stay, the lined face before her widened into a smile. "I didn't mean with me, Pebble. I meant with our young suitor. Do try to talk to him about something besides the past, won't you dear?"

Hopping down the steps of the stoop, she left humming, full of sugar and tea. But the only thing brimming in the hollow of Petra's stomach was more questions. How did she know about Dane? Or about her family? What were the Original Families? What had she meant by her father having 'moved back'? Head buzzing, she doubted she'd be able to sleep.

But exhaustion won the day. So overcome was she, that she didn't reawaken until Jinks jumped onto the bed, and pawed at her body until she twisted into the position he wanted her in to promote his maximum comfort. Opening one eye, annoyed, she caught a look at her alarm clock, sending blankets and cat into the air. Petra jumped from bed to shower and into a casual dress in five minutes, and was braiding her long honey colored hair when the second knock of the day sounded on the front door.

She tripped down the stairs, two, then three at a

time and then paused, composing herself before opening the heavy oak door. Dane had one hand up as though he were about to knock, but then smiled, and lowered his hand slowly. Something in the slowness told Petra he had thought to grab her for a hug or maybe a quick kiss on the cheek greeting but hadn't made up his mind quickly enough. She returned the smile, briefly, her cheeks still burning from the shower and the run down the stairs—and now from seeing him.

She turned around, thinking to lead him into the study to show him the notes she'd written up. That was why he was here, wasn't it? She hadn't heard his tread behind her, and she turned around, finding him precisely where she had left him, hovering in the doorway, one arm extended.

"Wait there, Petra!" He called, a smile playing on his lips. "The book can wait, I think. It's only 3 o'clock, and today is too nice to sit inside. I thought maybe...we could go apple picking?" He looked like a little boy. "And I thought it might help for me to give you a little tour of the area, as you are...unfamiliar with it. So that when Nerissa mentions anything about the mainland, you have a better layout in your mind. Maybe it will help...jog your memory."

She didn't need any reason beyond he wanted her to come with him, and so by the time he'd finished his sentence she'd already shrugged on her jacket and laced up her little brown boots.

She thought to tell him about her visitor that morning, but, a feeling of caution stopped her. She wasn't certain what exactly gave her pause, but in the quiet, pleasant car ride to the orchard, she didn't let the words pass the gate of her lips. When they arrived, Petra stepped out of the sleek black car, a touch over-posh, and she drank in the raw beginnings of autumn in the air. The whole scene that greeted her was dressed in flashes of oranges and reds of the coming season. He'd opened her door and offered his hand to help her out, and Petra felt like a duchess alighting from a carriage in some Victorian Romance novel. The orchard was vast with trees standing sentinel in rows, dripping apples like rubies, row after row into the horizon. She smiled, and she knew it was the happiest she'd been in a long time. Gleeful. Joyful. Filled to brimming. She was reminded of childhood, something tugging on her memory, though she knew not what. She could see tow-headed children, carrying wooden baskets beneath the apple trees, eating as many apples as they dropped into the wicker. Sticky hands and sticky faces. Her and Toby. And then the memory ended. Just a flash, a few scenes from the cinema of her life—or her imagination—and then they were gone.

"Petra—are you ok?" Dane was a few steps ahead of her, he'd turned around, his eyebrows knitted.

"Fine. Sorry. Bit of déjà-vu, I guess. Though, I'm certain I've never been here before."

His brow furrowed, and she noticed that he avoided her eyes. "Never been to Marr's? It's the best. No other orchard in the state to match it."

The sound of his voice was pleasant, but she hardly took in the words. There was something strange in his tone, something spooky niggling at her. Memories, or shreds of them filtered into her mind like the sun filtered through the trees. Dane was still talking, and she was walking alongside him, but her mind was somewhere else. There had been a time once, it was only a few years past, but it felt like a lifetime ago. Once when she had been regarded as a kind of rockstar in the linguistic world. She had been mouthy and brash, with a devil-may-care attitude for the status quo. Her books and lectures had been popular not only for her research, but also for her singular voice that came through loudly in her writing. Who was that woman? Where had she snuck off to? She wanted so much in this moment to wear a little bit of that woman on her skin, to say something amusing or to catch Dane's eye with easy flirtation. But it was like grabbing at sunbeams, gone, gone, not able to be grasped.

That woman had vanished. Had folded herself into Evan Ripley, had been drawn to the only fire that she saw that was brighter than the one that burned inside her own ambition. And she'd scorched herself. It was unfair to say that he had burned her. She'd done it herself, she'd seen all the signs, she'd laughed off all the warnings. But she wouldn't think about that now, not with the sun shining and Dane by her side. The story of her and Evan was a mire filled with blades. Even to wade in it was to emerge with bleeding cuts.

The crisp air, the familiar way Dane touched her elbow, the way his hand almost held hers…she grabbed fast to the moment. There were enough shadows to dwell upon back at the cottage, today she was in the sun.

Petra turned her attention back fully on Dane, who fortunately hadn't seemed to notice her introspective silence.

"…and another time when we came, my parents

and I, there had been a bad harvest. Freak chills in the summer. You wouldn't believe it, but only this variety survived." He gestured to a strange apple that was white. Petra peered closer to get a better look. It was truly white, with a green stem. Dane plucked one off the tree and took a hearty bite, showing Petra the flesh within. Strange to behold, everywhere his fingers touched turned a bright, healthy red. Where his mouth had bitten, the edges of the skin had gone red also, exposing the usual yellowy-white apple flesh.

"How peculiar." Petra stepped forward and took the fruit into her own hands.

Dane nodded knowingly. "That it is. They only grow here, at Marr's. Something in the soil, or the fresh water. Put Marr's on the map, they did. And they're the very devil to transport. They only stay white until they're touched. Something about a chemical or some such on human skin, though picking with gloves doesn't seem to help either. But they're hardy."

"What are they called?" Petra was turning the apple around in her hands, watching with fascination as the white skin melted to red with her touch.

"Blood Birch." Dane said, smiling.

"Rather gruesome name." The corners of Petra's mouth turned down, a thought drifting into her mind.

"What is it?" Dane had noticed her expression and had taken the apple out of her hands so that he could take another bite.

"Well, I thought the apple was familiar somehow, but now I'm wondering if it isn't from something I read in Nerissa's diary…"

Dane laughed, and then apologized, waving her on to continue. Petra made a face and then spoke. "You haven't read it yet, but Nerissa and her brothers have a special spot in the forest, where they planted three twined Apple Birch trees—which is not a tree I've ever heard of. Just a detail that caught my attention, I suppose, from reading the words, the birch thing popped into my mind. I've probably been too long indoors is all." Petra felt her cheeks pink with embarrassment.

They were both filling their baskets now, reaching up, admiring the vibrancy or striations on an apple before twisting it off and placing it in the baskets. Dane was thoughtful for a moment. Pensive, almost brooding. He bit his lip and answered the thoughts she hadn't given voice to.

"That seems to happen, doesn't it? My mother read to me so much as a child, that sometimes I puzzle over which memories are my own, and which are simply stories that I read, that I co-opted into being my own."

Petra tilted her head and smiled. A real smile, not the guarded ones she usually donned.

"Perhaps it doesn't matter. Stories become a part of you. Like Peter Pan and his shadow, the tales and the past have a way of waiting to be stitched on."

They both grinned, and Petra felt a lightness in her chest. The past had always been a place she knew she should escape from. A dusty, must-filled place of black and white. But with Dane, it filled with color, as it did inside her head, and she felt as though they shared the past, the stories, the mysteries, that lay behind. She didn't have to be ashamed to dwell comfortably there.

"That reminds me", Dane said as they walked between the trees, "I did a little digging downtown and I found our friend, Samuel Proper. Not too much to go on, I'm afraid, but he did exist, and he did have a general store and a wife named Margaret."

"But, that's wonderful!" Petra exclaimed, the possibilities of authentication popping into her head, the same rush she had felt for research, back when she was that other woman, that bolder Petra. He spoke for some minutes about the quality of the records and the way he had tracked them down, and then the wind changed.

The afternoon had grown colder, but their conversation had not cooled. They spoke of foreign cities and University, their parents, well, her Dad and his parents, then books and music. Petra could almost see the woman she'd been before, glimmers of her anyway. Boisterous and confident, until, without thinking, she brought Mrs. Garzing into the conversation.

She had almost forgotten the lady's visit. Had let slip her mind that she had decided not to bring her up with Dane. She had almost, in fact, convinced herself that the whole thing had been a strange dream. But the conversation had turned to Traverston, and she'd remembered the Original Families, and with them, Mrs. Garzing.

"Do you know anything about the "Original Families"? I had a rather strange visit from my neighbor, Mrs. Margaret Garzing? Do you know her?"

Dane's smile fell, and he began studying the branch before him with forced concentration. When he did respond, with a weak shake of the head, Petra continued speaking.

"You do know her? She said she's always lived here…"

Her words trailed off, as Dane's features had grown harder.

"Dane?"

"Hmm?" He replied, his eyes not meeting hers.

"Do you know her? Have I said something wrong?"

He sighed audibly and closed his eyes. "Yes. Everyone knows Crazy Maggie."

Petra bristled. She didn't like how eccentric old women always got labeled as crazy. She always thought it seemed very Salem for people to immediately label people who didn't fit norms as 'crazy'. Besides, at the rate she was going she could be "Crazy Petra" one day in the future.

"Oh, well, she seemed a little odd, but nice." Petra spoke quietly, pushing down her reaction to his changing mood.

Dane nodded, but did not meet her eyes. He muttered something about pumpkins and wandered off in another direction, handing both baskets to Petra. She stood for a moment, feeling foolish, before walking to the cash register housed within a big, red barn that had "Marr's" painted in broad white letters above the opened doors.

An older woman smiled at her from the back of the barn and called out that she'd be with her in a minute before disappearing through a doorway. Petra approached the counter, confused, because there was already somebody there to assist her.

The man at the register was about Petra's age with gold hair, and clear open features. His eyes were a soft velvet brown and his smile was infectious. She found herself beaming for no other reason than he was doing the same.

"Hello, there! You're back!" His eyes smiled too, and though he could have as easily been twelve as he was thirty, the lines from grinning were already marking his features.

"I don't think we've ever met." Petra replied, wondering if his statement was a come-on. "I haven't lived here too long, and I keep mostly to myself, so I know I haven't been here."

The man continued to smile, but he didn't move to ring her up. They stared at each other, and Petra looked beyond his grin and noticed his broad chest and handsome boyish features, though they were different than Dane's. He was country cream and sunshine and his hair was the golden red of the apples in the basket. He had tilted his chin up, and seemed to be considering, when he suddenly slapped a hand on the wooden counter and flashed white teeth at her gleefully.

"Sometimes I get confused, but I know I'm not mistaken. You're Pebble! Pebble Roccia. I knew I remembered! Though, Jesus, it's been…shit. 25 years? Same hair though—and same eyes!"

"I'm sorry, you must be mistaken. I mean, that's me, Petra Roccia, but I only moved here last year after my father…"

And for the second time that day, someone spoke the same words. "Moved back here, you mean. We… we used to play together. You, me, Tobias, Daner…? We were inseparable. My mom used to watch us, while your parents were…busy?"

As he spoke, Petra had flashes in her mind. A little tow-headed boy pouring sand on her head, playing chase with Toby.

Toby. Even thinking his name still hurt.

"I'm sorry, like I said, I think you are mistaken. I don't recall…"

His face fell for the smallest moment, and then was shining again. "Ah, well, let me re-introduce myself, Thomas. Thomas Marr."

She reached to shake his hand, but he was walking away. "Sorry, gotta run out to the orchard. My mom will help you check out. It was great to see you again, Petra. I will definitely see you around!" He was smiling, big and bright and the light of the afternoon sun seemed to swallow him up when he stepped outside.

Petra heard footsteps from the back of the store, and turned her head to see the same older woman she had first seen when she walked in.

"Sorry to have kept you waiting." The woman said, and Petra recognized the smile. It was the same as her son's.

"No problem, I was kept entertained." Petra waved away the apology, and the woman smiled again, though a little oddly this time.

"Oh, well, good. Is this your first time at the orchard?"

Petra laughed a little, and when the woman gave her another strange look, Petra answered. "I thought so, but I am not too sure anymore."

The woman studied her for a moment, and put a hand on her hip. "You do look familiar."

Petra nodded her head. "I think I used to know your son?" she offered the explanation helpfully, and the woman before her froze, her face cloudy, and searched her face.

"It *is* you. Petra. Never thought I'd see you again. It's like…seeing a ghost. Welcome home, chickadee."

The way the woman said it, Petra had the impression that she'd been called the pet name before, and with the same voice. She reached back into the history of her mind, grasping for a memory of this woman that would not come.

The woman, Mrs. Marr, had bagged up the apples, but refused money. She said very little, only sneaking glances up at Petra now and again, and smiling, though it was a sad smile that held secrets that Petra couldn't discern.

For her own part, Petra was spooked. Three people knew her, Thomas had claimed Dane was a childhood friend as well. Or perhaps it was someone else with the nickname 'Daner'? Surely?

Petra asked a few polite questions about the orchard, and the woman answered, though she seemed ever more downcast that Petra didn't already know the answers.

A shadow fell across the light streaming in through the door, and Petra turned back to see if it was Dane or Thomas heading back to the barn. Relief washed over her when she realized it was Dane. She was ready to go home, the sunshine of the day had shone lights in parts of her past she couldn't recall, leaving her in shadow.

"Is that Dane?" Mrs. Marr asked, her voice even smaller than it had been.

"Yes, Dane Fintan. We're collaborating on a research on local history."

Mrs. Marr smiled, but it was uncertain, and her brows were furrowed with an emotion Petra didn't understand. "Oh, not...recent history?"

"No, no, hundreds of years ago." Petra reassured

her, though what she was reassuring her of, she had no idea.

"Good. It's…nice to see you two back together. It's almost like it was…before. I never thought your father should have taken you away, you know. We needed you. You needed us. It was…wrong of him."

Petra's startled expression must have hit Mrs. Marr in the right place, because she quickly realized she had made an error. "I'm sorry, I shouldn't have said anything. It's just such a surprise seeing you here, after all this time. Please, come visit me in town, sometime. I'd love to talk. Really. And best of luck on the research." She wrote her address on a slip of register paper and thrust it into one of the bags of apples before Petra could say anything.

She turned and began walking away. Petra had gotten almost to the door, and Dane only a few yards away. She turned around to wave goodbye at the strange woman, a woman that may or may not have been important to her at some time.

"I do hope you both finish your project before he leaves. " She called out, though quietly.

"What?" Petra called back, she could already see Dane's apologetic grin coming toward her. "Before he moves, to be closer to Allie?" Mrs. Marr smiled again, as though she had made her point clear and Petra would understand.

Her stomach dropped, though if it was from hearing about a strange woman named Allie, or the idea that she, Petra was not a newcomer to Traverston at all—she did not know.

Diary Of Nerissa Swifte

It is unlike me to be disturbed much by the weather. I perfectly understand that without the chill of winter, the heat of the summer sun is less sweet. That the birth of a new spring, will mature, ripen and then flame vibrantly and die. Winter is the death of a year, a mourning—but it brings with it the promise of that same rebirth, the reminders of the joy that lies ahead.

I have always thought too that there was a certain delight in layering blankets atop the bed and the cats pawing their way beneath them as we sleep. This is my first winter alone, living in my little cottage, and I have discovered that there is something magic in the roar of the fire in the hearth, battling the cold and throwing light and shadows onto the faces of those sitting before it.

No, as a woman who understands and appreciates the way life and death lay in each other's shadow, the changes in the weather have never affected me much.

Excepting of course, now, suddenly, when they do.

This cold is not like the chills I thought I knew well. Instead, it creeps into my bones, to the very core of me, and will not thaw. It sits in my stomach and gnaws in my breast. No matter how briskly I walk, or how many blankets I sleep beneath, it stays with me. Though I had written before of the Lady in the Trees, Magda, the Lady of the Woods, I was unsure I would seek her out. She is not a witch or descended from the faerie, as I am, at least I do not think. She is simply old, and full of her own strange magic, and I think, quite mad.

Some call her Grandmother Oak, and others Mother Woods. I suppose it does not matter which as she will respond to any. She lives out here in the forest as I do, but her shelter is much smaller, more primitive and she survives on what she forages and on the charity of the islanders.

She is mad, truly. But in madness, lies wisdom.

There is scarce a soul living that has not gone looking for her, searching out that wisdom. My Da met with her before he took my mother to wife. He says she told him that he would have one sharp pain that would cleave his heart, but that he would also have three stitches to sew it back again. She warned him that it would still leak sadness into his soul if the threads became loose, or if he were to lose a stitch, it would break again. And so, she spoke true. Mother is gone, but Phin, Fisher and I remain, holding his heart together.

As I said, what some see as madness is also true philosophy. It depends, I suppose, on one's ability to perceive beyond the ordinary.

When I asked to move out into the woods, to live

apart in my own cottage, Da went again to see Mother Woods. She told him if he did build the cottage with his own hands, he would never leave my heart. But if he refused me, then my heart would soon leave his roof. And though I cannot conceive that I would ever love him less, she did speak true again. For there is not a day that passes that I do not cherish my Da.

But I? For myself I have only asked her wisdom twice. The first was years ago, and I find that my hand trembles to write of it. But the second was two summers past, when Fisher took Annette to wife. She did not even look at me, did Mother Oak. She looked only to the sky and sang to herself. As I turned to walk away, she cackled and told me there was poison, and if we did not watch it most carefully, it would spill into Fisher's mouth, and from there jump from his lips onto those of all he loved. I did not look back, but continued walking. I had left some autumn apples in a bowl as a gift, but nothing more.

I had resolved that day that thereafter I would not do anything to cause Fisher pain, even if I did not think his choice of wife sound. Poison can be tricky. It may stick to the throats of those who would speak it. If I tried to poison Fisher's mind against Annette, it might taint me as well.

Da says we should not seek out truth because it is warm and cozy, because it is not. It seldom makes a body feel those things. Instead, truth should be searched for because it is hard and cold like iron. And just as heavy to carry. But it is in that burden that we are freed.

And so, yesterday evening I left the bedside of

Mrs. Rollingbrooke, who, unlike her husband, rest his soul, will recover, and my feet found the path to Magda.

There are not many who venture out to the Lady in the Trees now. Many are afraid. To be honest, it is ignorant, I think, not to be. My bones froze and my chest and stomach felt hollow and cold, and this propelled me, gave me the strength to move forward toward her. Her shelter is a small lean-to whose fire puts out no more smoke than a man's pipe. I heard her even before I saw the smoke, singing in an ancient tongue, or a nonsense language. Either or both. I daresay she heard my step, though the fairy blood of my mother makes my tread soft as a whisper on the snow. But I heard her cackle, and swallowing my trepidation, I stopped and stood in place, waiting.

I did not wait long.

"Come in, Nerissa Swifte. I knew your foot would find my door."

She cackled again, a low creaking wind through the branches kind of laugh, and squaring my shoulders, I entered.

I wish I had something complimentary to say of Mother Woods, but though I squint my eyes and strain to think, nothing kind leaps to my thoughts. The shelter was unbearably cold, but for the fire on one side, that if I drew too near was impossibly sweltering. The old woman looked just as I had seen her before Fisher was married, but her clothes were more ragged, her skin soiled. I marveled to think that within a few years this woman would return to the earth, and the dirt and grime on her body now was only preparation.

I cannot fathom how, but it seemed she read my

thoughts. "Return to the earth" she'd said, "No, my dear, we will all be drowned 'neath the waves. Not me, though. Death comes not for me!" She cackled again, revealing even, if yellowed, teeth. Her eyes were cloudy like milk poured into water. And I studied her, and pondered her words before speaking. "'Why will we all perish in the waves?" I'd asked. To which she replied only, "I would ask you that, Mistress Swifte, for you will earnestly believe it is your own doing!"

Her eyes closed for a moment and her breath grew shallow. Old age, lines upon her face, the loss of the freshness of youth, these things do not trouble me. So when I write she is ugly, or proclaim her ancient, it is more to examine the life she has chosen. Any here on the island would give her leave to sleep in their home or in their loft. It is she who had made herself the strange forest creature that she is. I turned to go, thinking she must sleep, but her dry, rasping laugh, like crumbling leaves, rang out behind me.

"You would leave so soon? You have not even heard what you came to know."

"I have no time for riddles or games…" I began, but the expression on her face silenced me. She looked oddly…pained?

"Riddles? Games? I speak only what I see. The truth of what I know. It is not my fault if you do not see the same as I." All of this was uttered quietly, and her strange cream and glass eyes stared endlessly into the fire, hypnotized by the leaping flames. Suddenly, she turned both of them on me, seeing and unseeing. Holding my gaze and seeing past me in the same moment. Seeing into the future? Or looking back at the past? Perhaps.

"This fire, it is your answer. Too far away you

shiver, too close, you burn. But if you stray far from it for too long, it will die without you to feed it. Its leaping and crackling and glow dissolved into oblivion. Blackness. Death!"

She smiled her yellow smile at me, as if she had performed a trick. And perhaps she had. I reached into my heavy cloak and removed a jar of honey, placing it on the ground of the shelter. It was fine honey, from my own bees, and I was loath to leave it. Her advice seemed no wisdom at all. I had known in coming how cryptic and and shadowed her responses were, never knowing until later precisely what her mutterings meant. But Magda heard the glass of the honey jar touch the stones on the hard floor and nodded. She looked again into the flames and spoke.

"Do not set the jar too close to the fire, the honey will boil over, and when I look back to the jar, what was once full and sweet will have gone."

She cackled once more and shut her eyes. Her breath became shallow again, and this time, I scurried out of the foul smelling hut and back again to the snug tidiness of clove scent of my own cabin. She speaks strangely, of course, but to me, her meaning became clear. There will come a calamity, and perhaps the ruin of something. My future? My family? My closeness with Fisher, or the island? And also, there is sweetness coming to me that I am to treasure. Good and bad, bitter and sweet and all dressed up in the gauzy mutterings of a madwoman whom we islanders trust our futures with.

The meeting has left me thoughtful. I am bone weary from the work I have been called to these weeks, and if I cannot admit it here, where can I? I miss my father's hearth. I have not had a mother for almost as long as my memory reaches back, and Annette is not a sister to me. And so I long for the steady companionship of my men. Of Phineas and Da, and of course, Fisher. A night like tonight, with the wind howling and the snow falling in white shrouds, Phin and Da are at the fire, reading or playing the fiddle. Fisher plays the flute, but of course that hangs near his own hearth now, across the island, and its music is no longer for me.

But then, later, when the moon peeks out from behind the clouds, they will all meet at the water's edge, strip to their flesh and take to the water. Swimming in the places the ice hasn't touched yet. Water so cold it would kill another man. Though for a Swifte, it would kill them not to swim in that water.

For a moment, I thought I heard a rapping on my door. This cottage is not large, but from my seat here, staring down into my book of days, I could have sworn I heard it. Not a timid sound, but a knock. But then the wind screams and the panes of my windows shudder and gasp at the force of keeping that cold out. Oh! And it has sounded again! And although I am filled with unusual nervousness, for I can think of no one that would seek me out on a night like tonight but for ill, I must go and open the front door to be sure I do not lock a body out in the cold.

9

MAZEGERRY:

a daydreamer; someone who acts without thinking.

Blinking and running her fingers over the transcribed pages, Petra turned the page in the diary. A whole new entry stood on the next leaf. The writing loopier, larger, less firmly inked onto the page. It looked as though Mistress Swifte's fingers had flown over the letters, gliding easily through the hasty coding of the words. She looked at the clock, barely midnight, and knew sleep was not waiting in her bed just yet. Instead she would have racing thoughts, a lump of disappointment and confusion about her own past, and Dane's strange behavior that day, as bedfellows.

She stood up, stretching, and made her way to the kitchen. She put the kettle on to boil, her throat tight and dry from the long hours of mouthing the translation, without the aid of water, tea or wine. She padded back to the study and copied down the new words from the last entry. The instrument Fisher played which resembled a flute in Petra's mind was written as **flane**. Petra could see a dark haired man playing it, could almost hear the strange and haunting music playing in her own little cottage.

The second word she added to the growing collection was **misdazy**. The word was used several times to describe the Lady in the Trees, and the meaning Petra understood was perplexing. It was something like lunacy but not quite. A mixture of method and madness, or ravings and prognostication. The word gave her an odd shudder, and Petra tried to ignore the other shudderings that had plagued her all evening. As engrossed as she had been in the diary, she could not help but dwell on Dane's face after seeing she had been speaking with Mrs. Marr. It had been odd, and his behavior even stranger. He had come back to her house, true, and read the pages, but had hardly said a word about them, and then promptly left.

She had wanted to tell him her thoughts, and maybe even share that she thought that magic was possible. That she thought she remembered something like magic, that she still felt it sometimes in her mind when a word revealed itself, or in the itching she got on the back of her scalp before something wonderful happened. She had wanted to share these things, to see his smile as she told him, but his reaction to her today had pulled her back, like the tide. And if she was being honest, she was glad. She had only ever discussed her magic with two other people and they were both gone now. Toby, of course, because he believed in witches and fairies too. How he would have loved this book, and the words within it. And Evan, Goddammit, Evan. She hated thinking of him, but also a part of her enjoyed the searing pain that memories of him brought with it.

Zaps of electrical currents that left burns inside her chest, where the pieces of her heart still sat, scattered. Evan, who had ruined her. Who had ruined himself. Who had convinced her without trying that magic was nonsense and it was nowhere to be found in the world. Not after what he did, what he almost did, what he succeeded in doing.

Though, the fact that she was still here, writing, collecting the words at all was a kind of magic. A miracle.

Petra capped her pen as the teapot whistled. After fetching the tea, Petra popped her fingers, gave her neck a little half-hearted massage, and went on to the next entry in the diary. Anything to keep her mind from the secrets her parents might have hidden, to guard herself from the painful talons of the memories of Evan. And, finally, to keep her thoughts from sailing off to capture and embrace Dane Fintan.

Diary Of Nerissa Swifte

I have picked up and replaced my quill several times. Each attempt to write thwarted by my inability to organize my thoughts. I had thought my last meeting with Fisher strange, and my visit to Magda stranger still. So what words would adequately explain the knock on my door?

I had risen, if for no other reason than to prove to myself that I was not afraid. And even upon opening the door I confess, I was not. I cannot name the emotion, for I had never felt its like before that moment.

It was he, Alarence. He stepped in as I opened the cottage door, swiftly closing the cold out. His eyes were of a man walking in his slumber, and I could feel the cold coming from him. It seemed to radiate, just as heat does from a fire. I found myself tongue-twisted, for though I knew him on sight, he was also new to my eyes. No more the pitying sight of illness, but instead, I saw that he was tall, and robust. It was an image of strength and vitality, and though it was frigid outside, and he was cold to the core, it somehow had not touched him. And just as I was in mid-marvel of him, he spoke.

"I…I beg your pardon, Mistress Swifte. I know not why I am here."

Of course, I have heard stranger things, so I took off his coat, admired his broad shoulders, and led him to the chair nearest the fire and bade him explain.

He did not speak for some moments, allowing his tongue to thaw. Tabby jumped onto his lap, unceremoniously, and Mr. Attwater glanced over the shadows and light that danced off the wall of my books, his eyes searching out the titles and almost imperceptibly nodding when he recognized or approved of one or another. I am inordinately proud of my collection, and strain as I might I could not think of an action he could have begun with that would have pleased me more. But finally, he snatched his eyes away from the shelves and shifted his position in the chair, looked at me fleetingly, and looked back and spoke to the fire before him.

"I was lying in my bed, as I have taken trouble to rest more since my illness. But though I closed my eyes, and counted, and recited poetry in my mind—I could not sleep. For when I would close my eyes, your face would appear. Silver hair like moonbeams…the tiny forest fairy to whom I owe my life."

Again, I do not have the words to explain what this sentiment did to me. I had known from the first moment that he was my truest love, just as I can see the future husband of any woman. But it was not until that moment, those words, that I truly felt the power of that bond. The way two souls call to one another without reason or understanding, this is perhaps the greatest of all magics. There is no healing art that I possess, or curse that I have heard of that has the power that love does. Even as I write these words, these words that drip with sentimentality, I know they are true.

I realized that I had been holding my breath, and when I released it, it made a great sound between a cry and a sigh, and I coughed to cover my embarrassment. I am loath to admit it, but Mr. Attwater is the first man to make me feel... apprehension? My Da taught me to stand toe to toe with any man, for the fairy blood is in my veins, after all, and that is a creature above men. Though I do not know how much of what Da says comes from his own fancies, I think a woman is entitled to much more than men give them. And the bold ones among us take what we will and speak our minds. To our own detriment, to be sure, but it is worth it to unlock the words that would lay heavily unspoken on the tongue.

But, I have wandered from the tale at hand.

Mr. Attwater said no more of his thoughts of me, proclaimed nothing else, declared naught, yet the bond still swayed easily between us. I asked him instead of where he came from, and what he did in Travers Town, and his eyes lit as he began his tale.

It was all I could do not to grab my book of days as he began. His words to me were like gemstones, and I dared not move a smidgen lest one jewel fail to fall in my eager ears. Better than Robinson Crusoe! Better than Mr. Pope!

I have a mind for stories, and so I think I remember all that he told me, and I shall set it down here, so that I might relive Mr. Attwater's adventures on cold nights this winter. I will write it all as he told it, or as closely as I remember it.

"Come from? It would be simpler to tell you where I am a stranger. It is not a complicated question you ask, but I fear I have no easy answer. My sister Margaret would tell you Boston, and for her that would be true. Meg never looked beyond her own nose, and how my father allowed her to be married to such a man as Samuel Proper, all the way out west to Travers Town, I cannot guess. I see that wrinkle in your forehead, but do not mistake me. I say nothing against the place, it is my type of wild entirely. It is only that Meg and I are sunshine and darkness, water and rock, unalike completely.

You asked where I am from, and I would tell you truly, nowhere. Every place my foot has trodden and the places I've only read about could all be my home. But in truth, I feel that it no longer matters from whence I came, and instead only that I made my way here. A queer thing to say, you might be thinking. But an odd and wondrous blanket—the feeling of belonging. Warm and stretching just right over one's body, covering all the cold and vulnerable places— don't you find?

You smile, but I see your eyes. They are always looking at my hands. Even as I lay ill, and you worked your enchantments on me, your eyes always found their way to these hands. You have guessed that I am a scholar. I use these hands to write and draw. To sketch the natural world and the mysteries I find within it. I will see my way to publishing a book, but I tell you now—there are some things that I have seen that I will not write in that book. Some phenomena and fantasy that I will keep to myself for my own eyes and heart. Men have a way of squashing down the magic in the world, don't they? They like it to be ordinary, easy to understand, black and white with no grey—or god forbid violet, cerulean or rose! Ah, I see the flicker in your eyes. You would like to hear my secrets. And, you are in luck, for I have a mind to tell them to you, as you are one of them. To my eyes, you are the most marvelous of them all." He smiled then, a small upturn of his lips that betrayed his true feelings for me.

"Do not blush. I am not flattering you, but instead stating a fact. I'm a scholar, didn't you hear?" Again, that smile!

"I left Boston thirteen years ago, just before my fourteenth year. My father had wished for me to take over his tavern business. And a good offer it was, indeed. Right on the water, near the docks, the prices too plum for regular sailors, so instead it attracted in ship captains and officers and visiting aristocrats from anywhere you could throw a pin at a map. People with strange accents and unusual smells. They told tales of jungles and pashas, religious ceremonies and stolen princesses. They spoke of cargoes of gold and silver and the taste of the wine in Spain. But though it was profitable, I am not my father's son. I didn't want to hear someone else's stories of adventure, I wanted to tell my own. My mother was a wild thing, like a butterfly he captured in a net. My heart is the twin of her own, and so the moment I felt myself a man, I left. I hopped a ship and disembarked in Marseilles, but I did not tarry there long. I did not tarry anywhere. As I wandered, I would stay in a place as long as I had use for it. I was fortunate to find learned men who took me on as their apprentice in printing, writing and art. They gave me access to books and ideas and probed my mind until it was as sharp as their own. From there, I followed my ears to more unusual places. Listening for tales that would entice me. Men would come to the towns, speaking of secluded villages, where a giant held court, or cities where people kept bears as pets. A man spoke of a woman with two heads, and a clearing where only dwarves lived in the houses. To these places I went, and sometimes, they proved true. The woman did not truly have two heads, but instead a face on both sides of one. One side was fair and sweet, and the other twisted and horrifying to behold. I then came back to these Americas and found places where the townspeople slept all day and woke at dusk to labor through the night. After that, I came upon a tribe of natives that could only speak by singing, and so sweet was the sound that they lived in a melodious harmony. I journeyed long and saw many wondrous sights and people. But I did not think to find real magic in the world, until I came here."

He grew silent, and I did not speak either. I weighed his words and played the pictures he had drawn for me with them over and over in my mind, trying to see it all as he had. We sat comfortably for some time, and then I told him of my brothers and Da. I told him of the legends surrounding the island and our family. He nodded in agreement, but I pushed away his confidence in my story, telling him I did not believe all of it myself.

When darkness faded into the light of early morning, he seemed to gradually come back to himself. He apologized for the late visit and long hours, but I had scarcely felt the time pass. After promising never to come again at such an hour, and expressing regret for the type of talk that must surely follow an unsupervised visit of the kind might bring me, he left. Even as I tried to wave away his concerns, telling him it mattered not what people said, he stalked out glumly, as though he had done a great wrong. Though his eyes did not turn back to my figure in the doorway as he walked down the path, I know full well that these promises not to return are empty ones. Not because he is untrustworthy, but because none of us can battle destiny. And he is mine.

As I write, I think of the way he speaks and looks at me. As if I am a living enchantment myself. I must confess I have never cared for the word 'witch'. Nor enchantress. I am simply Nerissa, imbued with extra senses, maybe. Perhaps gifted with a sharper and more intricately woven bond to the the world around me. I know the plants, I can see people's natures and desires and I do not mistake the duty of Death as he walks among us. If this is a witch, then I am guilty. But I think, like Mr. Attwater, if others spent more time looking about them, they would see the whole world was sprinkled with magic and mystery. And they would be less likely to try and banish it from their sight when it was found.

Enough for now. It grows colder and I am tired after being out of bed all night. For all the warmth Alarence brought me, the coldness in my chest turns to ice. I have a mind to speak with Fisher, about this pain in my heart, as there can only be on reason for it —that his is heavy too.

10

PIGGESNYE:

a sweetheart; a term of endearment.

When she finally slept, she dreamt of Nerissa Swifte. A woman with such a mixture of darkness and light within her that Petra's mind couldn't quite make her out. Moonbeam mysteries and the words her quill had bitten into the pages. The words swarmed about Nerissa and Petra reached out in her slumber, trying to pluck them from the air and keep them for herself. Her words. Their words.

She saw the strange broad shouldered man with his wavy straw colored hair sitting at the fire. The intensity of his eyes, the sights they had seen in his travels—eyes that Nerissa had called unremarkable. But that was not true, No man ever turned such eyes on Petra. No woman could see the longing and danger in those eyes and call them "unremarkably hazel". Unless that woman was Nerissa Swifte. In her dream, she turned, her own ordinary hazel eyes looking into the deep quicksilver of Nerissa's and she could easily see, trapped there as she was in those grey pools, how this woman was called *witch*.

She woke with the word on her lips, her sheets tangled and clear morning daylight streaming through the window. Peering out, she saw fingers of frost had gently touched the grass and leaves, and even now the sun was melting away its chilly caress. Just as the details of the dream melted from her mind, no matter how desperately she clung to them.

She rose and showered, letting the warm water beat against her chest, trying to think of a good reason to step out of the water and begin her day. When the warm water started to drift cooler and cooler, she sighed, and turned off the tap and toweled off in the achingly cold, blue-tiled bathroom. The house always felt familiar, as though she had known it before, and she wondered now if it was because she had, somehow, known it before. The cottage felt like an old aunt that she hadn't seen since she was a child, but vaguely recognized and remembered fondly. She'd always chalked it up to the house being filled with her father's things, things she had grown up amongst. But, now, after Thomas Marr and his mother, she wondered if there was more to it. If this was her home. If she remembered it because she had to, because it was a part of her. But then why hadn't she known it at once?

Had Toby known this cottage? Why couldn't she remember?

She selected a sturdy wool cardigan and a dress that accentuated her small waist. The diary entry and the frayed remnants of her dream lingered in her mind, and she found herself dressing with more care as a result. The warmth of Nerissa's fire, the intensity of the couple's attraction. Petra wanted to be beautiful for someone, even if it was only herself.

She peeked into the study after curling her long waves, and spied Jinks, who merely yawned in her direction and curled into a tighter ball. She started to sit down on the couch, her hands reaching for her notes, but mid-sit, she changed her mind. She had too much garbling her thoughts at the moment to do translations and gather new words.

Stepping into her cozy little kitchen, black and white tile and wrought iron bistro chairs, she grabbed an apple from yesterday's outing, and dumped some kibble into the cat's dish. Tying on a scarf, she walked out her front door without another thought, into the late morning sunshine.

There was something about being near the lake, some scent, some bounciness to the air. It was an instantly invigorating feeling. Perspective, point-of-view, paradigm shift. Petra could feel the change, but could not anticipate where it would lead her. She followed the lane, through the trees, and she tried to see the trail with new eyes. Or, rather, she attempted to see it with younger eyes.

Had she known this place as a child? For it would be more likely, wouldn't it? Out of doors would have called to her as a child. She and Toby, not unlike Nerissa and her brothers, would have been out exploring, climbing trees, in their own little world.

But was it familiar to her of old? Or was it only familiar because she had followed this same path when she had first come, brooding over her father, wondering why she had come to this lonely place. She shook her curls side to side, hoping to dislodge the cobwebbed barriers that held back the truth. She didn't know. Petra paused and looked around her. She was truly in the forest now. She could not see her little cottage for the trees, nor could yet see the cottage that she knew belonged to Mrs. Garzing. Such a strange woman, somehow kind and unsettling at the same time.

Her thoughts worked their way over to Dane, and she stopped to pick up a stone from the path. It was small and smooth like an egg or a large marble. But it was cloudy white, and it reminded Petra of a snow globe, or iced wintry window panes. Her dad had always picked up stones, too. He never really commented on it, and she had never asked, but it had always seemed as though he were looking for something in particular. He'd bend down on the beach, or in middle of the street if he spied something promising. Sometimes he'd put it right back down, and other times he'd look it over, bring it in close for inspection and place it in his pocket. She never knew what he did with the ones he kept. She brought this little stone closer to her own eye and tried to focus on the whorls of white within it, but an image of Dane with a willowy model type hanging off his arm came to mind, and exhaling heavily she placed the stone in the pocket of her cardigan.

Petra had no idea of what this Allie looked like, and there were larger concerns for her to be anxious about, but she couldn't help thinking about it. She was probably beautiful with sex appeal and probably some super-charged career. Someone like Dane, or someone like Dane if he hadn't a pet interest in his mother's old book. She kicked the newly fallen leaves with her shiny patent flats. Disastrous. Preposterous. Calamitous and tragic. She always fell too quickly and for the wrong man. Petra wished she had Nerissa's powers, to know the man that was meant for her—wouldn't that make life simpler?

"Take it easy on those leaves! Whatever did they do to you?"

A cheerful voice called out from down the path. Petra had just kicked again, angrily, sending leaves flying up in the air, into the wind, which concealed the figure on the trail for a moment, and then swirling, the wind dropped them somewhere new.

Petra blinked rapidly, and put her hand to her chest. She thought she was seeing a ghost. Alarence Attwater, here? But no, the man down the path grew closer and she saw a flash of white, charmingly crooked teeth and straight red-gold hair that belonged to Thomas Marr. His stature and his coloring were so like the man from the diary…aha. Petra brought the heel of her hand to her forehead. Of course! Her mind had probably conjured Thomas Marr from her memory to play the part of Nerissa's beau in her dreams. She knew it must be so, but a tiny voice within her whispered "no, it was Alarence you saw", but Petra shushed her thoughts and met Thomas' smile with her own.

"Hello, Mr. Marr, how are you?" She asked brightly, hoping her expression matched her genuine gladness to see a friendly face. She tugged her cardigan a little closer all the same, for it felt as though it had grown a little colder, suddenly, and it also helped cover her awkwardness.

"Very well, Petra. I'd be better yet if you called me 'Tom' or 'Tomcat' as you used to." He noticed her frown and added, "Ahh, yes, you don't remember, yet. So until then, 'Tom', if you please. I was hoping to run into you this morning, but what brings you out?"

Petra closed both of her eyes for a moment, trying to shut out his insistence that they were known to one another. She forced herself to smile and answer.

"Just walking, clearing my head." She paused and thought for a moment, and then added, "You are correct, Mr...I mean, Tom. I don't recall, and I wonder if you might...illuminate me? Maybe it would remind me of...er, jar a memory loose?"

She glanced sidelong at him, and saw him bite his lip, thinking. The great bulk of him beside her seemed strangely insubstantial, and suddenly she felt the urge to reach out and touch him, to steady herself, to reassure him, or her? She didn't know, and so she fought the impulse, shaking her head. Crazy. Everything was up in the air.

"Of course." He answered, oblivious to her inner insanities. "I just don't understand why Dane hasn't said anything to you about it. Thick as thieves you were. And, if you don't mind my saying, I find it hard to believe you could forget. Although...I suppose, death is one of those things, the mind doesn't... accept well."

Her first instinct was to ask how he knew about Dane, but realized his mother must have mentioned something after she left the orchard. The rest of his statement gave her that same chilly feeling, and she gripped the cardigan tighter, as if the action would make it more substantial. "Yes, ah, odd, indeed that he didn't mention it. But there you are, I suppose. He hasn't said a thing about it." Dear, God, she thought, I'm rambling like an old woman.

Thick as thieves? That sounded...intimate. Close. It sounded like something someone *would* mention. She worked to set her expression as neutral though, and Tom smiled at her. They walked for a few moments, their feet crushing the fallen leaves with a satisfying, crunch, crunch, crunch. Birds sang and twittered above them., their wings disturbing the branches softly overhead. It was, for all intents and purposes, a lovely, normal autumn day.

Except, that she felt somehow that the sky was falling around her.

Finally, after a few more steps, when he still hadn't responded to her entreaty to enlighten her of her past. She was beginning to think he'd forgotten she'd asked him to in the first place, and then he swallowed, and spoke.

"I'm not sure where to begin. My memory is… different than it once was. I don't remember the first time I saw you, or when we met. In my mind, you were just always living in that cottage. My first memories have no beginning. Kind of like, anything when you're young. There is no start, things just…are. And for me, Roccia's living in Rock Cottage just always…was."

Petra could feel her brow creasing, and her mouth turn downwards into a frown. It made no sense. None. He went on though, not seeing the expression on her face. "I knew it was you on sight, and I guess, in a way I was waiting for you to come back. Apple picking was your favorite time of year, and so, I just knew some day you'd come back for it. You and Toby and Dane would always get caught by my dad, all three of you shimmied up an apple tree, sticky handed." He grinned as though he were seeing the memory in front of his face.

Petra silently looked down at her hands, trying to imagine them climbing an apple tree with a young Dane Fintan. In her imagination, he'd had freckles as a boy. Was it a memory? Or just a fancy?

Tom was still speaking, warming to his topic, as they continued on, crunch, crunch, crunch through the leaves.

"Always reading somethin'. Head in a book and telling stories like you wouldn't believe. Well, I didn't believe, not then anyway. You were a princess that had been captured as a baby, and hidden away in our town, or your family used to live underground until you found a ladder leading up to the the world above. Crazy stuff, but entertaining. It was definitely… quieter when you left. But, everything seemed to go quiet after Toby…after we…" He stopped speaking and ran a hand through his hair. "Does anything sound familiar?"

"No." Petra said quietly. "How old was I, when I left?"

"Hmm, well, I was 9, when it happened. So I guess, you would have been…7? Maybe? You'd have to ask Dane, you two are of an age."

"I don't remember a thing. I know it's strange, but there was a tragedy. I only remember a few things from my childhood. Bits and flashes."

Tom nodded his head knowingly, and Petra wondered if he already knew what had happened. She decided she wanted to speak the words, even if he did already know. To say them. Words were power, after all, and if she kept them inside they would control her.

"My mother was driving my brother to baseball. I don't know why…but they skidded on the road, wrapped around a tree. They both died instantly. I… guess I kind of went dark after that for a few years.

So, everything you say is strange and new to me. And I don't know whether it is true or not." She gave him a half smile and shrugged, but whipped her head back up, upon seeing the expression on his face.

"Well, that's certainly not the truth. Whoever told you that left a choice few things out."

Petra stared, confused.

"You really don't know? I thought maybe you didn't, thought maybe it was why I was waiting for you here....shit. I thought that you knew. I hoped that you did. Oh, Petra. I don't know what to say. I'm so sorry."

He cleared his throat and made a decision, strong emotion clouding his features. "Petra, there's so much more to it. I was in the car too, and so was Dane. You were the one who found the accident, you...found the bodies. And your mother...she didn't die. Toby died, and not instantly. Your mom, she was drunk, Petra. I'm so sorry, but she didn't die. She went to prison, and then you and your dad left. Just closed up the cottage and left. When your mom died in jail a few years ago, your dad came back, opened Rock Cottage back up, acted like he had never left. Like there were no ghosts following him, no ghosts haunting the woods around his cottage. He just came back, and so we thought...we thought you knew."

Petra was shaking her head back and forth, back and forth, hand on her heart, her face crumpled in a sob that she would not let escape.

"No, you're wrong. She's dead. She died in the accident. I wasn't there..."

Tom's eyes were full of pity, and he turned toward her on the trail, and for a moment she thought he would grab her and hold her tight, but he seemed to think better of it, and instead, held her gaze, locked into her, and spoke straight to her anguish. "Petra, you were there. You pulled Toby from the wreckage. They found you, holding him. There's a picture of you in the paper, standing at the scene. I don't tell you to torment you, I promise. But you need to remember who you were, and your life here."

"No, no, no." Petra chanted, and grabbed a hold of her elbows, hugging herself tight. She felt the fit coming on, felt the shadows that she had left behind darkening her vision, filling her mind, and suddenly, the same freezing cold feeling came over her, and she pulled her cardigan around herself, tighter still, and somehow in the action, the fit subsided. She looked up and realized they were at the cemetery. The realization should have added even more fear and weight to her flagging spirits, but strangely, she felt buoyed. Toby was nearby. She could feel him.

She wanted suddenly for Tom to embrace her, but he did not, just stood silently by as she gazed out over the rows of stones, the promise of no more tomorrows. And strangely, his presence alone gave comfort, although she still did not remember him. She didn't cry, she couldn't, but she allowed herself to just stand, and be held by the moment. Nothing felt real, and yet something in his words rang true. For a moment she wished Dane was there, that his arms were wrapped about her shoulders, cooing a metronome of "it's okay, it's okay, it's okay…" in her ears.

The coldness of Tom beside her made the hair on her neck rise.

"Do you want to see him?" He asked quietly.

She pulled herself from her thoughts, she knew exactly whom he meant, but she wanted to hear him say it. "Who?" she asked, her voice thick.

"Toby." He said simply, his eyes studying her, and also looking beyond her.

She looked out on the gravestones stretching long and wide, one section at the back ornately carved and blackened with age. He led her down a path in the sunshine, the noon-time sun too bright and cheerful for such a place. Under a birch tree, he pointed, and she walked forward to gaze at the place her brother's body had come to rest. She stared for a moment, trying to fit the enormity of what Toby was, what he meant to her, into this tiny square of ground.

Tobias Salvatore Roccia
Beloved Son and Brother
Too bright for this world, he was called back to the heavens,
There he waits patiently for those he loved most

Petra was certain that her father had written the epitaph. And it was true. All of the memories she did have of her childhood were Toby. Toby holding her hand during scary movies, or Toby reading her stories before bed. Watching Toby run, so fast. He was always sunshine in her memory, illuminating the dark places where shadows lived.

She had never been to the cemetery. One because she avoided them as a rule, and two because she had taken great pains to live as a hermit this past year, and even more so when her father died. She wondered, as she gazed at the hard stone, how much of her memory had been purposefully manipulated by her father. Had he been protecting her? Her mother...not dead. Her whole life she had always thought of her mom as another victim of the accident, but according to Tom, she was the author of it. The careless cause of her own son's death. Drunk. Drunk with babies in her car. Petra had never seen her father drink. Not a sip, not a shot, not a drop. And now she knew why.

Tom had left her side, was tarrying at a grave near the gates. Cemeteries meant different things for different people, and she had almost forgotten that all of these other stones represented someone who had been loved and lost by those they left behind. She wondered distractedly whom Tom mourned, whether he mourned Toby as well.

Either way, Petra was glad of the privacy. Strangely, the grave did not affect her as she had anticipated it would. She had never asked where Toby was buried, nor her mother, when she was a child. She had simply...disconnected. They were dead, and that was it, and they were nowhere. But now she wondered why. Why did she never want to know?

Perhaps, it was because even though it was peaceful here and the birch was shady and tall, it didn't feel like Toby was here. Not really. His bones were down in the coffin, permanent eight year old bones, but he wasn't here. He wasn't anywhere.

Except in her memories.

The birch swayed in a sudden wind and she felt chilled, but she did not pull the cardigan closer. She couldn't be as cold as Toby was, as cold as death beneath the earth.

She palmed the milky white stone from her cardigan pocket, and rubbed it between her fingers, half expecting it to turn red like the strange Blood

Birch apples from the orchard. But it did not, it remained a stone of frost, or bone, or the milky-murky depths of a fortune teller's crystal ball. She placed it on the headstone as they do in Jewish cemeteries, saw that there were other stones there already. She wondered if they had been left by her father. A token to say that they came. That she had come. Petra was here. Petra had visited and mourned, had never stopped mourning. Petra was here, finally.

Her father had been cremated. He'd asked to be scattered in the waves of the lake, which she had done. Petra liked best the waves by moonlight. The way the ribbon of light shifted and glittered in the darkness, lighting a path across the water. It was on that glowing path that she had scattered her father. She smiled, walking away from Toby's grave, wondering if Nerissa's Da, might also have returned to the lake after his death. The lake that meant so much to both their families, though Petra hadn't known before.

She met Tom at the gate, giving him a nod. He nodded back, smiling, but seemingly lost in his own thoughts. They didn't speak for a few moments, until clearing his throat, he spoke.

"I'd seen you in town a few times, you know?"

Petra shook her head. "No, I was not aware. Why didn't you say anything?"

Tom considered a moment. "I'm not sure. I saw you, and knew you immediately. But, it seemed best if you came to me first. If I waited until you were... more ready. It was a hard thing that took you away from here. I needed to be certain that...you were prepared for the past, I guess. It can be a hard place to look back on."

"Yes, I understand." Petra said, although she wasn't completely sure that she did. She looked up from her little shoes and found that they were returned to the back of her property, her sweet little cottage winking at her in the distance. She hadn't realized he had been leading her back home.

He reached down and nearly squeezed her hand, but didn't. His hand instead came up and rubbed his neck, as his eyes searched the distance. When he turned his eyes back on her though, they were intense and direct. "Thought perhaps you had a few things to mull over now. I expect that you feel a little heavier than when you left this morning."

Petra nodded, unable to tear her eyes from his, noting the way he looked at her, the heat of his gaze.

"Thank you, you're right. I'm properly shocked at the moment, but I'm certain the chaos of it all will come soon enough."

He looked worried for a moment. Worried about her, she realized and she offered him a small smile to reassure him that she simply needed some time to think and feel about all of these new revelations about her life. A few pinpricks of dread tingled at her temples and down her arms, warnings of the fits she had fought so hard to master. But she swallowed them down and smiled more brightly.

"If I need anything, I promise to call the orchard."

"Just come find me." He said. "I'll be out walking, keeping an eye out for a Petra in distress." He winked and Petra laughed. He leaned in quickly and kissed her cheek, though it was so swift and so light that she hadn't felt it.

He began walking away, but turned around to call back to her. "Go and visit my mom sometime. It would be good…for both of you, I think."

Petra waved and walked toward her back door, when a response occurred to her, and she again turned back to ask one final question.

"Tom, is my mother buried…"

"She's in Settler's Bay. Just up the coast." He answered, before she even finished the sentence. "You can visit if you like, I could take you."

"I'll remember. Thank you. Again." She looked down at the ground, and then back up at him, unsure what to say, but he was gone. He had obviously loped off quickly while she was stuck in thoughts of the dead mother she hadn't known. The dead mother who killed her brother. She knew suddenly that she wouldn't ever visit her mother's grave. She didn't need to.

Slowly, feeling a decade older, she turned back around once again and walked to the door, stepping into the coolness of the kitchen. She drank down a glass of water from the tap, then another, and walked into the living room, ready to curl into a ball and weep. Just to get everything out. All the emotion, all confusion and frustration of the news from the past two days. She knew what happened when you kept poison like that bottled in. She had seen what that did to a person. Had lived it. Had survived it.

Too much. Too much. Evan had told her to let go of the past, but he had never understood. It was the past that wouldn't let go of *her*.

Stepping into the living room, her eyes landed on a form stretched out on the couch. The same couch she'd planned to bawl on.

"Did you forget our date?" Dane asked. His mouth was smiling, but his eyes were troubled.

Her first impulse, pathetically, was giddiness to see him lying so casually on her couch. A scene of domesticity that made her heart leap, especially after the sour taste the day had left in her mouth thus far. But then, she reminded herself that this was a man who had been concealing things from her. A man who had kept her own past and their connection a secret. A man with a girlfriend named Allie, whom he was moving in with soon, apparently. A man who could have filled in all kinds of gaps for her. A word here, or an admission there, a reminder of something that could have triggered her memory, possibly. But he hadn't. And now, with the new eyes she had crafted, she looked and saw an intruder. A man who had trespassed into her home, and her life with his strange diary.

A diary that now paled in strangeness to the events of her own life.

But still, she focused her mind, thinking, *interloper, invader, housebreaker, liar.* And with her mind made up, she replied to him.

"What are you doing in my house?!"

His eyes went wide with surprise and he stood up, words sputtering from his lips. Petra put her hands on her hips, waiting for his explanation, and for once, she was glad of her curves as they gave her a much more intimidating stance.

"Um, yes, about that. We...we had a date? And the door was...open?" He looked at her guiltily, like a boy caught with a sling shot near a broken window. His cool, unruffled composure had slipped.

"We did *not* have a date." Petra pronounced each word carefully, hands still on hips.

"Yes, well, I guess not technically, but…I've been over every day this week and I just thought we could…"

Petra sighed. She wasn't angry. It took more effort and energy to make herself so than to simply leave it be. Yes he'd broken into her life. Yes, she should be upset. But she wasn't, not really. And there were other things to be concerned with at the moment. So, she said simply,

"Forget it. Call first or at least make sure I'm home".

Dane sighed, running a hand through his glossy brown hair. "Right, I'm sorry. I don't think sometimes."

He looked so sheepish, Petra couldn't stop the smile on her face. He followed her into the study, where she handed over the most recent pages she'd transcribed. He took them eagerly, and sank into the wine colored leather chair, oblivious to anything else.

Petra sat down herself, decided perhaps to do a little more of the decoding while he was there. Carefully, pulling on the cotton gloves, she raised her pen to begin, when she felt his eyes on her in the corner.

She looked up and he cleared his throat, looking back to the notes.

"Where were you?" He asked quietly, with a feigned casual tone. Petra looked away and crinkled her forehead, annoyed.

"Is that your business?" She asked, her voice free

of the cool tone she'd used earlier, though it had taken some effort.

"Of course not. I'm sorry." He replied, but still his eyes searched out hers. Petra shook her head, and told him, though she hadn't meant to, and wasn't sure why she did.

"I went for a walk and came across Thomas Marr."

Dane had looked down at his lap, but Petra could tell he wasn't reading. "Oh, unpleasant, then."

"Not at all. Actually, he's…quite lovely, actually. In a strange way. You were friends growing up?" Petra asked the question carelessly, but her eyes were focused on his face, waiting for the answers to her next questions.

Dane's expression was strange and he looked at her as if she had said something very odd, indeed. But he kept his voice neutral. "With Thomas? Well, yes. It's a small community here. He was a few years older than me." He shifted in his chair, and had snatched his gaze back to his lap.

"Ahh…" The normal, sane part of Petra screamed, *I already know! Why are you hiding it from me? Why the subterfuge, why the secrecy? What else do you hide from me?* She wanted to demand answers. She wanted to scream and stomp. She needed to know why, if they had been so close, if he'd known what happened, known Toby, why didn't he say? And why, *why,* if it was a secret, did he seek her out still?

But some other part of her bade her keep silent. It had been so long since she had felt safe with someone. After Evan….she never knew if she'd feel safe ever again. Oh, God, Evan. It was odd, and all these questions did trouble her, but she wanted to hold close the friendship, to guard the feelings she had for him now. Something inside her offered that pause, whispering, "wait, wait", and so she said nothing. She simply picked up the pen, found her place, and fell into the tangled story of Nerissa Swifte, and beneath her witch's spells.

Her problems weren't going anywhere, she could face them later, when she was braver, when she had a little more magic beneath her skin.

Diary Of Nerissa Swifte

It has been a fair few days since I have picked up my quill. It has not been for lack of ideas, or events of which to recount in my little book, I assure you. No, I have found myself in almost constant occupation, with scarce a moment for sustenance or slumber. If I had imagined this winter would be spent warm and cozy at my fireside, Tabby purring and open books to peruse—this was fantasy. But, I suppose magic has a way of working on its own time, on its own terms. At least, I find that this is so.

After all, is it not magic that draws Alarence to me night after night? That hums vibrations of longing through my body when he is near? What would I do to have his lips on my own? What would I give to press my body into his, making us one? But it is only a glamour. Since it is only his memory that caresses my cheek, my own desires that visit me. The man himself has not returned yet. Or, if he has, I have not seen him.

For, as I have written, I have been occupied. There is so much illness come to this island that I cannot remember a winter like this one. There is not a family in the village that has not suffered. It is an ailment I've not seen before. Stealthy and secret, it steals the flush from the healthy and silences those who were hearty only hours before. It is times like these that magic, that healing is as much a gift as a curse.

The scared people of the island, I hear them whisper tales of the Wendigo, the tall and bony man-eater with tangled horns on his head and his skin pulled too tight over his face. They speak in hushed tones of the Creetarth, the life sipper, the shadow man who comes and drinks the life, the soul from children and hale men and women. The creatures are given life in these whispers, in these retellings, until they grow and take shape. I could never be as scared of these monsters as I am of those who believe in them. A man who is afraid is the most terrifying being of all.

And so, I confess that as much as I have always looked on death as a friend, I have also looked to my powers to cheat him when my herbs and elixirs have failed me. And so, many times in the past nights I have wished to have my old book of days, with its receipts and spells—returned to me.

I have thought of asking Phin or Fisher to attempt to search for it when they are on one of their late night swims, but the lake is too vast, its depths too murky and unfathomable. And I could not ask Fisher in any case. His heart is so heavy I fear he would plummet to the bottom.

But yes, I wish I had my old book. In it, I had written spells that seemed the most efficacious. The exact words, the tone and inflection, the attitude of thought and wishes that must accompany the spell. All aspects of casting are vital. Any ninny or charlatan can mumble the right words and stir the correct mixtures. To truly wield and work magic? This is skill, preparation, alchemy and of course, destiny. I do not like the word, 'witch' as I have written before. It is not my name for myself, nor how I think of my skills. Magic though, is in everything, and no matter if Da says I am the enchantress of the island or not, it takes no special being to work it. It takes only the right eyes to see the possibility of every thing in nature. Twist it this way, stir it that way, say the right incantation over the mix, and...magic.

But, witch...witch is dangerous. A word as dangerous as Wendigo or Creetarth. A word that suggests as much evil to those speaking it. It is a word that chills, that brings to mind malicious cackling and hexes. A word that summons darkness. I work only in the light. I heal, I protect, I see what others cannot. Although, I will admit, sometimes I see that which others *should* not.

With the aid of my tonics and a sprinkle and scattering of a few spells, a few mumbled charms, I have saved some. One young woman, newly married, smiled serenely through the grip of the disease as I spoke the healing words of a spell, and reached her hand out to me in gratitude. I know, or at least I hope, that not all on this island can be swayed from understanding my true intent, no matter the slander that is spread. But I find myself wary all the same. I am offered pinched looks in town as I make my way from house to house. There are some doors that do not welcome me, though I know I could alleviate the sickness of the sufferers within. Their coffins weigh heavily on me, provoking anger in my heart for Annette. For my brother's wife is their murderer, pouring poison in their ears so that they do not summon me when they need me.

And so, although my time has been full as of late, I know in my heart it could be more full, and though I am weary, I would that I were more so.

Though, it seems that Annette too has been busy, which brings my thoughts and my pen back to Fisher. Today, just before I picked up my quill, he came. And though his step is a familiar one, it rang strange on my path, which made me realize how long it had been since I had heard that specific sound. Too long.

He walked into my cottage a lost boy, Hansel to my Gretel of the fairytale, following breadcrumbs to my door. He collapsed in the chair by the fire, warming his hands. His hair was wet, and so I knew he came from the lake. His expression was drawn, his face creased with worry. My twin looked years older than me, years older since last I saw him.

I came behind him and put my hands on his shoulders, but lightly. He reached one raw red hand up to hold mine. He spoke then, quietly, of the past. The past is a magic place I think. It changes and shimmers in our minds, more radiant, perfect and larger than it really was. The past is rebuilt, reshaped for our own purposes. A pleasant place to visit, but dangerous to live in.

His words made me fear that moving back into the world of our history was precisely his aim. He talked of our childhood. Of carefree days of our mother, covered in sunshine, which is how we both see her in our memory. Before she left, and took some of that light with her. He told a few of Da's stories and reminisced about Phineas' birth, and then moved on to our childhood games, our secrets, all of our strange twin connections. I did not interrupt, could not, had I wanted to. The words tumbled out of him like a stream, wave after wave, and so I let him speak on. His voice grew hoarse, and his joy turned to sorrow, thick and choking in his throat. I knew he was coming to his purpose. Roundabout and taking the long way, but coming nearer every moment.

"Annette is pregnant." He whispered, finally, and he wept. I almost wept as well, but not for fear of her life as Fisher did, but fear for my own if anything should go amiss with the baby. "I cannot feel happiness, no matter how I will it. It matters not that you say you have seen her safely delivered, the knowledge pokes at me, pricks me until I feel that I bleed within."

My hand was limp within his grasping fingers, and I knew he waited for my response. When had this happened? My resolute and confident brother, now hanging on my breath, waiting for my words to tell him what to do. I had always thought his mind was closed to me because it was a mirror of my own, but if it had been in the past, it was most assuredly no longer. He turned his head to look up at me, fear clouding his features so that he appeared almost blurry. I looked away from those pleading eyes—they tore my heart so!—and gazed instead into the jumping flames of the fire. The response was automatic, a careful lie a mother might tell a frightened child. But he was no child, and I am no practiced liar. Fisher is a man, a man who was frightened of his own ability to create life, and I knew not the right words. I still do not, though I rack my mind to find them, even now.

"All will be well. Do not fret, Fisher. As I said, I see many fine sons in your future."

Shining eyes, those that a supplicant might turn on his savior, glowed up at me in the glow of the firelight.

"Truly, sister?" he'd asked, and I smiled, patting his hands. We spoke of other things after that, meaningless trifles, just enough to hear our own voices return to normal for a few moments. Da, the lake, the sickness on the island. I did not offer an unction to relieve morning sickness or promote health of the babe, and he did not ask for any, we both knew that Annette would never partake of any physick coming from my hands. I did not speak to Fisher of Mr. Attwater or of my troubles with some of those in town. In the past, my brother would have shouted my innocence from the town square. He would have called any man who spoke poorly of me to account, would have sank his fists into their bellies, his knuckles would have slammed jaws and broken noses—all for me to tend to after the anger had faded from the men. But that brash man was gone. His recklessness and easily bruised pride hidden too deeply for even me to find.

Da and Phin were more alike, I suppose. They would never stand up for me, nor take my part in the village. Da would shrug if I'd ever thought to have asked him. He'd say the islanders opinions were naught to him. He would puff on his pipe, and look toward the water, saying, "We are Swiftes. We belong to this island. There have always been Swiftes—to swim the depths of the lake and know her moods. To protect the people and watch over the island, with whispered spells and our own special magic. Until the island disappears forever, the Swiftes will remain upon her. No man can break our bond to this place, and so it matters not what any fool mumbles about us."

And so, when I walked Fisher to the door, bade him visit me soon, spoke our customary farewell, I reminded myself of this same truth. Over and over, as the tears came, I repeated, "I am Nerissa Swifte, I am Nerissa Swifte, I am Nerissa Swifte…" But the words and the power that should have been behind them did not stop the tears, nor did they prevent my stomach from sickening, heaving my small dinner onto the snow, marring its whiteness. It was not until I came back in and claimed my quill, writing out the events as they happened that my fear has fallen away some.

Yes, fear. I am frightened. Terrified. My stomach clenches and seizes, and I feel that this new feeling prognosticates evil for me. An evil I know not how to prevent.

I have determined to brave the ice and walk to the mainland. I must see Alarence again. Especially now when all on the island has become illness and darkness, closing in upon me from all sides.

In him, I will seek the light.

III

RODOMONTADE:
vainglorious boasting

As she finished writing the final heartbreaking words
of the translated diary entry, Petra looked up to see
the wine-leather chair empty. The transcribed pages
that Dane had been reading neatly piled up on the
desk, and the man himself nowhere to be seen. Petra
sighed, and stretched, feeling the weariness in her
arms and back from too long sitting in the same
attitude. She stood up, closing the diary carefully, her
mind on Nerissa's fear, and the sudden awareness that
she lived in a place with a strange past, the history of
which she was now reading and biding in. She
thought of the window she was being offered into
this other time. It was different than reading about it
in a soulless history book, or from the stories she so
often found in her researches, tidbits she ran across as
she looked for an old word to collect. This was a
personal account, and the images that Nerissa
conveyed were real for Petra. She felt she could see

the sick children, hear the cries of their wailing families. Despair like that did not often enter her modern world. But, in Nerissa's time the winter cold and the illness that traveled with it were a battle to be fought every year.

She slowly removed her gloves. She couldn't hear anything in the kitchen, and the realization pulled her swiftly back to the present. Petra wasn't sure if she wanted Dane to still be there...or not. A wall had been built between them somehow. A wall made from secrets and the past and truths unspoken. Could she have imagined their intimacy? She must have. That was just her style, wasn't it? Blindly falling for a handsome man who shows interest in her. She shuffled toward the door, still not knowing what would prove more heartbreaking—if he had left, or if he'd stayed. She stopped suddenly, reaching for the bookcase to steady herself. An idea had popped into her mind. Maybe he felt so close to her, maybe their intimacy had existed, but it was because they'd been comrades as children. She wasn't wrong, he had been friendly. He had been familiar, confidential and comfortable with her, but not because of a tangle of fresh feelings for her, but because of their shared past. And Petra had mistaken that familiarity with something more amorous. Her palm came swinging up to her forehead. Stupid. Idiotic. Absurd. Of course, that must be it.

But then why did he not reveal himself? Reveal their past?

The door to the study opened and Dane stepped in with two steaming mugs. "Hot cocoa", he said, his smile broad and contagious. "You were lost in the diary, and even though I called your name a few times, you didn't even look up, didn't seem to hear me at all."

Petra flushed, but didn't say anything.

"I took the liberty of making hot chocolate on the stove—I might have added a little nip of something at the end as well. I was as quiet as a mouse. Though, I'm certain you wouldn't have noticed either way, as you were so engrossed in Mistress Swifte." He winked at her and handed the cup over, sinking again into the leather chair. All at once, he had put her right back where she had been before, school-girl crushed and in his thrall. But not so much that she could shoo away the questions that lingered in her mind.

She resumed her seat too, sliding the notebook with her hastily written and newly collected words into the desk drawer. She might be falling for Dane Fintan, but the words were still hers. Hers alone.

Dane chatted amiably about the pages he had read and how fascinated he was with Nerissa. Petra smiled, she could completely understand that. She felt the same. Tipping his head back to take a swig from his mug, he pulled it away to reveal a hot cocoa mustache atop his upper lip, which was completely incongruous with the next words he would speak. His face turned solemn and he peered into his cup.

"I'm afraid, you know."

Petra was startled, perhaps this was the moment he would confess their past, illuminate the shadows he imagined her to be hovering under about her own childhood.

"Afraid of what, exactly?" She asked, her voice almost breathless, which embarrassed her, but it was too late. The words were out. He hadn't appeared to hear her question. He was staring intently at the white porcelain mug in his hands. Gone were all the traces of his earlier sunny mood.

"I'm afraid. I can't help but feel that something bad is about to happen. Something really, truly, terrible. In fact, we know a disaster is coming, and there's no way to warn…" He trailed off, his eyes coming upward to plead with Petra's.

"Dane, what do you mean 'something terrible'? Everything has been going well. We've made so much progress. Surely, there's nothing worse ahead than what has already happened."

Dane's eyes filled with confusion. "What can you mean? We both know that their island is going to disappear. How is that not worse than being called a witch and having a strange family? We have to figure that she died on that island, suddenly, tragically. Why else would she have left the diary behind? I'm afraid for Nerissa. I feel some…trepidation for her. No one is safe on the island, but something else, something extra is coming for her—I can feel it."

Petra's expression had turned from puzzlement to frustration and then resignation. His last words had brought an unexpected chill up her spine, as he gave voice to her own fears for Nerissa. But it was hard to believe that he hadn't been speaking about the present. About the two of them. Instead he was talking about the book, about a woman who had died over 200 years ago.

She shrugged, "Yes, the tone of her writing does seem to be presaging such a thing. And being a witch in any historical context usually ends badly."

"Yes, but..." Dane began, his expression struggling to fix itself as he searched for the words.

"But what? Even if we do find that something ghastly befalls her, there isn't anything we can do. It's past. Gone and done."

"I know." He sighed. "But I just don't feel that way about the past. To me...it's as if Nerissa's story is unfolding in real time, in tandem, all those years past. As if her history is simply a page I have not yet read. In that way, her past is my future."

He gave her a look of such intensity that Petra blushed. When she'd first met Dane, she'd thought him so buttoned up, so polished and refined. And while she still did, she was also offered the glimpses of what all those buttons and smartly pressed shirts were hiding, what they were holding back.

A heart like her own.

A heart that had been like her own even as children, though even that fact he had buttoned away. But the heart belonged to someone else, she reminded herself. It was not hers to uncover.

Her voice came out quiet and controlled, and she held emotion out of it—no simple task. "It's a strange thought about the past and future, but honestly, I feel the same as you. But do not fall in love with Nerissa, Dane. She'll only break your heart."

Her last sentence had been a weak attempt at levity, but Dane didn't sense the teasing in her words.

"That's just it..." His chin fell sighingly into his hand, and he brought the tip of his thumb to his front teeth as he curled up into the chair. He was staring at the wall of books in the study, an expression on his face that told Petra he was somewhere else. Some other place, some other time, And his next words told her, with some other person.

"How could you read her words and not be in love with her? How could you get to know her and not feel as though you'd loved her your whole life?"

One corner of his mouth turned upward into a small smile, and he looked back at Petra, whose cheeks pinked brightly, warming her face uncomfortably. She wasn't jealous. No, she couldn't be. Because again, she felt as he did. She only wished his shining eyes and proclamations were for her.

They drank their cocoa slowly, silence descending companionably in the room. It was a pleasant sort of quiet that sat between them and Petra perked her ears up to listen to the walls. She had always fancied that if one was quiet enough when surrounded by books, then one could hear them whisper the stories between the pages.

They finished, and they both stood up, taking their mugs to the kitchen. Dane filled both up with water, as if that was the same as washing them, and then turned to face Petra.

She had been standing behind him, fiddling with the collar of her dress, and when he turned around, he was facing her. So close. They both seemed surprised by their proximity but neither moved away. It felt like an age, but it could have been only a moment. Their eyes were locked, a small smudge of cocoa remained on his top lip. The light, almost-not-there freckles and the intense blue of his eyes, inches away. Blue like the water in the bay, blue as the darkness as it begins to fall. Something clicked inside Petra. A scrap of a remnant of a memory of those same eyes, those same freckles, sitting on a tree branch alongside of her. A small finger coming to lips signaling for quiet, two sets of small legs swaying back and forth silently beneath them. But the same eyes. The same freckles. The same sense of adventure and mischief, and comfort and closeness. And then it was gone. Memory or imagination? It didn't matter now. Because he was so close. So, achingly close.

Slowly, tentatively, he brought a hand up to her face, pulling it nearer his own, until Petra could feel the heat of his breath, could almost taste the spicy cinnamon from the cocoa. His other hand ran up her arm, and then down to her hip as he pulled her even closer to him. Petra was so close she could only see his eyes, the blueness drowning her, covering her completely.

But she stumbled back. She shook her head as much as a response to him as it was to her own heart.

"No, no, no" She whispered.

"Forgive me." His words were husky and came out in a mumble. His fingers came up and touched his lips, as though testing to be sure they really hadn't been kissed. His body slammed back against the kitchen counter, as though she had shoved him, and he turned his face so that his eyes were no longer boring into hers. "I'm…I'm sorry." He said, still looking away, "I thought there was…something between us."

Petra was staring at him in consternation. What did he mean? Of course there was something between them, they had known each other as children. They were both traveling into the past, sharing the secrets of their witch, Nerissa Swifte.

"There is something." Petra finally said. "Of

course there is! Sometimes it feels like it is so strong as to be almost tangible. But…Dane…I know. I know about Allie."

His eyebrow shot up quizzically and he seemed to grow red with, if not anger, some other strong emotion whose name failed Petra. She was so tangled up in their almost moment that words fled from her. Her only refuge, her greatest power.

"Allegra? What does she have to do with anything?"

Petra gasped, pushing Dane away forcefully, and began to pace the kitchen. All instructions and tips from the grief counselor flown from her mind.

"What does she have to do with anything? What does she have to do with anything? What kind of person do you take me for? Do you seriously think I'd be okay with her being in your life? Or am I the one you'd choose to keep secret? What am I? Some pathetic fling?"

Her voice had grown more and more hysterical, and she felt the familiar shift of her anger growing too large to handle. Petra was a captive of strong emotion, or had been since Evan. Whatever had kept the feelings locked up since Toby died—that lock had fallen away, rusted, been torn off violently after Evan. It was why she preferred and pursued solitude. She was prone to these fits of temper, crying jags, unrestrained laughter and fits comprised of a jumble of all three.

It didn't matter what precisely had broken down the gates of her calm, because the feelings themselves had absorbed her. No time for deep breathing or quiet reflection or concentrating on a moment that brought her joy. And although a small voice inside of her, deep, deep down, whispered to keep calm, it was too late. She was in the thrall of the fit.

"Too much, too much, too much…" she chanted quietly. She crumpled onto the tile floor and hugged her knees to her chest. Dane was speaking, but she couldn't hear the words. She stared straight at her knees, focused intently on the fabric of her dress. Her mind was cruel. It ran only a reel of her darkest moments. The darkness after death. The news that her father had died, and then his body in the casket, paper thin skin and chapped lips, unrecognizably gaunt and grey. Evan…leaving. All of the times he had, Oh God, all of the times he had hurt her. Her hand came up and gently, almost not even touching it, her fingers skimmed the smooth line of the scar from the bottom of her ear to the thin skin of her throat, and she remembered. She made herself remember. She thought of the latest information, the secrets, her retreat from the world, and instead of her skirt, she saw again the plate before her eyes, and she suddenly wished she *had* smashed it that day. The day she'd met Dane.

Petra finally looked up, though her lips still formed the words, "Too much, too much, too much…" and tears blurred her vision. It left as rapidly as it came on, her mouth forming the words more and more slowly until her lips were still and her tears were drying. He had not moved from where she had pushed him, but when he saw that the episode was over, he walked to the sink and handed her a glass of water. He slowly sat down on the tile next to her and pulled his fingers through her hair. It was not a romantic gesture, but a comforting, fatherly one. Against her better judgement, Petra relaxed into his hands combing through her hair. They sat thus for some moments, silent but for the cacophonous echoes of her outburst vibrating around them.

Sighing, he pulled Petra a little closer to him and began to braid her long honey hair. His voice, quiet, and she could sense, in deep concentration, spoke from behind her.

"My daughter, Allegra, always calms down when I touch her hair, and since she is a dramatic child, I have learned a fair number of braids through the years."

Petra shut her eyelids and she was glad he could not see her face, for she could feel her cheeks redden alarmingly with embarrassment. "Oh, I...when I heard you were going to move to be with Allie, I assumed..."

"I know what you assumed." His gruff voice said from behind her. "What kind of man do *you* think *I* am?"

The slight tug and tickle of her hair being braided stopped, and she tentatively reached back for it, pulling it forward to examine his handiwork. It was a fishtail braid, and something about it made her want to cry again. It was something about the tenderness that had gone into the plaits of the hair, as if he had left a little of himself in the twists.

"Fishtail." He said quietly, his voice still behind her. "Allegra's latest demand. And I thought it was fitting for our island enchantress and her aquatic family."

Petra turned around now, their eyes meeting once again. "I'm sorry."

She spoke low and simply, her customary high-handed tone no longer a shield against her true feelings. They both knew she had let him in, behind her walls. "I'm sorry for that...display. And also for the false assumption."

His smooth smile flashed instantly to his features. "We all have our moments. It's completely fine. I just expect the same treatment if I ever have a fit of my own..." He raised an eyebrow and pointed at her face playfully."...and believe you me, it will happen."

Petra smiled now, full and sincerely.

"So, you...you don't have a girlfriend?" She asked shyly, everything inside of her fidgeting not to roll her own eyes. She sounded twelve.

"Let's just say that I'm working on it." Dane replied, leaning close, closer, looking at her eyes and then her lips. Finally he brought his mouth to hers and kissed her softly. Just a faint flutter of a butterfly's wing. Slowly, his mouth opened and Petra was leaning into him. She was caught completely in the snares of the kiss, in the past she'd shared with the boy that had become this man, and she surrendered to the possibilities of a future. All that mattered were his lips and his strong arms and the warmth of them both cocooning her in a moment that existed away from words and time.

This kiss ended, and breathless, they drew away.

"Well, I, should be going." Dane said, his words odd and almost impersonal. Petra hated how men could do that. How was it possible to chill so quickly after a boil?

"I would like to return tomorrow? If possible? Will you have more pages completed?" His voice was hopeful, but again, slightly distant.

"What if I don't?" Petra asked, more a challenge than a real query.

"Well, then, I could...come the next day? Or, we could... I could make you dinner, perhaps?"

"Yes, well, lovely, yeah." Petra replied, pleased and a little breathless still.

He stood up abruptly and was suddenly in a rush to be gone. Petra could feel it in his movements, and the feeling of unease seemed to hover about him like a fog. She stood up as well, awkwardly, and he leaned forward to give her a hasty kiss on the cheek and walked briskly toward the door.

"Until tomorrow" he said, his voice a trifle overloud, and Petra heard the front door click shut a moment later. So intimate, and then so...distant. Odd. And somehow they had both avoided all conversation of their childhood, of Toby...of Allegra's mother, of Petra's own mother—of anything of any real import. A strange dance that moved too erratically for Petra to learn the steps to. She wasn't certain how she felt. She still tingled from the intensity of the kiss, but disappointment felt heavy in her chest. She couldn't think about it. There were too many other mysteries, too many missing pieces from these other puzzles. She breathed deeply and counted as the counselor had taught her, and when she heard the knock on the door, she smiled. Petra knew she shouldn't have worried. He was already back to apologize for being strange.

She pinched her cheeks and raced to the door. "Couldn't stay away..." she began, before her smile fell. It was not Dane at the door, but the unusual Mrs. Garzing, her eyes communicating that she knew precisely what Petra was thinking.

Diary Of Nerissa Swifte

Much has happened. Last night, I ventured over to the mainland. Darkness had fallen, and I was loath to leave my warm hearth: my cheerful little fire, my crackling logs. Tabby was curled into a tight ball on the lap of my skirt, and I myself had been near dozing. It had been another taxing day spent among the ill. It is an unusual pestilence that has crept onto Traversint. It slinks and lurks in doorways and hovers and skulks menacingly over all on the island. Though I have given of myself tirelessly, Annette's words have mixed with chance to poison the island against me. I did not think to see it happen. After all the lives I have saved, the fevers I have broken, the pains I have eased—all forgotten.

I left the Weatherly household, (all within healthy and mending, mind you!) to find   all other doors firmly barred to me. I could see distrustful eyes watching me through windows, and   hear the ugly whispered words that floated through the keyholes.

Locks turned as I passed, and it seemed somehow to grow still colder as I walked.

I stopped only at Mistress Blue's cottage, her youngest being frail and needing more care than some. Varvara Blue and I were of an age, and she had been a companion of mine as children, like her cousin Searc. Although she had married at 15, her husband had died the past winter and I took trouble to stop by and offer whatever succor I could the year round. If there were any hearth that would welcome me, I knew it to be hers.

She did open the door, but only a crack. Just a large enough slit to tell me in a shaking voice to go away. The tone of her entreaty was sad, but filled with fear. I bade her look me in the eye, to remember my many kindnesses and our past friendship. I bade her look me in the eye, for the sake of her ailing children, but she could not do it. When I asked why that I—me —Nerissa Swifte—should be turned away when I have never done naught but heal and comfort—her response silenced me. Da was wrong mayhap when he said that the island needed the Swiftes. Perhaps it is instead the Swiftes that need the island. Mistress Blue told me that there was much talk. Talk of how I benefit from other's misfortunes. Words about town that I live well because others do suffer. I asked her if she would be satisfied if I was instead begging in the street? Should I ask for no payment for my healing arts? She then chilled me. She asked why it was that no Swifte ever falls ill. Why for Swifte men to be born with the good fortune of a caul and for the women to have gleaming starlight hair and sway with magic o'er the island?

She said it was wicked, and a small voice whimpered inside the cottage. The door slammed shut in my face then, as though I were a thief or a vagrant, and not a trusted friend.

And so I had returned to my cottage, deep in the wood, far away from accusing eyes or wagging tongues. With no one but Tabby, my friendly fire and the warmth of my mother's quilt. But, though I had found solace in my cozy home, I could not find rest. Something pulled on my breast—as though a rope were attached to me, and it tugged with more and more force upon me until I could not but go for the insistence of it. It was a bitter night out of doors, and the forest held no warmth within it—and even less is to be found upon the ice which I would needs cross to travel to Travers Town. But, as I have written before, the cold holds no terror for me, I have only to step quicker on my way to escape it.

All the same, I wore an old pair of Fisher's flannel breeches under my heavy skirts, and added an extra shawl beneath my woolen mantle. The looking glass above my writing desk showed a very lumbering sort of bear-shaped woman, with silver blonde hair poking out like icicles. But it was only a glimpse, for my feet were already on a path that my mind knew not. My destination known only to my heart, which propelled me ever forward. Through the sugared pines and the crisp steps through the snow, I came to the water's edge. Water has never been my element, as it is to my men folk, but it has always been a friend to me, and so I have never feared the vast depth of the blue, nor have I thought much of the horrors of falling through knives of glass into the frozen water. The terror for me lay in wondering where my feet led. The alarm of the hunch that began to form in my mind, and the trepidation that I was correct.

One step after the other, even as I heard the crackle and shifting of the ice beneath my feet. I continued on despite a sudden loss of balance when I felt it buckle and chip. I did not falter, my breaths coming out as smoke in the frosty night air but I never once thought of turning around.

The darkness about me seemed absolute, as though I had wandered beneath a blanket of black with only the sound of my steps and the puffs of my own breathing as companions in the night. The moon hid, and I felt that it was on purpose to lend more mystery to my errand. Soon the small lights of those still not abed in the tiny harbor village twinkled before me, just pin-pricks of light in the night. A fire seen through a window or a candle on a nightstand. And soon, as I walked ever forward, a figure became discernible in the darkness. I could only see the same smoky puffs of breath coming from a mouth, and a deeper blackness in the shape of a man standing amidst the powder white snow. Closer, closer, I came until the rope about my person seemed too tight, the tension so strong, that it might lift me off my feet entirely.

Until I felt myself soaring, flying into the arms of the man that stood in the dark. My mouth pressed into his, my hand about his neck, and over the great expanse of his shoulders. His breath was warm on my cheek and on my lips, and his own desperate hands were around my waist and around my shoulders, pulling me closer and closer. I know not how we came to his bed, for my eyes took in only he that summoned me there. The force that had pulled me to him did not slacken until our bodies knew one another, until we twined and became as one.

As I write, I feel as though it was a kind of

madness, and that I have skipped over the words that give this scene sense. But although I search the breadth and length of my vocabulary, I can think of no other words. Is it nonsense to claim our souls knew one another? To say that perhaps it was out of our control? That is how it feels, indeed, there was nothing more right than the moment I felt his lips on mine, and knew that our bodies were made for loving one another. And when the act was finished, we began again. Less frenzied, and more sure of ourselves, and it was a kind of poetry to whisper his name—Alarence—aloud, and know he was mine to love.

Father Lemorale would take my willingness as proof of my evil. He would denounce me and name me wicked as he has always wanted to do. But I believe it is more wicked to betray my heart. My heart was created to love Alarence Attwater, and I would not hinder it in its purpose.

I have never known a man's touch, nor do I understand what called Alarence and I together last night, but now I hope that I shall never want for either. We spent the rest of the night in one another's arms, whispering secrets and telling stories of both of our lives, so much that I cannot imagine a time that my life was not filled with Alarence. I see all of his wanderings, and they are as my own memories. I told him of the Swiftes as he stroked my hair and kissed my neck. I watched his eyes grow wide with wonder when I spoke a few words to make a candle light on its own, or when I carelessly mumbled the spell to pull the blankets over our shoulders. What is love but secrets shared between hearts? What is more magic than finding oneself tucked within another's soul?

Even as my quill scratches these pages, I caution myself against being carried away by my feelings. For, although I have written that love is strong enchantment, it can also twist into a curse. I have only to think of my darling Fisher to have proof of that. But tonic or poison, it is a powerful thing, and so, although I let it flutter my breast and send the corners of my mouth ever upward, I am on guard.

I am Nerissa Swifte, protector and enchantress of this island, as my grandmother before me, and I will not forget it, nor lose myself.

It is morning now, and the soft grey glow of dawn led me back to my cozy cottage, the fire still cracking merrily with a spell I had left behind me. It is time now for me to sleep, and later I will return to town to see if there are any whose hearts have softened toward me. Or any that have grown desperate enough to look past the rumors. I cannot believe it possible that years of healing and potions could be undone with a few pernicious words spoken by a spiteful woman.

My hand is unsteady and my eyes blur with exhaustion. Though, truth be told, I can hardly believe I will be able to rest after the world has turned so many times for me this past night. And will continue to flip round and round, as I will return to my love, Alarence, this very night.

12
NATTER:
to talk incessantly

The expression on Mrs. Garzing's face unnerved her, though for what reason, Petra could not precisely discern.

She was not scowling, nor did she seem angry. In fact, no negative feeling whatsoever was etched onto her lined face. It was simply something in the suddenness of her visit. As though she had been waiting for Dane to leave, watching, biding her time until she could spring herself upon Petra when she was quite alone.

Even with this odd suspicion pricking at her, Petra conceded there was nothing menacing in the old woman's manner. Instead, she was simply odd. And since Petra was odd herself, she supposed it was hardly something to hold against someone else. If Petra wasn't careful she'd end up an eccentric old lady too, and she couldn't imagine she'd be half so pleasant as Mrs. Garzing when she got there.

"…sorry?" Petra caught herself. She had no idea how long she'd made her neighbor stand silently on her front stoop while she allowed her own thoughts to get swirl about.

"No trouble at all, Pebble. Lost in thought you were. Can't be helped, can't be helped, I'm sure. I'm sure it can't. Are you up to a neighborly visit? I suppose there is no sense in asking, really, to be sure. For I am already here, visiting, as it were."

Her tone was polite, but it held a hint of… something. It made her feel yet again that the old woman had been watching, listening…or at the very least, had seen Dane leave.

Petra brought the tiny woman in, and glanced behind her as she led, taking in the oddly sleek white hair that swung behind her in an ungainly Rapunzel-like braid. They came to the kitchen and Petra put on the kettle, placing the sugar bowl firmly in front of Margaret Garzing, who flashed a set of teeth much too straight and white for all the sweets she swallowed.

They talked of nothing at first. Polite banalities, making the correct noises to indicate interest and agreement in the appropriate pauses in conversation. It was obvious that both women had something more absorbing on their minds, grabbing the lion's share of their attention. For Petra, it was Dane's revelations and the warmth of his mouth on hers, and she suspected that whatever was on Mrs. Garzing's mind was the real reason for her visit. But whatever that was, Petra couldn't begin to imagine.

Now that she had more information of her own past here, she thought perhaps she could tentatively steer the tiny woman who was now loudly smacking her lips on the spooned sugar and milk tea sludge around to that avenue of conversation. When the next lull presented itself, she pounced.

"Mrs. Garzing…"

"Call me Maggie, dear." She cut in, a faint milky mustache around her mouth.

"Ah, yes, Margaret. I had forgotten that was your given name, I'm sorry."

"It's not, but you can call me by it." She grinned at Petra, who couldn't erase the confused look from her face. So, instead, she stood up to fetch and refill the teapot while she re-formed her questions.

"Right. Yes, okay, Maggie. You said you knew me as a child. Did you then also know my…" the word caught in Petra's throat, trying to snag a sob, but she would not allow it, and so she forced it out with a croak. "…brother. My brother Toby? Or my mother?"

The painful lump in her throat that had hindered the words of her question now descended to sit on top of her heart as she waited for the old woman's answer. Mrs. Garzing sat back in her chair and raised her eyes to the ceiling, as though she were reading from a script that had been affixed above her head. Finally, she answered.

"Toby? Of course, a fine boy. Still is. No one better. Your mother? What was her name? Something silly? Yes, Gemma. Yes, I knew her. Didn't like her. Very….brooding. Not my cup of tea. Not at all."

She looked back at Petra, and smiled again, holding her cup out for more tea. "Do you have any muffins? Or perhaps cookies? I'm mad for cookies."

Still reeling from this new set of revelations, Petra walked like an automaton to the pantry. She didn't know why, for she knew she hadn't any baked goods of any kind. She barely had anything to eat at all.

"Let me guess? Sugar cookies?"

Her tone was sarcastic and she wished the words back , but Mrs. Garzing didn't hear the implied jab.

"Oh no. Unless it's Christmas, of course. Of course then, sugar cookies it is. But I am partial to butterscotch."

Petra was about to apologize and shrug, explain that she hadn't any, but in the middle of her pantry sat a tray of cookies, still warm. Again, robot-like, she picked up the tray, half expecting it to disappear, and carried it to the table.

"Here they are then, but….I'm afraid this will sound strange…"

"Perfect." replied Mrs. Garzing, not waiting for the end of Petra's statement. "Chocolate chip. I wouldn't worry too much about from whence they came, Pebble. The important thing is that they're here."

Petra could almost feel another fit hovering about her. She was confused, her emotions were raw and rollercoastered, she was imagining things, surely. She excused herself, briefly, and went into her bedroom. She screamed into her pillow, and then took three deep breaths, shook the nonsense out of her head, and walked back down the stairs.

When she returned to the kitchen, she was calmer, but determined to ignore the cookies, which were now mostly eaten, except for a partially chewed piece that seemed to have no chocolate chips, which remained forlornly on the tray.

"Saved you a nip." Mrs. Garzing said, her eyes not meeting Petra's, in a guilty child-like way. She was paging through a notebook, her concentration taken over by the writings on the page. Petra's notebook.

Her private notebook that contained the diary translations.

Her mouth dropped in horror as crumbs and sticky fingers thumbed through her pages. She had no voice, and for the second time that day, no words.

Maragaret's small, gnarled fingers worried the corners of the pages, and—horror of horrors—Petra watched in agony as Mrs. Garzing reached one bony fingertip to her mouth, bringing it back down to turn a precious page. In this action, Petra's immobility released into a flurry of words and movements in order to save her notebook.

In one deft move, she snatched the pages from Mrs. Garzing, seizing it one handed and pulling it close to her chest, cradling it. She hadn't realized until then how possessive she had become of the book. The translations contained Nerissa, after all. And to have a strange woman pawing through the private thoughts of one she admired so deeply felt like a violation. And not just of Nerissa, but of Petra. How had she ever agreed to publish this diary?

"I'm sorry, Pebble. These ancient eyes thought the notebook was an old friend. One of your father's notebooks. Your father always did have the most interesting tomes and thrilling notes on them, didn't he? Bless his soul. The most wonderful books haunting his library, don't you find?"

Petra's earlier panic was subsiding, realization that the old woman had no idea what she was looking at, had only been interested in the notes because it was something she thought she recognized. Margaret's eyes were looking beyond Petra, back to the past, though whether it was a memory of her father, or one of the woman's own faraway reminisces, she couldn't guess.

She stood up, suddenly, disturbing the china on the little bistro table, and dusted the crumbs from her sleeves and long black skirt, and Petra noticed again how bird-like and frail the old woman was. Her features were somehow ageless and ancient in the same glance. It was the second time she had visited Petra, and yet, she still knew nothing of her. What was her life? How old was she? Why did she remain in Traverston if she could go anywhere she wished? And what had she known of her father, her family, her past?

She was moved to ask, but Margaret was already bowing her way out the door, clucking courtesies and thanking Petra for the tea. She bestowed a feathery kiss on Petra's cheek, and hastened out the door, promising to return soon, and giving a vague warning about ghosts in the library. She slipped out quickly before Petra could sputter any questions beyond her own confused lips.

But, besides the odd comments about ghosts, something Margaret had said niggled at her. Petra ran a hand over the braid Dane had plaited in her waves, finding knots and snarls that would need to be brushed out. What was it? She started running water into the teacup, watching the grains of sugar float upward, when it dawned on her. Her father's books. Mrs. Garzing had mentioned the library and that her father had owned interesting tomes and notebooks. Had she meant the books themselves were rare? Or that her father kept notebooks about his reading that were somehow unusual? Either possibility was intriguing. Petra had never gone though the library. When she had first arrived in Traverston, she was a shell of herself—after Evan, and then the loss of her father, the inheriting of this cottage in the middle of the woods. She was still mending. Her cuts still raw, physically and emotionally. She had lived with the numbness for so long that she hadn't really even seen the books. She knew they were there, but she hadn't seen them as individual entities, but instead as the complete amalgam of 'her father's library'. They had been a sad reminder of the life she had left behind, of the life her father had left behind. And although she had known real loss, she also felt keenly the million other tiny cuts. The every day death. The deaths of a relationship, or of the version of herself she had used to know. The vanishing of a part of her life that she would never see again. Many, numerous, infinitesimal deaths that cut into her like daggers, until she looked at her own reflection and perceived that she had been sculpted into a form that was unrecognizable from the woman she had used to see peering back at her from the looking glass.

Still, Margaret's comment about her father's library had struck a resounding chord. She marched into the library to take a good look at the books she'd barely seen in all the time she'd been living there.

Her first thought stepping onto the worn Persian rug, breathing in that musty vanilla and paper scent, was how glad she was to be out of the kitchen. There had been too much strangeness in there today. The oddness of it all stuck to her like cobwebs. Dane's passionate kiss was caught in her hair, and Mrs. Garzing's sugar-sticky fingers flipping through her notebook were still clinging to her sleeve. The library wiped all of the cloying memories away, the words and thoughts and ideas of the books worked to filter out the confusions and disappointments of the day.

Books always seem to do so. Clear the mind, revive the senses, massage away the tensions, leaving the mind free, and then capturing it within the pages of a story.

Petra took a moment to clear her own mind, and took a deep breath, listening again for the sounds of the books. She was certain now that they had been speaking to her earlier, whispering their stories to her in the silence. She ran a finger along the spines, moving slowly, not reading the titles just yet. Odder and stranger, she had lived here for over a year, and she'd never thought to peek at these books. It had felt…wrong, somehow. Each page of each book had a different image of her father's face imprinted into it. He had lived a moment between the covers of these books, and to disturb them felt as though she was losing some ghostly part of him. If she opened the cover the minute part of him that had been captured by the book would float out and away, and it would mark her grief fresh. And, it did seem like a kind of trespass. Our books are a reflection of ourselves, after all. One cannot dwell within a novel's pages without something of the words rubbing off onto our palms, our eyelashes, our souls.

And vice versa.

But now, with her fingers trailing along the spines, she paused and without looking, plucked a book from the shelf. It did not smell or feel particularly old, but still contained that vanilla and ink scent that she knew loved so well. She opened her eyes and saw that it was one of hers. ***American Slang 1750-1850, Dr. Petra Roccia.***

She paged through, seeing *Apple Dumpling Shop*, a charming term for a woman's bosom, *Snabbled,* meaning, killed in battle, and then finally flipped to *Znees*, (frost) her favorite of all. She'd had such a ball researching this book. She'd traveled all over the country, tracking sources and rare books, elderly gentlemen and ladies who could remember their great grandmother saying such a thing, or who possessed a letter of their great-uncle's, in which was written such a thing. Lost idioms, lost phrases and turns of speech —she had searched them out and brought the treasures that were those lost words back into the gleam of light. That had been when her star had begun its ascent. Before Evan. Before her heart shattered. She opened the fly-leaf on the back cover to see the smiling black and white headshot they'd used for her biography. She didn't look that much different, except the eyes. The eyes always gave a person away. Her eyes had seen a lot since that picture. A lot of sadness.

Petra was seized suddenly by another cloud of melancholy, though this was one she successfully derailed before it became a full-blown fit. She breathed in deeply and counted as her therapist had taught, and she reached for another book, paged through, and then grabbed another. Besides the photo of herself on the back of her own book, there were no other photos in the house. Petra's father had never had them. She had always thought it was because the pictures of the two of them would be too much display of the family that was missing. Dead and, as Petra now knew, locked away.

The murdered and the murderer, as it were, though it felt like a punch in the gut to think of it that way.

So, it was eerie to find a photo of Toby, the edge of the picture a bit crumpled and worn from being frequently held, inside of one of her later books, farther along the shelf. Tucked inside, ***Funerary and Mourning Customs: A Linguistic Exploration,*** she found Toby. It made her cold all over, her fingers so cold they almost burned. Her father had stuck her brother in a funeral book? Her funeral research? So morbid, and sad. But if he was obviously often looking at the photo, why did he hide it? What possible reason was there?

So many puzzles, so many secrets. They seemed like cankers in her mouth, all the more painful when she worried at them, yet she was unable to let them heal. She couldn't forget about them because she didn't know from whence they came. Her life had been complicated enough before without all of these new sores to tend to. It wasn't a pretty analogy, but it was apt. For cankerous was how the mysteries and lies felt. Painful, ugly things that once pricked would pus and dribble and had now infected her thoughts so that she was feverish thinking of them.

She replaced the book but noted where she had taken it from. Petra already had a perfect picture of Toby in her mind, an image the snapshot stuck in the pages could never equal. No two-dimensional printed and faded copy of him could match the living breathing brother of her memories. The smell of him, the warmth of him, his voice quieting her tears when her mother was yelling, screaming, in another room. All the same, she didn't want to forget where she'd found it. In case she needed it. In case it was a clue.

Clues. Could they be considered thus if they weren't left behind, bread-crumb like to be found? Evidence, hint, indication, tip—from the late Middle English *clew* meaning 'ball of thread' —the means to guide one through a labyrinth.

A labyrinth. A maze, warren, network of passages, entanglement. From Greek, *laburinthus*, the maze constructed to house the minotaur of legend. Yes, this photo was a piece of a thread, a line that would help her through the passages, from the darkness and back out into the light.

But Petra had dwelled in darkness so long, she wasn't sure she could stand the brightness that she might find.

She glanced back at the book that held Toby within its pages, and then toward the door that led to the kitchen. A kitchen where a mug sat, still partially sticky with sugar. A kitchen where she had momentarily lost herself, her mysteries, in Dane's kiss.

And then her eyes lit back onto her notebook, waiting patiently on the overly large oak desk, sidled up next to the diary. Nerissa's diary. Somehow it all connected. The secrets began in Traversint, hundreds of years past, and they led to Petra, but...a Petra of tomorrow. A Petra whose job it was to sleuth out what was hidden in the past, and the raw wounds that had been left behind in Petra's childhood. She walked quietly, as though she might scare off the books, and sat down gingerly in her father's chair. Carefully, she drew her gloves on, and resolved to read until she had another thread to follow.

And then she'd need to see a man about some apples. Thomas Marr, the man who first made her aware of the mutterings lurking below the whispers of her own sorrow.

Diary Of Nerissa Swifte

I have became a creature of darkness. Coming alert and awake with the fall of night. The sun rises, the sun sets. Day breaks, it crests, it rises mightily into the sky. But night—night falls. It sneaks, stealthily, it tiptoes in on velvet shoes, clothing the world in sable and onyx. But this has become my element. To be hidden by the embrace of midnight, and to flee from the promise of golden day.

And never have I felt so powerful.

Like the Swifte men who were crafted carefully for the caress of the waves, I am made for the glow of moonlight. It puts the flash of lightning in my eyes and in my fingertips. It glances violently off my silver-blonde tresses, confirming me as a daughter of the dark. It is in this attitude that I arrive to Alarence each night. I cannot have enough of him. He is the delicacy I crave, the quench of my thirst, the only sight for my eyes. He is, in truth, a comely man, but when I look upon him, I see him not at all. But instead, the light within him. The light of his spirit, of his soul. A torch that grows brighter when added to the dark of my own.

Each night we make love. With our bodies, with our hearts, our minds, and I leave him before the sun can catch me. Indeed, the sun always finds me back in my own bed, and that same sun is none the wiser that I have gone anywhere since it left with the daylight the day before.

Before it is supposed that I have run mad, I most solemnly profess that I have not. It is an idyll for Alarence and I. All love begins with new love, and so I must cling to it as it lasts. For soon, all love is tested, and I have cause to think ours will be tested before too many more moons.

I gaze into a little silver hand-mirror, a love token from my sweetheart. Our initials are engraved with swoops and swirls, looping letters etched into the edge of the glass by his own strong hands. Hands that I loved from the first, hands that I know well. He says it is a gift given in hopes that each time my visage is reflected within, I will see what he loves most in this world. Pretty words from my love, and I will treasure them for their sentiment.

But, I must close up my little book, for night is shuffling in, and I must away—until the purple ribbons of dawn call me back to my cottage.

13

MISMARROW:

to mismatch two things together incorrectly

Petra peered into the diary, darkness falling just as stealthily outside her own windows, and she tried to understand the words she had begun to read. The previous entry was more whimsical, almost musical and melodious in its tone. And then she had turned the page to find a hasty, crabbed scrawl, so different from Nerissa's usual writing that for a moment she could not believe it belonged to the same woman she knew and admired.

Oh, rot. She didn't know Nerissa Swifte. She was long dead, as vanished as the island she had lived upon. But she knew her writing, felt the swirls and tittles, the swooshes and crossed letters in her heart. She realized she should seek out more information on Samuel Proper, as Dane had begun to do. Perhaps there were blueprints, or a map of the old town lurking somewhere. There had to be a...remnant of Alarence Attwater, or Meg Proper or...perhaps, just maybe something of Nerissa? Somewhere? She would have to ask Dane…she felt her face grow red with only the thought of him. She shook her head, erasing the tender memories from her mind, and turned back to the diary in her gloved hands.

Petra bit her lip. She had to admit she was apprehensive about continuing to translate it. Nervous. Anxious. Worried. Agitated. Distressed. Most definitely on edge at the idea. There was so much fresh tumult in her own life, she wasn't certain she could shake the joy she received in reading about Nerissa's new love. Wishing it was her own.

She set the book aside momentarily, and tended to her growing list of words.

Navamorrin, she had translated as *new love*. But the way Nerissa had used it had seemed more like a state of being, or a force upon the body. But the other word bothered her. As much as words were her own power her own solace and confidantes, one word had defied her usual automatic processing. Petra had written, "never had she felt so powerful" but powerful was not quite right. It was lacking in dynamism and passion for what Nerissa's emotion suggested. The word **Fravelin**, was difficult for Petra to even imagine in her own mind. It was something like being so filled with your own happiness, so aware of your own gifts that you became in some way unbreakable. Larger than life. Powerful was so puny a word for such an emotion—but it was the best Petra could do at the moment.

She cracked her knuckles one by one, enjoying the satisfying pops that issued from each, and set her face with determination. She owed it to Nerissa to carry on reading the words of her life, no matter the path they led her down.

In reading her words, living her story, Petra brought the woman back to life, if only to dwell within her own mind.

Words were powerful, Petra thought, not for the first time, as she poised her pen over the naked page. Each word was a breath of life.

Words were *fravelin*, she thought, and she felt somehow, somewhere, Nerissa Swifte would agree.

Diary Of Nerissa Swifte

I reckoned it possible that my fingers would not obey the torrents of my thoughts. That the events, the storm of the past hours would be locked within me. Even now, as I release the whirlwind into my book of days, my precious little book, I am unsure if there is wisdom in such a tempest being set free from the confines of my mind. Will it clear my thoughts or only roil and stir up more confusion and chaos?

Last night, as I had written, I followed the string on my heart to its twin, and I spent the moonlight twined completely with Alarence. It is less than a full day since those moments, and yet it is lifetimes ago. He had spoken of leaving this place, or taking me with him on his travels. And though I long to see the wide world with my own eyes, to experience the wonders that lay beyond my front door—for all of that, Traversint is my home. And more than that, it is my dominion. I am the healer and protector of

Traversint, whether it is truth or legend, I feel the mark of the place upon me, in my very blood. And my mark upon it. To be separated from it forever more? 'T'would be the death of me—and I was soon to learn such a separation could be the death of me in truth. Even if the islanders continue to banish me from their presence, even if the malady that ravages here takes them all into the arms of my misunderstood friend, Death, I must abide here. This island and I will cease if I were to leave. I did not tell all of this to Alarence when first he spoke of it. No, I allowed his fantasies and dreams of a future together to enfold me. To robe me with hope as his words, like a thousand kisses pressed against my skin. I pretended that it was all possible. That there was no destiny to contend with. No responsibilities to fulfill, only the whims of my own heart. I imagined—though it was wicked— that there was no Da, no Fisher or Phin. No villagers or islanders, no maladies to cure, no babes to help deliver, no island at all. Just myself and Alarence and the wide world for us to wander as we wished. It was a pleasant fiction, and I held it close like a flame I did not want the wind to blow out, as I walked home in the pre-dawn purple-grey of the morning.

The shock, then, of arriving back to my snug cottage was immense. Although I had not outright told Alarence, my love, my heart, that I nay could could go with him, I had whispered the words in my heart. To come upon my home, my retreat, that my brothers and father had built for me with their own sweat and their own hands—to find my blankets torn to pieces and my dresses shredded to rags. My kitchen swirled into a chaos of crockery shards and broken glass. A autumn's worth of canning and provisions scattered on the floor, chairs splintered and books torn. Tabby was nowhere to be found, and this diary I believed to be as lost to me as the one that had dropped to the bottom of the lake.

I stayed only a few moments, stunned and mouth agape, calling softly for Tabby in a half-voice. My eyes searched the wreckage constantly for a remnant, something safe from the destruction. I found only a few underthings, and a dress I had pressed beneath the mattress long ago for some forgotten reason. My small box of herbs had survived too, and that only because it was kept in a safe place, wrapped inside of a scarlet cape that belonged to my mother.

I heard a twig snap in the forest, and suddenly the wood was no longer an escape, but felt dangerous. I did not wonder why this was done to me, or by whom. The islanders, poisoned by a few words and recent sickness, believed my powers evil, when they had only ever been used in their service. My healing used for their health, and the prosperity of our shared island home.

My words, my claims of innocence would not matter now. Poison cannot be drawn out as easily and quickly as it is taken in.

I ran then, my eyes wild and my gleaming hair flying behind me like snowflakes in the wind. I was a flurry incarnate, for I felt myself frozen, numbed past feeling by the betrayal. I clutched my belongings to my chest, my treasures. I ran first to the twined Apple Birch, but saw no one. Instead I saw a notch, very new, very fresh, the tree still weeping from the wound. No one else might have seen it, but it was a signal to run, and so I went to the only place I could think of, the safest and most powerful place on the island.

My Da's home is ancient. It is large, but gnarled and twisted as though it were an enormous tree trunk that continues to grow. Da says it is made from sea and sky and that is where the first man fish and his fairy wife made their home. Living together as they did in neither water nor heaven, but with the power of both. The house changes as it grows, and as the people within it change, so do the shape of the rooms. An enchanted place, and it is said that the tree the home is carved from anchors the island on the lake, and that as long as Swifte's dwell within, all will be well.

It had been difficult to leave a place so warm, so filled with family and...magic. Truly magic, for there is no other word. But it was even more difficult to return, knowing my cottage was no more.

Phineas opened the door before my knock, and silently took my things, placing them gently on the table before presenting me with mulled wine. I fell to shaking, and tears fell from my eyes, though, in truth, I could not feel anything. So much had changed, and in only a few short hours. One moment I was in Alarence's arms, the world paused in its turning around our bodies. We were the universe and life itself bent before us. And then, my heart had pushed against his desires to keep me, to take me on his adventures, to live them by his side. The cottage, my things, the people—my people, my friends! Turned against me. Phin and Da did not ask what had happened, they knew. I had not told them, but they knew.

Da shook his head back and forth, back and forth, looking more heartbroken than even I. He was unwilling or incapable of believing what had transpired. He muttered, "There have always been Swiftes, always been Swiftes, always been Swiftes…" over and over under his breath, like an inhale and an exhale. As though the repetition was the only thing triggering his breath.

Phin was speaking to me, pleading with me to hide, making urgent plans to get me to safety, to remove me from the world of the island. My heart did leap, I must admit, at the thought that I might, after all, join Alarence, that fate was clearing a way for my dreams to come true. But Da, he put a hand up, and looked at us both, stopping all thought and all plans with one glance.

His voice was low and full of ghosts. I could see the swirling phantom memories and memories of memories sounding from his throat.

"It is time" he began, the words slamming into me with unexplainable force. "Time that I told you the full legend of our families." Confusion had gripped me, and my stomach sank. When my eyes found Phineas', I knew he too did not understand. The stories, the tales of fairy and fish, our destiny on the island—what more could there be?

Da motioned for us to sit in the chairs. They were solid stone, and very special to him. He had told us from childhood that our Great-GrandDa had found them at the bottom of the lake. That they had once belonged to the chieftain of all of the lake people, and that more magic had touched these stone thrones than I or my brothers could imagine. They were not usually used for sitting, and again, my stomach sank, for I knew there was something terrible about my family's secret.

Da went to the window and looked out, a light came into his eyes, and he stepped quickly to the door, opening it to reveal the figure he had seen approaching.

It was Fisher. Relief flooded me, though I had not recognized before that I was afraid for him. He had changed so much as of late—but deep inside I knew the intrepid Fisher lived somewhere, and it was that Fisher that I feared for. If the island was on edge, there was always a chance they would turn on my twin, my other half, my second soul.

He rushed to embrace me, dropping Tabby and this, my book of days, my hand mirror, and a few of my notes on spells and herbals at my feet. The cat scurried to the fire side, and I held my brother close to my heart. "I went to the birch…" I began, but Da cut me off, motioning for my silence.

"We haven't much time, and this story must be known to all of you. I did not think to see this day, else I would have told the tale long ago. I pushed the telling of it away, and away and away and now it is upon me, and I have no more space to push it."

Fisher sat quietly beside me, and both of my brothers grasped my fingers. Our Da was not known to be a serious man, always jolly and laughing. His tone alone sent shivers through us.

I have taken pains to recount his words as he spoke them, though without the lilt and gravel of his voice I cannot hope to replicate them.

"It is true that we are born from the lake and the sky. That a combined magic runs rapidly in Swifte blood. But the union of our forefathers was not without price. Nothing can be given or rewarded without price. And the greater the gift, the higher the debt that must be paid, and the Swiftes have a gift most precious.

When a man from the lake and a fairy from the air looked upon one another in love, they made their life on this land. But this island had to be created. It did not exist, and with their enchantments, they conjured it into being. They could not go and simply build their home on any shore, they needed an island. Land that grows amidst water and heaven, surrounded on all sides by both. I do not know what magic they used, but they created Traversint, which was called by another name at that time. An island of soft green with trees and flowers, creeks and springs. A place of so much beauty and color that neither of the lovers would miss their former lives beneath the waves or in the clouds.

But a spirit saw what they had done. An old spirit, older than the lovers, almost older than the lake or the sky. He had protected this area since time began, and when he saw their island, a place created for themselves for their own happiness—he was displeased. He thought the lovers selfish, using their magic for their own desires, creating a life of isolation and plenty.

And so he cursed them for their thoughtlessness and self serving. He brought people to the island; sick, poor, those that needed a little of the beauty of the island for their own souls. And he put a spell on the lovers. Never could they leave the island they had created. Forever would they live to help and heal the humans of the island. The daughter of the isle was doubly cursed. For if the fairy enchantress ever left for more than 3 days, the island and all of the people upon it would sink into the lake, never to be seen again. Whomever had defied the spirit would live forever, knowing that they had the deaths of all the island on their hands. Immortality without love or forgiveness."

Da finished, his voice breaking. He sat down on his old wooden chair and turned his face toward the fire. In the light of the flames and the darkness of the shadows, I noticed how old he looked, and now how full of concern, for us, his children. Our futures on the island seemed less secure, and if his unbelievable tale can be believed, the curse of the Swiftes would soon come for a reckoning. Or at least that was the thread of my thoughts that stitched through my mind.

Tabby stirred at the fire, picking her head up and squinting toward the window. She caught my attention, my little cat, though I cannot say why. So even as Fisher was squeezing my hand and my brothers questioned my suddenly silent father about the story, I knew to be afraid.

I knew they were coming for me, knew they would take me. Mayhap they would burn me. The mainlanders would not do such a thing, the practice being out of taste for some years. But the islanders were strange folk. More readily attuned to the supernatural.

But I said nothing, only staring into the golden green eyes of Tabby, until finally I pulled Fisher's coarse and callused hand to my lips and whispered for him to bring me my book of days, and to keep my cat safe. Pointless requests. Responsibilities I needn't have asked him for.

But then the door flew open, like a cannon shot, and my brothers jumped to their feet. Their black hair took on an even greater wildness, and their cold black eyes turned to ice. I could see my Fisher, the old Fisher, in the set of his jaw, and the violence in his stance, and he did not falter even when Annette stepped into the room. Phineas too, looked more man than boy. I think they might have tried to fight every man in town—even kill them. But it was my Da that made my mind up.

His face, covered by his hands as though he could not bear to look upon the scene. Silent sobs that racked his once larger-than-life frame. Black hair faded to iron grey. "Not my children…" He said it quietly, so quietly, only Tabby and I could hear it above the chaos and fear and anger of the townspeople that had come.

I stood up at once, understanding. I could not watch as rage filled Fisher, making him more animal than man. I could not stand by and allow Phin, my baby brother, to leave childhood behind in a storm of blows. And I could not break Da's heart. It had been broken when our mother left, it could not be torn again this night.

"I will go." I said. And though I spoke quietly, every man and woman grew silent at the sound of my voice. "Your quarrel is with me, not my family. I will go, willingly. But leave the Swiftes in peace."

Father Lemorale stepped forward with the oldest Rollingbrook, a young man I remembered from the deathbed of his father. Annette stood with a few of the wives, and though her expression was of revenge and wickedness the other women did not meet my eyes at all. Instead, they looked to the stone floor, and frowned as though they did not like to be there.

Fisher and Phin were struck dumb, and Da did not remove his face from his hands. I walked with Mr. Rollingbrook, acting the part of the constable, who mercifully waited until we were outside the door to place me in shackles. Annette fairly skipped down the snowy path, though I noted the rest of the party was somber. There were sideways glances and wrinkled brows aplenty, each man and woman seeming to be deep in thought about what they had done. I could not tell if it was that they believed so strongly in my guilt, or because they had doubts about the steps they had taken. I still do not know.

I fought back tears. Feelings had finally been restored to me, and the shock of finding my cottage and my life torn to shreds thawed into pain. Tears pricked like needles, but I blinked them back. I am a Swifte, I can will myself to strength.

Mr. Rollingbrook walked me to this cell, only one of two for the infrequent and few prisoners ever seen on this island. He was neither kind nor unkind when he locked the door and strode down the passage, leaving me in darkness. Instead he was indifferent, which somehow was the most painful of all. I searched my mind for some moments, but could recall almost nothing of the walk from Da's to the gaol. A blur of trees and flickering firelight from the houses we passed. Instead, I turned my mind to the warmth of Alarence's bed, and the feeling of his mouth pressed to mine in ardor, and the memories warmed my heart for some moments. But soon after, the cold of the night set in, and the stones beneath me were blocks of ice. I could see nothing but a finger of moonlight, such is the angle of my cell, and my lip began to tremble. For though it is true that I do not feel the cold as keenly as some, being myself made from the coldness of the deep lake and brisk north wind air, and frozen light of the moon, it still has power over me. Cold's fingertips still graze against my skin and prick and prod at my flesh. As I wrote some months ago, I knew it to be a cold and difficult winter from the start—though I could not have known how the cold would sink into the marrow of my bones, nor the extent of the difficulties before me.

As I began to despair, a bundle was pushed through the grate far above me. No voice, no sound, save for soft fabric falling to the stone floor. I looked up, squinting, but could see no one, but I knew immediately who it had been. Fisher, dear Fisher, my heart and soul. The bundle was my red cape, and his own black one of miniver, and very warm. They had been wound tightly about 3 tallow candles, flint, my book of days, and some pemmican to eat. Though I did not know the contents for certain until I lit the candle.

I waited until morning to write in this book, not wanting to waste the light. It is grey dawn now, and I have been writing in the dim light. Between my cape and my brother's, I passed a not completely frozen night, and was warmed further by his kindness. I have seen no one since the night before, nor heard anything. My stomach is growling, though I conserve the food, not knowing the islander's plans. It did occur to my tortured mind that they needn't burn me, or give me a trial at all. They could simply hope I would freeze to death or starve me—or a malicious combination of both. I am terrified to consider such things, especially of those I once considered friends. Of those whose lives I fought for against illness, and though it may have been a curse to care for the sick and poor of Traversint, for me it had been a calling of pleasure and purpose. But I must quiet these thoughts and think only of the travails of the moment. For the islanders, it is easier to ignore a problem than face it, so mayhap they will forget me, allow me to wither and my heart to stop, frozen in death.

But, Fisher—Phin—Da....they would not allow that, surely?

My mind turns to Alarence again, and...oh! Hark, a sound of keys in a lock down the passage, I must hide these ramblings, and hope to discover my fate.

14

MISSLIENESS:
*a feeling of loneliness caused by missing someone
you care for*

She set aside Nerissa's diary, long after midnight. She'd read and re-read over the list of words she'd collected. She'd added, **Gardaween,** which she'd translated awkwardly in her notes. Instead of a one word substitution for the term, she set about describing the specifics of the Swifte's responsibilities on the island. The stone thrones, the **Krilance,** as Nerissa referred to them, had been vivid in Petra's mind as she read the words on the page. She could almost feel their power, even as she was not there in that moment, but instead, hundreds of years in the future. Their majesty resonated still, through Nerissa's swoops and whorls of ink. It was this more than anything she'd read so far that had finally convinced her, to her core, that Dane, for all his secrets, was right.

There was magic in this place.

Or, there had been, many years ago.

She had wanted to keep reading, to continue taking down the record of Nerissa's words, her personal collection of the rare almost an afterthought now. Instead, it was Nerissa herself that Petra yearned for. The essence of her bravery, her confidence, her zeal for life and love, even amidst obstacles.

But sleep weighted her eyelids and tired her cramping fingers until, all at once, it had stolen over her. And later she'd awoken, her head in her own notebook, looking out on a grey dawn not unlike the one Nerissa had described in her latest entry.

She'd showered and dressed, her mind still made up to pay a visit to Mr. Marr, Thomas, who would hopefully light her way in the darkness in which she found herself about her own past. She took the same path as before, admiring the golds and reds and fiery oranges of the season. The world seemed brighter today, and she found herself straining to see the lake that she knew must lie just beyond the trees. And once, when she had paused in hope of glimpsing glittering sunlight on the glassy blue, she was joined by a familiar voice.

"You won't find it" Thomas said, his voice light with amusement.

"Find what?" Petra didn't turn around to greet him, her eyes still trying to search out a flicker of blue, or the ripple of a wave.

"The lake. It's not there. Well, it is, I suppose, but it's impossible to see. The land ascends gradually and is dappled with trees. It's such a small incline that the eye hardly notices it."

"Oh, well, shit." Petra said, making a click with her tongue, snapping her fingers. "You caught me out."

She turned to face him, and was surprised to see the smile on his face.

"What?" She asked, suddenly self-conscious.

"Oh, nothing…" He began, but her squinting disbelief caused him to roll his eyes and change his response. "That's a familiar mannerism is all. You and Toby both, would do that almost constantly. The click and the snap, usually followed by an exasperated exhale. One of you was always disappointed about something. A curfew, getting caught for mischief, coming home with a coat or shoes missing, something."

They had fallen in step as he spoke, their strides matched, although he was much taller. Petra looked over at Thomas, and for some reason his face looked…younger. Softer, somehow. It was probably a trick of the morning light, or maybe her own memories of him as a boy beginning to surface. Petra realized that they had not properly greeted one another, but somehow it seemed unnecessary, and oddly familiar, although, she remembered it was not really familiar at all. "Tell me about him" she said, quietly, her faced pointed straight ahead down the path, though she did not know which direction they were now walking in.

Thomas sighed and scratched his straw-colored hair. "He was bossy, but not as much as you. Everyone demurred to the two of you. He was the fastest runner, but a very sore loser at games. He was a great pitcher though, best on the team. Toby always had that book with him, was always reading it, writing in it, don't remember what it was, now. He liked to tell jokes, though I've no idea where he heard any of them. He always seemed to know a new one. Let me see, hm, well, he had infinite patience, a slow temper, and he was always convinced he was going to catch a raccoon or a squirrel and keep it as a pet. As if your mother would ever have allowed that!"

Thomas bit his lip, realizing his error. "Sorry, I...I shouldn't have brought up your mom."

"It's all right." Petra exhaled, and with a very small voice, then asked, "Will you tell me about her, too?"

Thomas gave her a small, sad smile. "Of course, but you'd be better off asking my mom. You have to remember, kids don't often notice much about their friend's mothers." He rubbed his chin and then crossed his arms over his chest, as though protecting himself from the words he was about to speak.

"She was pretty, like you, but she was less... vibrant. She seemed, I don't know...preoccupied? Bored? Unhappy? I'm not sure, it was like she wasn't all there or as enthusiastic as other parents. She dressed...really fancy, and went away all the time. I only know because when she came home your folks would fight and that's when we'd find you and Toby in the orchard. And Dane, of course."

"Why do you say, 'of course'?" Petra asked.

Thomas shrugged his shoulders, and spread his hands apart as though it were difficult to put into words. "Because he always followed your steps. Wherever you were, Dane was also." Thomas' voice was full of confusion as he explained.

"I take it...he hasn't told you yet?"

Petra shook her head not trusting herself to speak. "Strange..." Thomas said, and then was silent.

They walked for some time, in silence, their route taking them to a coastal path where Petra's eyes could wander over the beige-golden sand and out over the water, the blue continuing on seemingly forever.

Infinity. Never-ending. Petra's eyes searched that blue horizon, hoping for a signal, a sign, a hint, a clue... something that would tell her where the island had stood. She wasn't certain if she was hoping for magic glitter or an enchanted x-marks-the-spot, but she received neither. Which was just as well, she'd had enough fits of nerves and moods these past days, she definitely didn't need to add a supernatural event to the mix.

Petra looked again to Thomas, a question on her lips, but it froze and died there before she asked it. There was something...odd about him. She realized she had never asked him what his life had been while she had been away. When they weren't speaking his face was almost a mask, and his eyes were looking at distant sights, distant memories, perhaps. Darkness was inside Thomas, just as it lived within her, and she didn't like to ask him about whatever it was that fixed his attention so firmly and made stone of his features. Everyone was allowed their own ghosts, she supposed.

Petra hadn't thought that perhaps Thomas was walking somewhere specific. Being out wandering herself, and rather selfish, she simply assumed that he'd appeared because she had been looking for him. By the time she realized he was headed somewhere, she found that she had rather forwardly tagged along. They were on a small avenue, just outside the cheerful downtown, only a few short streets away from Love's shop—and Dane.

There were only a few stately brick madams on the avenue. Perfect posture and iron-gated, looking so much like prim school marms, that Petra stood up a little straighter as she stepped. "I'm sorry, are you...

visiting someone?" It occurred to Petra that she hadn't the slightest idea where Thomas Marr lived, and she could very well be hounding the poor man home. Which was not only awkward but also disconcerting. She couldn't imagine the affable Thomas Marr living in one of these houses. So when he informed her that his mother lived here, and that he'd thought she might have better answers to some of Petra's questions than he did, Petra relaxed and followed him up the walkway to the stoop.

She was confused when he stepped out of the way, urging her to go on up, without him. "But why? Why aren't you coming in?" She asked, and he shook his head and laughed. He had business in town, he told her, and he would see his mother later. He reminded her of his mother's invitation for Petra to visit, and then gave her another lighter than wind faux-kiss on the cheek and disappeared down the street, whistling a tune that faded as he walked away.

Odd, Petra though. Unusual. Mysterious. But, she shrugged. She was here now. She bounded up the steps and onto the front stoop, and knocked on the door before she had a moment to change her own mind. The house was an expansive Tudor-style brick, not large enough to be a mansion, but too grand be called a house. Before she could knock a second time, Mrs. Marr answered the door and commanded her shoes off, her voice somehow sweet as she did so. She then ushered Petra into an inviting and multi-colored front room, a fire chattering away in the hearth.

Petra sat on the edge of a small couch, and she ran her hand admiringly over the gold brocaded upholstery. It was an old piece, and for its finery was rather more classic than flashy. She hadn't a moment to inspect Thomas' mother until she bustled back in with two cups of tea. Petra hadn't studied her too much in their first encounter, and so took a moment now to do so. She was as tall as Petra, and slim, with long chestnut-bronze hair and fair skin. Petra knew she had to be in her early sixties, but the woman before her was as timeless as her elegant home and furniture. She wasn't gaudy or gauche, but instead possessed the well-aged film star kind of beauty. A Meryl Streep or Raquel Welch type. Petra thought of Thomas' face and looked at the woman before her and sighed. Good genes, indeed.

Elizabeth Marr smiled and greeted Petra, and then left the room once again to grab some snacks, even though Petra assured her she wasn't the least bit hungry. She was left alone, and she stood up as the other woman quit the room, and looked around. Baroque paintings hung in ornate frames, and no less than six cats slumbered on registers and curled up on couches. The Persian rug was blood red and midnight blue, and Petra didn't think she'd ever been within a room that felt so warm and inviting. For all of its pomp and beauty, it felt like home, though no home she'd ever lived in. She envied Thomas, suddenly. The orchard and his mother with her just-the-right sweetness and her lovely vibrant home. She'd had something like that once, when Toby was alive.

Before her mother killed him.

Hadn't she? She'd been happy and whole once, right?

Elizabeth re-entered and sat down on a chair across from Petra, a cat appearing suddenly next to her, looping around her legs before popping casually onto her lap. She was smiling and though the woman did not embrace her, Petra felt as though she had been been given a hug all the same.

Elizabeth Marr looked at her appraisingly and her eyes crinkled in the corners. "Well, you don't look like either of your parents. You're much prettier and your hair is lighter."

The older woman reached out and touched a strand of Petra's honey colored hair and sighed, "Welcome home, Pet." Her voice was soft, and then she motioned toward the small sandwiches she had brought in on a silver-plate tray.

Petra thought she'd have a million questions for this woman, who had known her parents, known her as a child, but when Elizabeth handed over the photo album, she couldn't speak at all. Of course it was mostly Thomas, and a much younger sister Petra hadn't known, or had forgotten about. Elizabeth said her daughter was in college down-state when she saw Petra staring hard at the picture of a young Thomas, holding an infant in his arms. Among the pictures of Thomas though, there were glimpses of Dane and Petra and all of them together in the orchard. Running, climbing, chomping apples, or hiding behind trees, little faces poking out from behind the trunks. And Toby. Toby picking up Petra piggy-back, or Toby chasing after Dane and Petra. Toby and Thomas sitting reading, or all of the boys playing catch while Petra read. She couldn't take her eyes off the boys, her boys, and herself. Her younger, happier, carefree self. Had she been carefree? Well, if not carefree, not careworn. And Dane, with the same smile and the spatter of warm freckles like kisses from the sun on his cheeks. Even as a child she had loved him. She could see it in the pictures. The way they sat so close to each other, their arms touching, wanting to be in contact at all times, even if it was just their legs alongside each other on the same tree branch. And Thomas, older than the rest of them, and almost creeping into manhood. He was…the same as now, but brighter. Finally, Toby. He glowed like the sun itself. Her big, strong, amazing older brother. Brother and best friend and parent and confidant. Her whole world. She was emptier every time she looked away from the photo. How could someone so bright, so shining and new and wonderful…be gone? It was like the sun disappearing.

She turned the pages of the photos, there were maybe thirty or so, on just five pages, and something stuck out to her. At first she couldn't place what it was. She just had an itch, a niggling that there was something in the photos that bothered her. As she turned back and forth, searching for the thing that had caught her subconscious, Elizabeth talked.

Petra listened as carefully as she could as she searched, but heard only vague details that brought to mind a very blurry, fogged childhood that was still outside her grasp.

"Your mother, she didn't have many friends in town. She wasn't from around here, and the gossip was she gave your Dad hell for bringing her. She wouldn't work, wouldn't socialize, and I'm not sure I ever saw her outside of the grocery store. But, your father loved it here; we knew each other as children, you know."

Petra looked up from the photo album, "No, I didn't know. I hadn't realized he grew up here." Elizabeth's eyes widened.

"Yes, of course. Roccias have always been in Traverston, same as my family, the Brooksides. And my husband's people, of course. Most people who are born around here, well, they don't want to leave. The Lost Families, The Original Families."

Petra started to ask her to explain what she meant as she still didn't understand what these original families were, but Elizabeth had already moved on.

"I don't mean that people never leave; many of us went away for university, including your father, of course. But, people have a way of finding their way back. Like Olive's Dane, and you. And some never get the opportunity to go and come back at all." She gestured toward the photos and smiled at Petra again and sipped her own tea.

Petra smiled back, and looked down at the photos, her head buzzing with the past and Dane and destiny —when she caught it. She looked back over each picture, the pages of the album slapping together as she furiously flipped them back and forth. It was there. The same book, in every picture of Toby.

"What is this?" She asked, holding the album up for Elizabeth to see, her finger pointing determinedly on the protective plastic. "What book is this? Why does Toby have it with him?"

It was red and small, and it was in his hands or at his feet, or on the edge of every shot. Elizabeth looked at the photos, drawing them close for inspection, a puzzled expression on her features. She clapped her hand to her forehead, and said, "Oh, I know—it was...a dictionary. No! A thesaurus." Her face was lit up; Petra leaned in, expectantly, to her animated hostess.

"You really don't remember, do you, lovey? Well, I have to say I envy you a little; sometimes I wish I could forget. We all lost...so much that day. But, yes, it was...a little thesaurus. Your brother had a row with your mother? I think? Your father told me about it at the time; we had still...remained friends, even though it was difficult after his marriage. The whole town kind of turned against him, your mother being so unfriendly and all. But anyway, your mother had said something...unpleasant or unkind about Toby's vocabulary. I'm sure I have no idea what it was. Afterward, he bought the thesaurus at one of the library sales, where they sell their old stock, or excess books, worn copies, you know? I only remember because I'd asked him about it. He liked to use the words he learned, you see. And write down new words that weren't in the thesaurus in the back or on the pages."

Her lip tugged upward at the memory. "I thought it was just...darling. I'd ask him his word of the day when I saw you two at the orchard. Do you remember, Pet?"

"Not really, but, kind of. Is that strange? I think I remember the book. I can almost see it in his hands. Maybe a memory of Thomas teasing him about it? Faintly? I'm not sure, the memory is there but its not." Ripples, fireworks, small flames ignited in her mind at discovering the book. She swallowed all the feelings down and smiled pleasantly, "He didn't seem to care though, if I remember anything. Toby never cared what people thought."

Elizabeth smiled and nodded.

"A pair of wild indians..." Petra said softly, and then shook her head. "I'm sorry, I don't know why I just said that."

Elizabeth smiled again, more brightly. "I do. Your father used to call you and Toby that."

Petra's eyes widened and she shook her head, jumbling all the new information around in her mind. She was still wandering through fog.

"What can you tell me about the Lost Families?" she asked and Elizabeth closed up the book and hugged it to her chest. The older woman stood up and placed the album on a shelf nearby.

"Well, there's not much to it, though, for some reason or another people are shy to talk about it in town. The Lost Families, or The Original Families, are those of us who have been here since the beginning. Think of it like the Founding Fathers of Traverston or something like. Some say we are remnants of the survivors of the island that vanished; others say there was no island and our families have just been in one place too long and our brains have gone soft. But, it's a point of pride, and...a kind of secret, I suppose. There's something....bad luck about being one of the originals, or so they say. And, well, I guess you and I can easily believe it, huh?"

She didn't say any more, but Petra didn't press. Yes, she'd had a run of bad luck, tragedies aplenty, and she didn't need to ask this woman what hers had been. Everyone was entitled to their ghosts, as she'd said before.

She stayed and talked for another half hour or so. She listened to Elizabeth's proud recounting of her younger daughter's college exploits and they spoke a little more of Petra's career in writing. Elizabeth Marr didn't speak about the accident, or Toby, or her son Thomas again though, except to say that she missed him. Which made Petra a little frustrated with him for not visiting his mother. But Petra was oddly glad that no more was said about the boys, as she couldn't think of anything else to say about the past, not at the moment.

But, a glance at her watch told her it was time to head out, perhaps stop by Love's, though she was unsure what she would say to Dane after their kiss. Was he really going to make her dinner? Had all of it really happened? She hadn't heard from him all day, and now she'd seen photographic proof of their past together, it was even more difficult to pretend she didn't know—or to understand his reasons for omitting the truth. A truth he had to know she needed from him.

She said goodbye at the door, giving Elizabeth a kiss on the cheek and promising to visit again. She hadn't wanted to overreact, or say anything untoward in her presence, but Toby and his thesaurus had exploded her small, safe world wide open. She'd made his childhood hobby her life's work. She retreated into the books, had hidden herself away in them, in a way covering herself with the blanket of a forgotten memory of her dead brother. When had she stopped reading the books for their stories, and instead just for the words, the words she could steal from them and hold hostage to herself, solely for the power they gave to her?

She pointed her feet toward Love's, suddenly unsure about almost everything in her life, but surprisingly, fine with it.

Diary Of Nerissa Swifte

Alas, the jangling keys brought forth no news at all. Only a meager hunk of bread and a withered apple. I was heartened to see that the bread was still edible, and not too miserly, thinking perhaps this was a sign of favor from the community. But then I recalled that this gaol cell has been occupied so seldom that it is more likely that my keeper does not even think to punish the inhabitants with moldy bread or none at all. Even in my present predicament, and all that I have seen of the changes in the islanders, I know in my heart that they are mostly decent, simple folk without malevolence.

The hours stretch on, and while I have a little daylight, I shall use it. I have decided to commit to paper a few of my memories, not in any order, but as they come. For certain events have suddenly become very dear, and there are some well-lived moments my mind has been dwelling upon. In addition, I will write of my time in this cold, little cell. In hopes that a record of these days will be preserved, whether for myself in my old age, or for other generations, to remember. It is in losing the past that one is doomed to repeat it, after all.

I have very few memories of my mother, but I remember she was not like me. Instead, in my memory, her visage and Annette's are the same. I do not think this was true, but so alike are they in their temperament that for me they have fused as one. Our Da doted on our mother, Adela, as she was called. But I cannot remember a time where she looked on him with the same love. There must have been one, but my mind cannot conjure it. We had been close, for a time, a short time. I think because Fisher was so obviously an oddity from the very beginning. The webbed fingers and toes, the shock of raven black hair and the strange bottomless black eyes that are as the depths of the lake—same as Da's. She thought it unnatural. But, for myself, many babies are born with downy white duck fluff hair that darkens as they age. So, perhaps mother thought I was…like her. Or, she hoped. But my hair never darkened. It grew silvery white and my eyes were polished by the years into a glimmering amethyst grey. My skin darkened in the sun and stayed that way. And so each year mother realized I was less like her than I had been the year before. More…unusual. And though my Da was pleased that my Swifte blood shone through so strongly, our mother shied away, she grew colder, more distant. And I saw something in her eyes… something like disgust. I was still a small child, but I knew that our mother hated us. And when Phineas was born, black-haired and bawling, webbed-toes wriggling into the world—she left. Da was mother and father to three unusual children whom his wife thought were monsters.

But, he is a good Da. He did not seem to blame her, though he has worn his heartache every day since. "Every body is ordinary." Da always says, "It is much better to be extraordinary. To twist the usual a bit." That's what Da says magic is, the twist of reality. It is nothing new, nor is it a trick or a cheat of circumstance. Instead, to live within the magic of the world is to see the possibilities beneath the surface. These were the lessons he told us, all of our days. "Look beyond, look beneath, see what might be."

We could see we were different of course, but I do not think we completely accepted our enchantments. 'Tis a hard thing indeed to admit to oneself that magic lies within you. I must confess I thought, and still think, of magic as a force anyone might possess. It is just a matter of seeing. I approach a sick child's bedside, and I see the sickness inside them, just as one might see the nose on their face. And then I think, "What if the sickness were a tangible thing? A shawl I might lift from them? Or perhaps it could gather together into a ball inside their chest and travel out their mouth in their next breath, and then it could flow out onto the wind, and blow away across the lake." I think this, and then I see it leaving, flying away on a breeze, and the child is well. Or I lift it from them like a too-heavy-blanket, and health comes back to their cheeks.

Seeing the possibilities. Twisting the moment in a different direction. This cannot be magic, truly? A few herbs that any good healer would know, mixed together to relieve pain, pressure, or to aid in breathing and then…a small twist of reality. I am no sorceress, am I? And yet, they call me a witch.

My cell grows colder, and I can only think it is perhaps the weather has turned more foul. I am grateful for the extra warmth more than ever, and though my fingers are red and stiff with cold, they will not yet cease writing. My thoughts are rolling like thunder through my mind, clamoring and howling to be set free onto the page before me.

Who else am I fixed on, but Alarence and Fisher. My brother and I made ourselves outcasts from the beginning. We always preferred one another's company, though sometimes we would spend a whole week without speaking, all of our conversation instead in glances or nods, following each other's steps about the island. Or sometimes, I would sit on the shore as he swam deep within the blue, and other times there were not enough words in the world to tell all the stories or ask all the questions we thought of. The other children in the village would watch us, sometimes trailing us over rock and through island streams. But we paid them no mind, they were nothing special, nothing to us at all. Indeed, I believe we frightened them. We did not romp and giggle as other children, no, we were…all intensity. If a thorn scraped down my arm, Fisher would scrape a thorn against his own, and we both would watch, silently, as the blood dripped and fell onto the forest floor. His blood and my blood, falling all over the dirt of this island, mixing a little of ourselves with our island, so that it was a part of us too. When he bled, I bled. When he cried, I cried. If I fell from the tree branches, his body would fall next to mine, the both of us wind-knocked and gasping for breath in pain.

The other children were not Swiftes, and so they were nothing to us. Fisher could swim and dive, jump and stride through water like a man falling through air. And I, I could see things others couldn't. I could hear the lie in their throats before they told it, and know when someone had found their soulmate. I could see death when he crept near and I heard the cries of heartbreak across the island, and some that carried beyond the waves. The wind whispers secrets to me, and the forest had always kept me safe.

I remember the first time we met Grandmother Oak, Fisher and I, and she was old even then. I had not known if she were human or creature, and I must admit, I am still not entirely certain. Fisher was affrighted of her, said she was not natural, that she did not belong on the island. I never knew what he meant, and still haven't a clue. Magda seems as much of the island as the tress or the earth at my feet—or myself. Our bones are made of the island, and when we die our bones will sink beneath the lake water and become part of Traversint again.

For some reason that I know not, that fear of Fisher's clings to my memory, and I cannot help but wonder why. Perhaps it is because I wonder if he is right. If mayhap she is a creature, as I am, she does not belong on this island. If what Da says is true— and I have ever known him to speak naught but the truth, if a little fancifully— then the Swiftes are the only unnatural, or perhaps, supernatural, beings that exist here on Traversint. It is our curse, our birthright, our unique destiny. So then, what could her purpose be here? What does it mean?

Or, it is possible that these are all musings of an over-exerted mind. Too little sleep and not enough light and the stone in my gut that is my desire for Alarence. The feeling of needing he whom I must release, as I mayhap will never leave this place or glimpse his face again. And though I know he is my match, I must allow him to leave this place, to return to his roving. To keep him safe, and to bring peace to my own mind, though I know there can be no peace for my heart. Not now.

I ramble. My teeth chatter and my thoughts spring unformed and nonsensical from my mind, moving in circles. What will become of me? What will they do to me? What of my family? The island? Alarence?

My memories of the past and the need to recount some of these recollections—these still nip at my writing hand. But the cell grows dimmer, and I have need of rest. I cannot yet see the glow of starlight through the darkness of this place, which my body and spirit are slowly fading into. Which leaves me only one option.

I must become the light.

15

RAGGLISH:
constantly changing and unpredictable

She had not walked to Love's after all. She had directed her feet that way, but with each step she thought of another reason to go home instead. Dane had said he was coming to her cottage that evening, after all. And though the plan had been made after the kiss and the awkward moments that followed, she was choosing to believe he would come.

The pictures in the album, the memories of her brother, they kindled the possibility of answers to her questions, and she didn't want to dam the information as it was flowing to her. And so, in a rare spirit of optimism, she decided to wait to see how things with Dane would play out. Petra had other mysteries to pursue—Dane could chase her for awhile.

Though, if she were being honest, she would need to admit that her new found optimism was convenient to her true intention. From the moment she had seen that little red thesaurus in the pages of Mrs. Marr's photo album, she'd had a strange tickle at the back of her head. A snapshot of a memory, of many memories. She felt certain that she had seen the book before, had held it, paged through it. But more than anything, the book conjured Toby. She wasn't sure if these memories were true, or if she had imagined them from seeing the album, but the tickle wasn't scratched by debating with herself or wondering. Petra knew she had to find that thesaurus. Knew it had to be somewhere in the library. It would have appeared insignificant, certainly. A simple, standard pocket thesaurus. The same kind found by the dozens in libraries and in schools and at bookstores. But *this* book carried Toby within its pages. To read this book, she felt, would be to have him return briefly, back to life. That's what books do, surely, bring to life those who live within the pages.

The cottage, when she returned, seemed colder and somehow more mysterious, as though she could finally sense the secrets that scurried within the walls and noiselessly across the floorboards. Secrets she had lived amongst and ignored, or had not suspected of such mischief. Whispers she had been ignorant of, oblivious to. Secrets that were kept from her, on purpose. But why? Why was it so imperative to keep her in the dark? She could understand her father's reasons. He had meant to keep her from the grief he so obviously suffered from, her own lost memories perhaps giving him the opportunity to do so. But, Dane…what reason could he have? Had her father asked it of him? It was all she could come up with, and it wasn't much.

Flicking the lights on in the library, she searched in the red-orange glow of the Tiffany lamp that dangled from the ceiling. A little red leather book, a little red leather book…her eyes moved frantically, racing across the spines of the books. She knew it was here in this room. Knew it absolutely, though Petra wasn't certain precisely how she knew. Maybe it called to her, a siren song, willing her to uncover it. She had meant to change into something else, in the expectation that Dane would, in fact, arrive as he said. But the hours wore on, and instead of dressing up, her skirt became heavy with dust and the remnants of something Jinks had been chewing in the library. Damn she-devil tabby cat. Petra's fingers too, were dirty, and she didn't even pause to imagine the state of her hair. She was too intent on her purpose, finding Toby, digging up Toby, uncovering him, finding the thesaurus.

Petra had never imagined she would ever think that anyone could own too many books, but her mind was very definitely altered on the subject by her father's collection. She had never fully appreciated the extent of it, and it wasn't until she'd been pawing through the books for some time that she realized that many of the books were on the same topic, or related to the same topic. Atlantis, hidden cities, finding Troy, the discovery of Pompeii, uncovering Herculaneum. Books about exploring shipwrecks and bog bodies and hidden treasures. Her father was looking for a lost civilization, a lost people, the find of a lifetime. Her father had been looking for Traversint.

Once the idea took hold in her mind, she couldn't budge it. Everything shifted, just a centimeter. She hadn't really known her father, her family, her past, her life. She had never really known herself, because her memories were built on something as ever-changing as the lake outside. It wasn't just Toby she was searching for, it was Petra.

As she searched for Toby's book, she worried at this new revelation like Jinks with a spider. Pawing at it and swatting it, never taking her mind from it for a moment. Was that why her father had moved back? Studying these books, these theories…was that what he had done all the while, secretly? Her father had been a teacher, and then a Professor of History at a community college, close to the townhouse they'd called home when they lived downstate. Was Traversint his passion project? Every new discovery she made, caused a feeling of hopelessness in Petra. But also, a feeling of hope.

The realization that her life was never what she had imagined it to be, the truth lingering just outside the door, and she'd never even thought to reach for the handle to invite it in. She hadn't been whole for twenty years. She wasn't only the linguistic best-selling author, she wasn't just the academic darling. But, she also was no longer the broken-hearted weakling who'd let one man leave splinters in her soul. Or rather, she was all of these, but she was more. She had a past. A story with a tragedy in it. But, for whatever reason, this knowledge gave her strength.

Her father had been searching for Traversint.

Well, like father like daughter, she supposed. Thanks to Nerissa, she was searching for it too. She sighed. That was all well and good, and she *was* glad to have found some much needed fearlessness in her current state, but none of that helped her find Toby's book.

Too many red leather bindings. She thought she'd finished a shelf, only to find another row behind the books she'd just looked through. She dug through the library, uncaring as to the spirits in the books she might be disturbing. She had one single focus, to find that piece of her past, that part of her brother, to glean from it whatever answers, whatever memories or notes or sensations that she could.

Her fingers now felt dry and her nose was in dire need of a good blow from the dust storm kicked up by the sleeping books she'd awoken. It had gone 8 o'clock, and she'd still found nothing. Her father had startlingly few reference books of any kind, it turned out. She was reaching behind a small shelf on her father's desk, after having gone through all the books in the front row, when her fingers clasped around something not at all book-shaped. It was cold, and rounded, and when she pulled it out and into sight, she saw that it was a cloudy white stone. It felt familiar, and looked familiar, just like the one she'd placed on Toby's grave. Without taking her eyes off it, she reached her other hand back where the stone had been and pulled out a book. The cover wasn't red exactly, but a kind of pinky-strawberry. She felt a shock, and couldn't bring herself to tear her eyes from book or stone. She'd found it. It had found her. It couldn't be the same rock; very likely it was just similar. There were probably scores of them all around the island. Most likely. Suddenly her excitement turned into apprehension, and she tucked the stone into the pocket of her skirt, and then patted the pocket, twice, thrice, needing to feel the cold of it knock against her leg through the thin fabric pocket.

Petra held the book in both hands now, and the shock hit her again, like static electricity when she touched it. It was possible that it was indeed, static. The room was dry and the books dusty. But she couldn't help thinking there was more to it. And turning the small book over slowly, she knew she was right even before she read the title. It was here, in her own palms. Toby. Toby's book. His hands had been where hers were now. If she closed her eyes just right, she could almost see his hands, beneath her own, a time-traveling touch that felt almost real.

Shaking, she ran her fingers over the faded cover and tears pricked at her eyelids. Traitor tears, coming when they weren't wanted. She opened the cover and saw *Toby Roccia* printed neatly in a confident hand. So like him, it was almost his voice in her mind. He had been proud of this book, she could tell, she could almost remember. Petra paged through, carefully, soaking in the words he had added boldly to the pages. New words he discovered, better synonyms for a term that he preferred. She could picture him, pencil in hand, chewing his bottom lip, reading and writing, finding the perfect words to describe his world. Toby's words for Toby's world, and now hers. Every moment her eyes scanned the pages was a stolen moment with her brother, moments she thought to never have again.

And then the knock sounded on the front door, and the feeling vanished. Though she had thought to be pleased that Dane had, indeed, come, instead she felt annoyed at the intrusion. As though she had been mid-conversation and had been rudely interrupted. Every step to the door echoed the pounding of blood in her veins. She was filled with…something. An emotion she couldn't identify, because she had never felt it before. The precipice of something, peering over into the chasm of the unknown. This was a moment that would change her, was changing her, even now. It was as though a decision had been made the last few days, or perhaps several years…or maybe even since the moment she realized that Toby was never coming home. A decision that was now, like Dane, waiting on the doorstep, waiting for her door to open.

And so, biting her lip, and running a hand from her eyes to chin and back up, she shrugged, walked to the front door and pulled the damn thing open.

Dane.

"Hey, hope you like pasta." He proffered a grocery bag in her direction. "And I hope you don't mind, but I am continuing my campaign to win over your cat with another can of the good stuff."

His smile was sheepish, uncertain. Petra hardly moved, barely reacted, as he stepped forward, tentatively kissing her mouth.

It was as though she had forgotten to wear an imaginary pair of glasses. He was blurry, past mixed with present. When she looked at Dane, he became, somehow, more dear to her. It wasn't his perfect posture and wide, muscular shoulders underneath his polished and pressed blazer. It was…a memory of those shoulders bare and covered in sand. Bony and pale skinned next to her brother's tan. It was that same glossy brown hair, but lighter and longer, unkempt and tousled about as he sped away on a bicycle. The freckles though, just the lightest sunbeam's blemish of freckles across his nose, they were the same in her memory and standing before her. She hadn't said a word, couldn't say a word. The memories, perhaps released by the touch of the book? Or by breaking down a wall within herself? Or maybe just by opening the door to destiny, inevitability, whatever. These memories swirled and spun, warming her and illuminating the room around her, which filled with still more memories from her past.

And she realized what Nerissa had meant about magic. It was everywhere, and in everything, if only your eyes knew how to see it.

She was seeing it now. Toby's shoes, kicked off at the door, haphazardly with her own muddled in between. The piano! Yes, a piano playing in the study, she had completely forgotten her father had played. He never had, not once, since Toby had died.

Fresh flowers in vases all over the house, the one thing she did remember about her mother. The piano, playing wildly, sometimes a mournful dirge, sometimes a bluesy jazz rag. Toby, sitting across a chair, his head on one arm rest and his legs hanging across the other, his feet tapping the air to the beat. All the while writing something in a little red book she wasn't allowed to read, and discouraged from even peeking at the covers of. Her home, her things, her family, in this house, the past and present existing simultaneously in her eyes—and Dane.

Dane who also existed in both worlds.

This time she stepped into him, his confused expression obvious, but not to Petra. Her recollections had taken but a moment, but Dane could see the change in her as plainly as her figure before him.

A woman, who had been beautiful but chipped. Intelligent, interesting, but blurred...was suddenly vibrant. And this, this second kiss was passion and longing and desire. It was past tragedy and sweet memory combined with hope for brighter things. It asked questions and gave answers and their bodies moved only closer together. The groceries were dropped and hands searched for cheeks to caress and waists to grip, and as the intensity and urgency grew, they clung to one another, simply to hold fast to the moment. Finally, breathless, they broke apart. Her eyes, clear and bright, peered into his. Those same lake blue pools, those dawn blue eyes, and she wondered, had she loved him her whole life? Had her heart always known his? Had part of her known and remembered, even when her mind had not?

She grabbed his hand and pulled him into the house, only pausing for him to pick up the bag. Instinctively, she headed toward the library. His voice behind her was far away, "Petra—what was that? Shouldn't we be going to...the kitchen?"

And the decision that she had known was coming, the jump into the chasm that she'd peered into, was suddenly not a decision any more. Besides, she had always been rubbish at keeping secrets.

She walked deliberately into the library and picked the thesaurus up off the desk where she'd left it, it felt warm, as though Toby had just been holding it, out in the sunshine, chewing one of Marr's apples.

She spun around, and holding it up like a talisman, she spoke quietly.

"Dane, I know everything."

And the groceries, again, dropped to the floor.

.

Diary Of Nerissa Swifte

They came in the night. Father Lemorale and a few men from the village. They came with dark looks and sharp tongues, tossing insinuations and accusations about as a dog would shake off water. Edward Wade, a fisherman whom I believed to be a friend of my father's, and Joshua Shore, the blacksmith, stood at the front of the group. The jeers and taunts of the men fell silent with one word from the priest, however.

He is cunning, I will own that. More clever than I had thought. He does not openly threaten me, nor does he make a show of his disdain. Instead, his is a quiet, secret hatred. He hints, he gestures, he asks questions of the group, guiding them along the path of his own prejudice. So skillfully does he lead this dance that the men believe the ideas to be their own, the thoughts their own creation. They do not see that he is their puppet-master, moving the cogs in their mind, twisting and warping them until their thoughts are his own. Is Father Lemorale Annette's creature? Or is she his? Surely, in either case, two minds more suited to one another I could not imagine, especially on a space of an island as small as this.

I was asleep. If it can be called that. Shivering and heavy lidded wakefulness in this prison below ground, carved into the earth of the island, deep enough so one might believe that the lake could start filling in from beneath the stones of the floor. It is never a true rest here, even when my body takes the shape of sleeping. But they came and they let themselves into my cell. Joseph Marsh used the tip of his boot to rouse me, though the cacophony of their movements had already woken me completely. They muttered, "witch" and hissed, "murderess", "demon", "satan's mistress", each insult a bit louder than the last, the men, not unlike boys, growing bolder because of the group. Men saying things they would never say if they were alone. Men that might help me if they did not become children in a herd when together. I had begun to think the men would do me violence when an unlikely savior stepped in.

The same Father Lemorale. Though, hero he was not. He urged the men silent, and within moments they were as docile and meek as whipped dogs. I could not understand his power then, and still find that I cannot. These men have seen me heal with their own eyes, yet the words of this priest with his invisible God give more proof than their own experiences.

After they quieted, he began remarking on the strangeness of my habits. "Do you notice that she lives alone away from the community? Do you see her inhuman hair? Her demon's eyes? Why is it that she is always present at the scene of tragedy? Why so often it is that where her foot trods, death follows?"

The questions were asked quietly, almost as though he were speaking to himself, and the men who had come with him almost vibrated with rage as they answered the questions in their own minds. Forgetting that they had always looked for my presence in their darkest hours. That they had rejoiced when I was able to heal, or breathed easier because it was my hands that eased a loved one into the final embrace of Death.

The priest continued, as though it pained him to say the words, "think on the noxious and perverse things we discovered in her cottage. Unsavory ingredients used, no doubt, to communicate with her dark master. She is but a woman, and knew not how to resist the evil, no doubt. Dark items for dark arts, gentlemen. This truly is a creature of the night, and it is a blessing we were able to restrain her before she endangered more islanders, or did more damage to her soul—if she has one. 'Tis noble of you who brought her in. She knows not the villainy of her relentless feeding off the good Christians on this island. Would you have justice? Would you give this woman justice? The fire might cleanse her of evil, gentleman. We might could save her, yet."

Again, so quietly, so casually spoken that one might imagine he was remarking on the weather or the day's catch. But the men's ears were tuned to his voice and the acclimation of 'aye' was loud and discordant through my cell.

He had proposed my murder, and made it seem righteous.

Though I am small, I stood up then, and I looked at each of them, full in their eyes. I wanted to make certain sure that they all saw that I knew them, and that I was looking into their soul, burning the shape and color of it onto my own. I would know them in this lifetime and the next. I will admit, I was not then angry. Nay, the anger came, but much later. I was bewildered. These men had been my friends, my people. But reflected back in their eyes I no longer saw their souls, but instead only the uniform beetle black of hate.

I, too, spoke low, and somehow managed to keep steady my voice. "You know me. All of you. You have known me from a babe. I grew up on this island. It is my home and that of my family, and their family— and on until the day Traversint rose from the lake, just as your families have been here. You know I never came to your homes with naught but kindness in my heart and health in my breath. What has twisted your hearts so? Who had mangled your minds? If you do this to me, the stain of it will curse your souls and that of your ancestors. You will live to feel shame for this act."

Some among the group had the decency to look uncertain, and a few turned their faces downward, kicking the dirt with their feet as though they had forgotten why they had come, were confused as to why they were there.

"Enough, enough." The priest's voice whispered again. "No more of that, Mistress Swifte. Even now you seek to curse us through your dark master. Your trial will be in three days time." He stuck three bony fingers and licked his lips, as though the idea of my humiliation was delicious. They left me then, slowly, more quietly than when they had come. Some of the men snuck glances in my direction, and their faces were inscrutable, which I have decided to take as a favorable sign. At least it not open hostility.

I sat shivering in the dark a while, considering my fate. It was so cold on the island, so very frigid, yet I knew I preferred the freeze to the licking flames of a fire.

And then, manna from heaven, two notes floated down from the window, and a hushed whisper. "All right, Nissa?" it said. And though I was not, the letters made everything so for a few moments at least. And so I had answered back, "all right", though I do not know if Phineas was still at the grate to hear me. If he and Fisher are not careful, I fear they too will be arrested.

But, pause, I shall lay my quill down a moment to read these epistles, which I have forced myself to set aside until this account was written. I hope they will warm my heart, for the writing has done nothing to give heat to these hands.

16
WINGLE
*to stagger or walk with difficulty while carrying
something heavy*

"What do you mean by, 'everything'?" He asked. Petra couldn't see his expression because he had bent down to pick up the grocery bag.

She had meant to catch him off guard, and though his reaction had confirmed for her that he had been concealing things—purposefully—his low, husky voice when he spoke those words made her feel as though she was not in control. Not as in-control as she'd imagined she would feel, at any rate.

He was facing her now, and he again was robed in his usual cloak of casual aloofness, but she could see the tightening in his jaw—and was that *fear* behind his eyes? He turned and headed toward the kitchen, forcing Petra to speak to his back.

"I mean precisely that. I know everything. I

remember. We have a past, you and I. We were childhood...friends. You, Toby, Thomas and I...we grew up together. So, I know that every day since we re-met in your shop that you have been lying to me, but I don't know why."

"Oh, yeah." His shoulders visibly relaxed.

"Oh yeah? Oh yeah?! That's all you have to say?"

Petra could feel the rage coming, but she took a breath and closed her eyes, visualizing the cottage as it would have been—when it was a home. Her home. She directed her mind toward what she hoped were hopeful, happy memories. She didn't have time or inclination for a sobbing, losing-herself-in-feelings fit right now. She needed answers.

He eyed her with concern for a moment, and when he could see she had mastered her emotion, Dane walked over to the counter and began unpacking the bag. After a moment of awkward silence, he turned around, facing her. His eyes pierced hers, and Petra realized she had no idea what to say next. She hadn't prepared. She ran her fingers under the bone of her jaw, feeling the smooth hot scar, the mottled, ruined flesh. A brand on her skin, his brand, her constant reminder. What had she expected from this conversation? Why would she ever imagine she was in control?

Dane cleared his throat, and bit the tip of his thumb, a gesture that comforted and alarmed her. He looked upward and ran his other hand through his hair, and clutched the back of his scalp, as though he needed something to hold fast to.

"Can we...just forget it?"

Petra wasn't sure what he meant. Forget what?

That she knew the truth? That there was truth? That they knew one another at all? And so she shook her head to all of those things. She was done with forgetting. He sighed, and his words tumbled out, an apology she had to sift through.

"I'm sorry I didn't tell you…but, I, well, you have to understand. I mean, please, understand, that the last time I saw you, you didn't know me."

"When…what are you talking…?" She started to ask, her words trailing off into oblivion as he talked over her confusion.

"Here. Of course. Here. After it happened. You… changed. And when your father came back, well, he let it be known that the Petra that Traverston had known had died alongside of Toby, to put it harshly. And…furthermore…" His voice was shaky, as though the next words he would speak were in a different language that he had read but had never tried to pronounce himself. "…well, that the Petra we had read about and that was doing so well with the interviews and book tours…that Petra was dead too. That if we saw you on the street or you came back to visit we wouldn't know you. And you wouldn't know us. Especially…me."

Petra could feel her brow furrow into ugly lines, and her mouth twist in confusion. Why? Why all the secrecy? What was she being protected from? But Dane wouldn't know the answers to these questions. They were her father's secrets, and he'd taken them with him into the earth.

So, instead, her question for Dane was, "Why you especially? I would have thought it would be you I'd most *remember*. Mrs. Marr had photos of us, you see." Petra offered this last sentence as way of explanation, but Dane shrugged it all off, and turned back to the groceries, his hands instantly finding the right pot he needed for the pasta and the shelf she kept the olive oil on. He'd said it was a gift, knowing where things were. Always knowing where things should be.

"I don't know why I said that. Forget it. I guess your Dad was wrong. You remember more than he thought, obviously."

He was distracted, nervous, choosing his words with extra care…and feigning nonchalance. This change in him surprised Petra. She realized that no matter the photographs or the memories, or even the feelings she had for this man, she didn't really know him. She'd given him the benefit of her doubts based on their magnetism and shared history. And now, even when confronted, cornered by the truth, he was trying to find his way back into the comfort of only facing the present, leaving behind their past, as if it disturbed him, or he was ashamed of it.

She didn't meet his eyes, and instead began fiddling with a wine bottle, awkwardly attempting to remove the cork, but succeeding only in breaking it before drawing it out. A pot crashed behind her.

Without thinking, she inhaled rapidly through her nose and her hands came to her face, her neck, warding off invisible blows, the bottle dropping with a thud onto the counter, and then with a second crash, to the floor. The glass didn't fly far but the scarlet wine oozed like blood, like her blood, all over the black and white tile. She stared at the bottle and the spilled wine, tears pricking her eyes and panic rising like bile.

She was conscious of Dane in the room, but her eyes didn't leave the wine. It was too familiar. Neither of them stooped to clean it, but instead, her mind fixated on strange things. She remembered the plate she had almost smashed, and that she hadn't. She wondered briefly about the loud crash-clang of Dane's pot, realizing he had smashed it to the floor on purpose, just as she had wished to do with the plate. A result of boiled over frustration and emotion. She thought of the wine and how it would, and probably already had, stained the grout in the tile. How even after she cleaned it, and sprayed bleach on it, some of the blood-red stain would remain, to remind her of this specific moment. A memento of the past as legible to her as Nerissa's words on the diary pages.

Dark blood red stains. Staining her tile and her thoughts and burning onto her eyes.

Was that the trouble with the past? That no matter how much one scrubbed or bleached or forced it down—the pain and the love of the past, it was stained like a tattoo, was cut into the soul like a scar *and it would never go away.*

She made herself look back at him, and when she did, she couldn't take her eyes away. How could she have forgotten him?

Dane wasn't looking at her though, wasn't sharing in her moment of epiphany. He was transfixed by the wine on the tile, the way that it disappeared on the black tiles and blared discordantly off the white. He, too, was reminded of blood. The memory of blood. So much blood, too much. How could anyone lose that much blood and live? They couldn't. They didn't. He shuddered and felt that he was going to be sick.

But then, he raised his chin to look at her, and his

eyes locked there. Why was it necessary to remember that past? Why couldn't they have created their own past and future? But most of all, why hadn't he stayed away from her? It would have been simple enough, even in a small town. He should have left already, moved closer to Allegra like his ex-wife still wanted him to do.

But, he knew the answer to that. He couldn't have stayed away. He had never wanted to. For him, it had always been Petra, somewhere, inside, he'd known, always.

And when he'd seen her, just over a year ago, in that hospital. He'd driven all night, but he didn't wait for her to wake up. He had needed only to see with his own eyes that she was living. And when he did, when he knew that she was alive— even if a little more of her had been murdered inside, just like him, that was enough. She was alive. She would live. If she was still living, then he was too.

That's all he needed to know.

Because he'd known, always.

Even when it had seemed impossible. When he lost her. When she was able to forget him. As if he hadn't existed. As though *they* had never existed, and the memories in his mind had been merely fantasies.

But if they were fantasies, it would make that *other* memory a nightmare. And a nightmare was still a dream from which one wakes—and there was no waking from that horror. No, he would live with that forever. And so part of him was jealous that she had forgotten him. He was envious that she could start over clean and white—and not bloodstained by the past as he was.

Until, that night in the hospital. Seeing her hooked

up helplessly to the machines with bloops and beeps and electricity running in the room that kept her wired and alive. Then, he saw that she *was* stained with blood. That she'd always been stained. That she hadn't escaped as they'd both pretended. And in that hospital bed, she'd been cut all over again, and the blood splattered her anew. He wished he could cover himself with her pain, and he had grasped her hand and willed it onto himself. But he was a coward, and did not stay for her eyes to open. She would have no idea he had been there at all. Which was fine by him. As long as she was alive. That was all he needed.

But now, he only wanted to be close to her, and so, he stepped around the glass and pulled her to him. Her body went so easily into the cold empty places, the places that needed her touch. He felt her breath exhale out, ragged with an emotion he couldn't name but knew too well.

"Why especially you?" Petra whispered into his blazer. And sighing, his eyes looked skyward, and he held her a little tighter, not knowing if she still would want to hold him when she heard the truth.

"Because...because you don't know everything, Petra."

One of her hands travelled slowly up his arm before reaching his shoulder, where she clung to the fabric as though the truth might blow her away.

"Then tell me." she whispered.

Diary Of Nerissa Swifte

I dreamt last night of the past. I find that these are the worst and most dreadful of dreams. They make one reach fingers out boldly clutching at possibilities that no longer exist in the moment.

I think it was the letter that brought the dream. One of my blessed letters yesterday was from Alarence, though how Phineas came by it, I cannot guess.

He wrote to me of rescue. Of life away from the island. He wrote of other waters and of people that would run toward my magic, with open arms. But, it was a letter, so I could not explain that if I were to leave, the magic would be lost. That in my prison I have come to realize that my magic, my powers, they flow from the island like a cool spring. To leave Traversint is to bring a bucket away from a well, and expect it to refill itself from the air.

But, it was not of Alarence and his offers that I dreamt.

My mind and memory did instead travel back, back, back to a time I try not to think not on.

Back to a time, where there lived a man named Searc.

He, too, had stumbled upon Traversint. His family were fishermen, looking for waters to make their own. The Rippley family were cousins to them, distantly, and so they had come to our island after good reports from their kin. Searc was a few years older than we, but Fish and I followed him about. He was good and kind. His family was jolly and filled with optimism in finding a new home—their place in the world.

Searc was flame-haired with a thin face and an aquiline nose. He was lithe like my brothers, but sturdier. His eyes were a grey-blue coldness—like chipped glass. But, we all lived for his smiles. I was naught but fourteen, and he perhaps, seventeen. I knew he was not meant for me, I could see it in his eyes. Or, rather, could not see it. His eyes held no reflection of children to come, just an ice-grey mirror. But, I fought my destiny. And when he asked me to marry him, I said I would, without understanding the finality of it, or what it meant, or how long a future could be. We resolved to wait until my 15th birthday, and I had even gone back to the hearth and told Da. He did not say nay to me, only shook his head, troubled.

It had not mattered to me that Searc could neither read nor write. It mattered not that we could not discuss stories or history or debate ideas. Searc and his family were well liked on the island. Ordinary, helpful folk with courage and boldness, all traits admired on our tiny island. Admired and expected for those that would live in such a strange, disconnected place.

The emptiness of his eyes should have told me. Or mayhap, I should have divined the meaning within the absence in them. But I was young, and his kisses were like sparks from a fire and his promises of the kind of life that most women craved—they were honey to me.

But, I am not a normal woman. I am the enchantress of Traversint.

And I knew that sweet, sweet Searc was not my destiny. He belonged to no one. But still I clung to him as though he were my own. He saw no one but me, though he was sturdy and good, and new. All of the things a lonely daughter of the island with her cap set to marriage wanted. But, he was no one's, and so he was mine.

He drowned one night in a sudden storm in the middle of the lake. It is not often that they come, but when they do, they are stealthy and merciless. And with a great swipe of fate's sword, the flame that was Searc was extinguished by the lake's waters.

There were no children in his eyes because he would never father them. My promise to marry him was never a promise at all, for I knew, somewhere inside myself that it was an empty one. You cannot promise a future that you don't have.

Why did he haunt my slumber last night as my body shivered on the cell floor? It is not that I still love him, for he exists only in the world of yesterday, a place where no one can return to for long, without the future sprinting on ahead. I can only think it is my spirit, wishing for the humdrum, ordinary life that Searc had offered me. The future that might have been, if I were not Nerissa Swifte, if there had been a destiny for Searc, if the the island and the magic of it didn't burn within me.

What if for me, life could be so simple? A steady man, children to coo and kiss, and no expectations of healing arts from the islanders. No whispers of evil to blacken my name. Surely, it would be vastly different.

Too different.

I, too, would be suspicious then of anyone different. Of anything powerful I didn't understand. I would tremble when illness came to the island, and cower in the face of forces I did not understand. Nothing is ever simple. No life is easier than another. Not really.

Which is why the dream woke me and bided near me in the early morning hours. He came to me from the folds of my memories, but it was not in truth, ever a choice on my path. Ordinary was not made for me, nor would it be simpler. Living against one's destiny is the most dangerous, difficult task of all. So no, Searc was s spot of sweetness, a breath of *what if?*, but my life is now. My destiny is this place. My heart is for Alarence Attwater. And I know now that the priest may try to rile the islanders, and though I can hear them planning what to do with me, the cruel grumblings crawling to my ears like spiders—I will not rage against the present. Nor will I fret over the past. It is done, and I am finished with it.

I will believe instead in the memory of the child, our child, that I saw in Alarence's eyes when first I saw him. The moment my eyes found his in the sickroom and I knew him for my own. I will be the light in my own darkness.

But hark—there are voices. Louder now that I am not lost in my own reflections. My heart is suddenly like lead in my chest. Cold washes over me. Voices, coming down the tunnel, through the corridor, and one of them—Fisher's!

The other, oh my stars, is Magda, the Lady in the Trees. But the voices are not of rescue—I must hide these pages, and quick. I know not the calamity that nears me.

17

SWEVEN
a vision or dream

Dinner had been subdued. Dane had entreated her to read the pages she had transcribed aloud, and every reference Nerissa made to the past had made him wince. Petra would have liked to have shared with him how close to the bone these same comments and observations cut her, but she could not. She could not bring herself to share anything more with him until he answered her questions.

She'd been certain he was going to make a full breast of it, but something had changed, his eyes had traveled back to the tile and he had stooped down, picking up the shards of the broken bottle. Petra's whole body had sighed and sagged as she stepped to the drawer stuffed with dishrags to sop up the spilled wine. She had read him the pages as he cooked, and she had admired the confidence of his hands on the skillet and with the spices. He had made this before. For whom? His ex-wife? His daughter? Surely.

Petra had bitten her cheek hard at the thought. It wasn't worthy of her. She had her own past to suss out, she needn't fret about his. Besides, it wasn't her damn business.

The ate in semi-silence. So many things bubbling and simmering between them. Confidences unshared, questions unasked. Until finally, with a clatter of his fork, Dane threw the cutlery down and his hands up in surrender. His forehead was all lines and worry and his eyes were desperate.

"Look, can't we just forget all about it? Can't we start new? Everything was going great... I thought. Didn't you think there was really something...special, between us? What does it matter if we knew one another before? We know each other now, again. Isn't that good enough?"

His eyes were pleading, and Petra wanted nothing more than to toss her plate across the room and throw herself into him. But she didn't.

"Yes! Things were great. I don't understand how the past ruins anything. Can't you see that part of what made this whole romance wonderful was that we had a shared past? That we'd meant so much to one another as children? And hell, the past brought us together again. The history of our parents, the island, Nerissa Swifte! We can't ignore the past just because...it hurts."

Petra could feel her own voice rising higher and higher, and she stopped speaking, thinking of the cool, calm, Nerissa had showed in prison. Her pragmatism. She would do well to learn a lesson from the woman's fortitude.

Dane sat, his head rocking slowly in his hands as though he were weighing a decision in his mind. When his voice spoke again, Petra nearly forgot all thoughts of calm, collectedness.

It was a sob, nearly a whimpering plea of one in torment. "Please, please, Pet. Please don't do this. We found each other again—isn't that enough? Does anything else matter?"

And though she wanted to hold his head to her chest and whisper, 'of course', and agree with him, she didn't. She yearned to soothe him, to hold him, but she could not. First, because she could not understand his resistance. His secretiveness still escaped her comprehension. What was it that he had yet to tell her? What else could there possibly be?

And furthermore, he was wrong. Something else did matter. More than anything else. And clearing her throat, she answered him with more conviction and confidence than she felt—sounding more like the Petra of old than she had in some time.

"Yes. Oh, yes. Something else *does* matter. Toby matters. His life matters. His death matters. My memories of him are just that—memories. And that's fine. That's where he belongs. But, I will not cast him aside, nor forget him—myself—or you and I. I have to remember, even if it is so that I may say a proper farewell." And though she'd said nothing she could imagine was unreasonable, the shudder of Dane's body across the table made her flinch. As though she was watching him being pricked with a needle, only to find that it was her doing the wounding.

He stood up and the chair fell over behind him. There was something wild in his eyes and Petra couldn't believe she'd ever thought of him as unflappable, impassive, unruffled, imperturbable. The man she was seeing lately was…boiling with passion, intensity, and strong emotion.

The heels of his hands squeezed at his temples and he grit his teeth. Spinning around, he took a violent leave of the cottage, as though another moment within the walls would make him explode. After collecting her scattered reactions, Petra followed.

But, he was already in his car, pulling out of her drive, the setting sun making its final exit from the autumn day in a riot of orange and red flames taking their last licks of the horizon. It was all so…dramatic.

Petra followed the lights of the sleek black car until it vanished. She'd come to Traverston to escape the memories of the city, to say goodbye to the father she should have been with in death. She'd stayed because it seemed a safe, sleepy place. She had been wrong of course. Lulled into false safety by appearances. She, who lived so neatly in the past, between the pages of her words—she was being forced to remember a carefully stowed nightmare. One that was neither safe nor magic. But instead, real and painful and dead.

She almost wished Evan were here now. She'd tell him he was wrong. One couldn't help but live in the past, surely. For your past stuck to you, stained you, like the wine between the kitchen tiles. It became a part of you, changing irrevocably the present and future self you were becoming.

What did Dane flee from? What possible reason would a man run from a death more than 20 years gone?

The crackle of the leaves behind her turned her around. For a split second, she thought it could be Dane, returned to explain, before she realized that was impossible, as she knew he was in the car, probably back to Traverston by now.

But the last rays of that same sunset caught the honey of his hair, so similar to her own, and again Petra was taken aback. It was a ghost. Toby.

The glare gone, she realized her error and smiled uncertainly. Not the spirit of Toby grown to manhood, but Thomas Marr instead.

"Tom, what are you doing here?" Petra had to force a little friendliness into her voice, but she *was* glad to see him. She wondered briefly how long he'd been about, and if he'd watched Dane's hasty retreat. In response to her question, he merely nodded, a small unreadable smile tugging his lips. He kicked the leaves lazily, and fixed his gaze on the distance, hand sitting easily on his hip.

Petra took a few steps forward, closing the large space between them to better read his features in the growing dark. "It was nice to meet your mother..." she began hesitantly.

His voice cut the air like a blade, though nothing he uttered seemed especially pointed; but it sliced the moment, nonetheless.

"Weather is changing." He said, his voice soft, but clear. "The wind is different, mind that."

Petra smiled, uncertainly, taking another step toward him. "Is that some kind of omen? Something to add to my almanac, perhaps?"

She reached to lay a hand on his arm, but he neither met her gaze or returned her smile, instead taking a sudden step back so that she was not touching him.

After a few more moments of darkness gathering, she could no longer stand it. The temperature was dropping and she desperately wanted to go in and phone Dane—to demand some answers and explanations for his strangeness. But something in Thomas' bizarre behavior kept her rooted, waiting.

Finally, he cleared his throat and spoke again, this time looking deep into her eyes, searching them. "I've tried to be a friend to you since you came. I had waited so long, here. And it gets harder and harder to stay. I've tried to draw you out, to show you that you are important to Traverston, even if you forgot it. That you were important to me."

"Tom, I...I don't understand." But he wasn't listening to her. A practiced speech sprouted from his mind, concealing his true thoughts. "Go to Mrs. Garzing. There is...I can't. There are things only she can explain."

Quickly, he leaned forward and gave her another breathy, almost kiss on the cheek. He smelled like apples and sunshine and home, a scent she never thought to recognize.

And he was gone, and like Dane's headlights, she stayed and listened to the sound of his lighter than air crackling footsteps, like wind over leaves, recede into the woods, vanishing into the ink of night.

She turned on her heel, confused, tired, exhausted, and ready to focus her mind on Nerissa's diary, if for no other reason than to forget the tumultuous and exasperating state of her own night. But there was also Toby's thesaurus and the call to Dane she ached to make—and was it too late to visit Margaret

Garzing? Did she even want to? Could she handle any more? Thomas had seemed so certain that she needed to.

The tears gathered in her eyes, fogging her vision, but not spilling over. She'd been so strong, so strong, she'd been doing so well. No fits at all, and now the breakdown was imminent. Brewing. Forthcoming. Impending. Unavoidable. Inescapable.

Until, through the veil of tears two headlights illuminated the front of her cottage, and she was no longer alone.

18

GALLIMAUFRY
a jumble or confused medley of things

And then, just when she thought he'd come back, he hadn't. The two headlights drove right on by without stopping, leaving Petra even more bereft.

She looked back to the cottage standing cozily behind her, could see the cheerful glow of the Tiffany lamp in the foyer. But it felt barred to her somehow. As though it waited for a future version of herself to welcome home. She couldn't go in now, she didn't deserve the welcome, not yet.

The night had grown bitterly cold, crisp darkness holding her in its arms. And, abruptly it occurred to her that she was headed to Mrs. Garzing's. A jolt, like an electric shock, ran through her body, and she could almost swear she could see sparks fly out from the ends of her hair. Something…clicked into place. An awareness, a certainty, though she couldn't quite grasp precisely what it was. Her senses were heightened and she knew something within her had changed.

A fine mist of the gentlest rain began, though, it did not seem to fall. Rather, it appeared around her suddenly. She did not need to pick her way or find the path, instead she allowed her mind to ruminate on whatever it chose, knowing instinctively that her feet had walked this path before, many times, even though her mind could not recall it.

She was surprised that the rage had passed, or, had faded, she didn't know which. She had been on the precipice, about to lose herself in the chaos of feeling, and then...nothing. Like a string pulled taut, almost to breaking, and then...slack appeared.

The Greek myth of Ananke came to mind. She had studied it in her post grad work, the phonemes of the Greek language and the evolving of the roots and words as they traveled across the Mediterranean and farther, always of particular interest to her. Ananke was the personification of compulsion, force, inevitability, necessity—fate. A woman so powerful, an entity and idea so mighty that gods paid her homage and knew they could not go against her.

Something about the deity's dynamism reminded Petra of Nerissa, and the idea of destiny itself calmed her in a way she hadn't expected. All of the pain, all the loss, all the lies, the success and the sadness, every secret and moment of her past led to this moment, and those that would follow.

She inhaled the night air deeply, the wetness of tree leaves and the familiar scent of earth—this earth. The soil of her childhood, the place where her roots had been planted all those years ago. She thought of Toby and his little red book, and Dane's skinny knees next to hers as they sat in the grass, and his freckles like stars in the sky above her. She thought of Thomas Marr and the way he'd always watched, quick with a smile, but never could quite break into their games, their trio. She frowned at the thought and pulled her sweater closer around her shoulder.

Her eyes made out a string of white lights, fairy lights on a small cottage, not even a quarter of the size of Petra's. Part of her wanted to run to the door, and demand the strange old woman tell her whatever secrets she held fast. And the other part tarried, slowing the rhythm of her steps through the crunching leaves on the forest path. What harm was there in delaying Ananke, the inevitable?

Her mind conjured the latest words collected, amassed, compiled, gathered—nay, hoarded—from the diary. Nerissa had spoken of being **pretroged** to Searc, which she had translated as 'promised to marry', but it was less like an engagement and more of a giving of consent. She could see the meaning in her mind, see the young Searc cupping Nerissa's dark face, the silver hair whipping about them as a powerless talisman against the fate she already knew from looking into his eyes. And the word she had written as 'memory' came from a different, more heartbreaking word in Nerissa's diary. **Nimraksha**. It was a word that had an ache that tied to the past, a memory, but one that sits on your heart like a stone. A word that evoked a feeling Petra knew very well.

It was that collected word that she had wanted to share with Dane over dinner. And now, raising a timid fist to the white-washed door, a beacon in the dark for all that would seek her, Petra feared that it was nimraksha that Mrs. Garzing would share with her.

The small, childlike ancient woman smiled through the lines in her face, her long white braid like a mirror of the moonlight, and pearly all-seeing, unseeing eyes met Petra's. Without a word she gestured for her to step from the tiny porch into the mysteries of the cabin.

Petra exhaled the night air from her lungs, raising her eyes to the rafters in the porch, glad the old woman hadn't fixed the holes and breaks in the wood planks so that she could take a last glimpse of the stars. Petra threw her head back and shook it lightly, feeling as though she could jostle all of her fears out her ears and out the ends of her fingertips.

Stepping in, she found a fire crackling and chattering, many sleeping cats, a wall full of books— and Dane Fintan, his face illuminated by the glow.

Diary Of Nerissa Swifte

I have heard it said that reunion is a sweeter joy than union. But I am now certain such a claim must be accompanied by a clear accounting of the circumstances. For it was a reunion for myself and my twin brother, but the setting of the event was less than fortuitous. Or joyful.

Coming in behind Fisher was Grandmother Oak, and her apathy at her own capture chilled me—but I've run ahead of my own narrative. If I am to organize my thoughts in a way that will aid me—that will act as an arrow to show me the direction of my life from this prison, then I must ink these tumbling thoughts in the chronology of which they took place, else I will be lost. More so than I find myself now.

I did not see who shoved Fisher into my cell, nor who did such violence to Magda as he knocked her head against the metal bars. Her teeth rattled and the sound of her skin breaking on the cruel iron was audible. And terrifying.

My brother had fairly flown to my arms, burying his face in the crook of my neck, as though he were my child. He quickly turned, though, to hear such a violence to one as old, as feared and revered as the Lady of the Woods was unthinkable. One could imagine it as one would imagine inflicting a great hurt on the lake. That is, not at all. She was a woman who had been born old, and had lived on the island since it first was conjured by the fairy and to imagine her existence as moving the same way as any normal woman's…this was nonsense. But, she bled and I could see the break of her ancient bones, but thankfully, I could glimpse no pain. Although, mayhap it was because I did not wish to find it.

I had not a moment to ruminate on it, however, as I was once again swept up in my brother's arms. He put his webbed hands on either side of my face, uncaring that I had not bathed in days, looking not at the dirt and grime on my face, but instead looking straight at my soul, the mirror of his own.

His eyes were cold, and the expression within froze me further than the stones of my prison had ever penetrated. There was blood coming from one of his ears, and mottled flesh on his face that I knew would soon become black and purple. He moved stiffly and winced with the effort of it. But, what tugged my heart most dreadfully was the deeper pain written on his countenance, but he did not speak of it. Instead, he whispered softly, and stepped over to Magda, a comforting arm about the old woman's shoulders.

"She is much hurt, I think." He began, moving his head about to try and locate some small source of light in the darkness from which to observe more closely the wounds we had heard inflicted. I was more used to the dark than they, but even I had trouble making out the details of the wounds they both sustained.

As I stepped forward to give aid, she laughed in response to the two of us. A small cobwebby thing that fluttered about the cell like a moth. "Hurt is only for bodies." She replied, cryptically, and laughed again.

Fisher's hand came to find mine in the darkness, and he squeezed lightly every few moments, as though checking that I was still there. I unclasped his hand from mine and stood before him, inspecting what I could, searching for blood or harm. "How came you here?" I had asked. I suppose I thought he had been planning my escape, and had been caught outside the little building that contained my cell, which had necessitated his arrest. Obviously, though, from the expression I could make out in the darkness, I saw I was in error. Very much so.

The look he gave me was oddly mistrustful, and it caught my breath. He eyed me warily, as though willing himself to be harder. But, he grasped my shoulders again and clung to me, pulling me down into his own world of blue. Something had happened, I knew, and I would have to wait until he could explain precisely what.

But the Lady of the Woods? Her long white hair hung about her eyes, her wrinkles and the dark hid all of her secrets. If her thoughts did show on her face, I could not read them there.

The passage outside the cell had grown quiet, no more the jangling of keys or the heavy breathing of the townsfolk, my keepers, our keepers.

I cleared my throat then, for I had come to realize now that Fisher had fallen under a spell of silent anger, looking somehow to me for guidance and illumination in the gloom surrounding us.

Grandmother Oak was a force of her own; she stood amongst the two of us, and yet was not a part of the events unfolding. As though they did not touch her. I threw my shoulders back and tossed the snarled strands of my hair to the side, and spoke, again, as it seemed my question had been ignored. Or too long considered.

"I said, how came you here? Fisher, my heart, how do you find yourself afoul of the town? I had thought Annette was their creature, and would surely protect you?" I then turned to Magda, and placing a hand gently on her arm, asked her the same. "How were you taken? And why? Have they mixed you in my troubles?" I did not really wonder at her answer; in truth, I was sorely surprised that they had not brought her days ago. She was a fixture of mysticism on the island. If I could be thought to be only a healer, and nay a witch, it was because of my skills in herbals and physick—healing arts that I had learned and practiced for the deliverance and good health of the island. But there was no mistaking the old woman's identity. She was a witch, who threw the bones and saw the future in the runes. She communicated with spirits and sacrificed to the fairies and the people of the water. Not my father or my brothers, but the first people of the lake, the true ones. She was lined and small, but sprightly, too full of vigor for an age as advanced as she surely had attained.

Oh, yes, if there was to be a burning, we two would burn. Or, I would, and she would escape by some enchanted means I know not.

Even in the shadows I saw pain steal across Fisher's features like a howling wind. "Oh, Nissa, we quarreled. Annette was…wild. It was as if…I had suddenly awoken, do you see? And my mood was black, my temper incontrollable. I…I was making ready to return to you, to bring you more candles, and some food to eat…" He stopped, ran his hand over his eyes and then his mouth, holding the words inside a moment longer before they could be unsaid.

"…I did her violence, Nissa. She became… grotesque to my eyes, and I lashed out, throwing her away from me, and into the wall opposite. She was some foul creature, a daemon! And it wasn't until she slumped into a heap on the floor that I recognized her. My wife, that I loved, that I do love. And not a daemon, but a woman—but a wicked one. With a cold heart that I do not know."

The cell grew quiet as I waited for him to finish. He was not crying, but he had not the master of his voice.

"I cannot explain it, except to say—I did not know her. I felt that I had not known her for some time. Her words were vicious and cruel. About you. About our family. About what she hoped to see….she hopes to see you burn, Niss. She called me your familiar and hinted that she would not tolerate my further association with a known witch and heretic. That I was not to see you again, though you were in this prison, under lock and key. She marveled at her own harsh power, her control over you and me—and in that moment, she was…she was a daemon! I swear it! For a moment, I thought I saw…"

He was lost and bewildered and I knew not how much sense was in his words, nor did I care. He sobbed in earnest then, his arms about me and his chin in my neck as we had cried together when our mother had left us. All those years ago.

A raspy voice sounded from Grandmother Oak's corner. "It would not be uncommon. All humans have daemons living inside them. Like little moths that fly in their mouths when they say something ignorant or cruel. Like spiders that crawl beneath fingernails when one commits an unkindness."

Her words sent shivers down my flesh, but she did not cease.

"Do enough and say enough that is rotten, and think enough that is evil and the daemons will feed and eat away the good that was there. Mark me, young Swifte, it was that which you saw on Annette's face." We watched her gnarled bony fingers like twigs before her face as she described them, and I clung to Fisher a little tighter. Fisher patted my hair, and swallowing down the truth of her words, continued.

"They were waiting outside the door. And I knew then that she had been playing with me all the while. She had already decided that I was of no more use to her, that I was not to be won to her side, that she would need to punish me. They grabbed me…they… tortured me, Nissa. And they brought me here—to you, which is a balm to any and all hurts."

I patted him and spoke some words from our childhood. Nonsense secrets that only we knew, or remembered knowing in another time. Soon, whether from trauma or exhaustion or both, he slept.

I see now that all I desire is to remove my brother from this prison. I have made peace with never gazing on my lover's face again, that there will be no proper farewell for Alarence and I, nor Phineas and my father. Fisher is all, though; as much as I love my family and Alarence, it is not difficult to believe that it will end thus. Fisher, my other half, my soul and heart's counterpart. If he can be saved, then is it not as though a piece of me is saved as well? It is a fair sacrifice, for me to die and he to live. For we live in each other. Perhaps I am writing nonsense. I have been thinking much on this as I listen to him sleep; we are back to back in the little cell, and I can hear his troubled slumber as I ink these words into my little book, my little quill scratch-scratching the page. Grandmother Oak, like me, does not sleep. We will sleep when our bodies are ash. Her eyes glint in the near-dark like Tabby's do. And ah, more than anything, I wish I had that roaring purr to give me comfort as my hands cramp and sting with the cold.

Hark, I can hear them gathering the twigs, I can hear them piling the wood, trying to find enough that is not over-damp. They will be glad when I confess, only too pleased to set Fisher free, for they hardly have enough kindling to smoke out the shadowy soot souls of we two tiny women.

In the end, I will fulfill my destiny. I shall never leave this island, unless some of my fire-singed flesh is carried aloft in the wind.

The island will be safe, and my brothers, and Alarence, my heart, will wander far, far from this place. That is all I can hope for.

From the corner, under the cloak of shadows, I think I hear Magda laugh her same dusty, cobwebbed laugh, but I cannot be certain. But, somehow, it will still echo throughout my foggy half-dreams this night.

19

SANGUINOLENT

tinged with blood, or a passion for bloodshed

"I don't understand" Petra stammered. "I was, I mean, Thomas said, well, I was told…"

"Yes, quite, I'm sure you were…sit down, Pebble. Do stop skittering about, you make an old woman dizzy." Mrs. Garzing laughed at her own words, and Petra swallowed and shook her head, as though it were an etch-a-sketch filled with errant lines and she needed to begin again.

She could see Dane clearly, but he kept his face steadfastly to the fire. Petra was unsure if she wanted him to look at her or if she preferred avoiding those lake blue eyes.

"Sit, sit, sit. Would you like tea, Pebble? Of course you would. With sugar? Oh, of course you do. Don't you worry, not as much in your cup as mine—you're sweet enough already." She laughed again, a thin spider's web shaking kind of laugh, and cleared her throat. "Now then, Dane, my dear, fetch the tea things from the kitchen like a good boy. We both know you don't need any help finding them, such a gifted boy. I think you'll find some oatmeal cookies in the pantry. Bring the plate, won't you lamb?"

The moment he stood up, she shimmied past him into the the large leather chair, and there sat enthroned, smiling oddly at Petra. They both watched as a stiff-backed and uncomfortable Dane plodded toward the kitchen, but there wasn't a moment for any of Petra's questions, instead Margaret firmly held the reins of conversation.

"There now, we can finally talk about the important things, you and I." Petra would have sworn her eyes twinkled, but the fire danced another direction and the effect was gone.

"Well, Pebble, what brings you out to my doorstep?" The question was not a question at all, and Petra felt as though whatever answer she gave, it would be the wrong response. False. Incorrect. Erroneous. Spurious. Inaccurate.

"Well, Thomas came by, suddenly…and well, he said to come…" The answer which came so immediately to her lips now seemed strange, as had Thomas' manner. Actually, everything about Thomas seemed…off. He looked so much like the way she imagined Alarence Attwater, and like Toby…or how Toby would have looked. She must be confused. She shook her head again, erasing the muddle of thoughts within her mind.

But Margaret Garzing simply sat back into the ancient, carved high-back chair. She managed to look at ease, though Petra thought it unbelievable it was possible in such a seat.

Dane re-entered the room, and she could feel his

eyes on her, surveying her, gauging her for signs of…
what? Had her fit the other day made such an
impression? He seemed afraid of her or unsure of
her, and she could feel rather than see the exchanged
glances between Dane and Margaret. When Petra did
decide to meet his eyes, he looked away, instead
pouring her tea, and busying himself with adding
spoonful upon heaping spoonful of sugar to Mrs.
Garzing's pink and yellow rose covered china. The
eternal blooms an idea of a memory of spring
captured for eternity on the thin china cup.

The fire crackled merrily and a log shifted,
releasing a series of pops into the room. The wind
outside sang a lament, and rain, like tears unable to be
held back, fell softly in the darkness. It reminded
Petra of crying alone into her pillow at the hospital
after Evan…and of the numerous other nights when
the pillowcase was the repository for her sorrow. As
if tears shed in the dark and dried before morning
didn't count, because the evidence of their short life
had vanished before the light could discover them.

Mrs. Garzing sat forward and fixed Petra with her
unnerving stare, grey and purple and orange in the
reflecting flames. She reached out tenderly and took
Petra's hand and spoke, her voice coming out
differently, somehow older and fiercer and her long
silver hair took on the glow of flames so that the
strands appeared to burn.

The effect silenced Petra, and reminded her in a
way of Nerissa Swifte, and of her own childhood,
and legends and fairytales that she'd forgotten—but
really never had.

"Let me tell you a story about a girl. A girl who lived in Traverston, and though she left, she carried the past with her always. Comforted herself with it and tortured herself with it so that her past was present, and her future, it too, lay in the past. Didn't it? Of course it did…"

Mrs. Garzing's Story

This girl wasn't ordinary, because no girl ever is. Her summers were full of sunshine and trees to climb and creeks to splash in. This girl had a brother, an Irish twin, just a year older than herself. And while the girl and the boy teased and fought as all siblings do, they also loved one another dearly. Their home was a cold place, full of fear and tension, and so they sought out the sunlight of the outside world, together.

The girl had a big imagination. She told stories and named the trees. She invented identities, telling her brother they were a kidnapped prince and princess, or that they had sprouted from the earth in the forest like moss on a log. Her brother was books and proof, science and evidence, always needing to find the root of the root of all things. They raised themselves and the town they lived in raised them and they found the world around them, overall, to be an interesting and exciting adventure. The children made friends easily, but had two special friends. Two others who seemed to share their differing passions for chaos and order. Imagination and intellect. But this girl, this girl was their leader. She chose which games they would play and assigned roles. She chose the trees to climb and the places to build forts and the best hiding places.

And they were all content.

But it cannot stay light indefinitely. The darkness they avoided at home would not be kept forever at bay.

As the children grew older, they were still inseparable, but they were no longer just a group of friends. They were growing up. Moving away from one another. They were boys, and she—a girl. And a time came that the boys were signed up for a baseball team by their well meaning fathers. The girl wanted to join too, but girls couldn't play baseball. Girls were made to play softball. So, this girl didn't play at all. She stuck to the woods and climbed trees, but the forest was quieter and brambles caught in her hair and without a leg up or friends to run with, her knees skinned more often and branches scratched her cheeks.

Her brother was unhappy, too. The shadow of his problems at home would steal over him more often, and his sister seemed to have taken the sunlight into the forest with her, along with his childhood happiness.

He escaped into his thesaurus, always trying to find the right words for how he felt, the words to give him power, the words to make him strong and brave. But he could never find the right ones to explain the pain inside of him. And he practiced daily at being this new older boy; hitting ball with bat and running,

running, running, though to where or at what, he never knew.

There was nothing special about the day. It wasn't especially warm, nor was it cold or raining. It wasn't an important game, just a team a few towns over. Nothing significant had happened except that his mother had been out late and his parents had fought about it. His father had called her something—a word he didn't know and he couldn't find it in his thesaurus either. But none of that was special. His parents always fought.

The boy had looked for his sister before they left. He'd checked her room and under the porch and on the roof, but she wasn't there. He'd hoped she'd go to the game—their friends had missed her around, he'd missed her lately. Things were less fun when she wasn't there.

But he couldn't find her.

The other two boys were already in the car when he walked up. His mother didn't look good. Her eyes were red and her eye make-up was smudged. Her dress was disheveled. Suddenly he was ashamed. Why couldn't another of their parents drive? Why did the rest of his team have to see her like this? And too quickly, she saw the expression on his face. She knew how he felt about her. Could *see* the way he felt about her.

"Don't look at me like that!" She'd spat at him, her eyes wild. Part of him was worried she'd now refuse to drive them to the game. The other part of him saw the panic on his friend's faces and hoped she wouldn't.

"What's a whore?" He'd asked, not sure why, but

knowing the word his father had used would hurt her. His mother looked away from him, and told him to get in the backseat. So, he had.

And one of his friends moved to the front seat.

The ride was silent, except for his mother muttering and the clink and roll of a few tea-brown beer bottles in the backseat. Every once in a while she drank out of plastic pop bottle, but he knew it wasn't soda inside.

He hated it when they had to ride with his mother. And he wished his sister was there, she was never quiet. Even when their mother was mad. Or when she acted odd, like she was now.

His mother drove erratically, the car moved too quickly, back and forth across lanes. But, still, no one spoke. It would be over soon. They would get to the field, and then he could forget about it. He wished he'd brought his red thesaurus. Maybe there was a better word for how he felt. Anxious. Frustrated. Embarrassed. Was there one word for all of those feelings?

Soon it would be over though.

And with a squeal and a crash, it was.

It was nice outside, he thought. It made him giggle, but it hurt to laugh. Blood came out instead of a laugh. He felt funny. Strange. Odd. Unusual. He almost laughed again, but only blood came out. His uniform was covered in it. He thought for a moment that he'd need a new one. But, then, it didn't matter. He was feeling tired suddenly. Weak. Exhausted.

It was a good thing his sister hadn't come to see

the game. She might've gotten hurt. It was better to be in the woods, he thought.

And then he was there himself.

And then he was nowhere at all.

20

WELKIN

the sky or the vault of heaven

The story Petra had heard was different. But it ended the same, as it must, for no matter how the story was told, Toby was dead.

"There were...more people in the car?" Petra asked. She knew the answer, and what's more, the memory tugged on something raw and unhealed. Something ignored for years. She knew who the people were.

"Yes, that's right. Four people in the car. Two walked away, but only one ever walked free."

Mrs. Garzing's gaze came over to find Dane, who stared at the fire with forced intensity. The rain fell harder against the panes, as if for dramatic effect.

"You." Petra said softly, almost to herself. Her hands slowly drifting up her arms, readying herself for the embrace she would need to give to hold herself together. She could already feel the tremors coming, the little cracks that would shake her to crumbling.

"You…you lived?" She asked him, and though he did not look at her, she saw his body go rigid as though she had spoken an incantation that turned him to stone.

Petrified.

Petra-fied.

"We switched seats." He said, his voice clear and controlled, his tone betraying nothing, which betrayed everything.

"Who else?" She asked, not allowing herself to consider the implications of his confession. She looked from one to the other. Dane, adamantly resisting her eyes, Mrs. Garzing's stare unwavering from her person. Neither answered.

So, Petra did. "Thomas. It had to be, but…"

"Thomas." Dane said, his voice final.

"But, I've seen him…"

"Yes, Pebble, strange isn't it?" Mrs. Garzing said. She tore her eyes from Petra for the first time to pour a spoonful into her mouth directly from the little sugar bowl.

Diary Of Nerissa Swifte

It is three days now since they last came bearing bread. Bread that began edible, and then of late, had become moldy and rotting. As though no new bread was being baked. For even in times of plenty there is not so much surplus made as to become stale or molded.

This was not the first sign that there is aught wrong on the island. Our jailer was grey, last he came, and seemed to grow paler before my eyes when he came with the meager victuals. His figure less sturdy, more translucent somehow. It is as though their aim in locking us away has gone awry. And instead of preserving themselves from our taint, it is we who are safeguarded from them. I did attempt to gather his attention, to tell him I wished to confess—in order that I might save Fisher—but the man only shook his head and walked away. They have no use for confessions. There will be no trial.

This little cell is dry enough, though it is ever colder, but I find the attitude within these walls the most chilling. Whatever spark that did ignite Fisher the night he saw through Annette's lies has since burned out, and instead he is now like a cat in a cage, yowling and snapping at anyone who speaks to him. It is tragic to see my strong, brave brother brought so low. His world had been crumpled and crushed like ink-stained parchment. His freedom and his beloved lake have been stolen from him.

Not I, nor for Grandmother Oak. I find that women seem to bear up under suffering. Perhaps it is because we have been taught that to be a woman is to be weak, and so our whole lives are spent trying to build up the lack of courage within ourselves. When the freeze of the cold is too much, I turn my mind to the warmth of memory. To the songs Da sang when a nightmare had ridden through my dreams. When I am frightened, I think of walking on the ice and the sickrooms I have walked into, never taking the sickness myself.

There is magic in memory, and within me. I will use this as my talisman. For I am the fairidie of Traversint, and though they may burn me for it, they can never take my magic. It is eternal.

I can feel the hum of power between Magda and I, and when I speak to her, we talk of herbs, and if spearmint or peppermint is better for a broken heart. We speak of coltsfoot and houndstongue and Indian Pipe and lamb's ear, and the right moon to pick them all under. We speak of sickness and death and how to cheat them—and what tastes better under the setting sun, wild black raspberries or clover honey?

The corners of our present do not touch us the same as it does Fisher. For we are women and that is our own magic too.

It has grown darker these past days and fewer whispers creep their way into my ears. The sun seems to have abandoned the island. The day is dark and night blinks in the same grey shadow. The wind howls and we all know not when to wake or sleep. Our bodies are weakened from lack of vittles and though I do what I am able to soothe Fisher's troubled heart and his broken spirit, I cannot stop the dreams that wait hovering like bats beneath my eyelids when I sleep.

I dream of strange things. Vivid, vibrant fantasies that are somehow not mad at all. I dream of the cries of a score, nay, a thousand, nay—a hundred thousand tabbies, just like my own. A sea of mewling, yowling cats, tiny bodies curled up in sleep or death, I know not which.

I dream of the island, overgrown and lush with greenery. Not a living soul but the birds and the rabbits and squirrels scampering from tree to tree. I hear the laughter of little beings of light. Are these fairies? Would I know them to look at them?

And sometimes, if I am not over-careful, the children come to me. Young boys, their bodies blood and gore, ripped and torn in places a body cannot be. Their little ghosts hovering above their broken bodies, their wails unanswered by the hand of death. He is not there to take them to the next place, he is gone. My old friend, Death, whom all fear, though none should! For these boys are proof are they not? How much more frightening is it to not be met by death? To wander and watch and relive the pain again and again?

The Word Collector ✧ A. Nolan

I know not if these are conjuring of an overly imaginative mind, if they are shades of the past, or, perhaps, if they are whispers of a future I will not see. But, it matters not, for they all terrify me, waking me with a sob in my throat and tears running well worn tracks down my cheek. It is then that Fisher reaches for me, and holds me close, as when we were children. He hums the songs our father used to sing and runs fingers through my matted hair, and for those moments, I am his child to care for.

He tells Da's stories then, when I cannot fall back asleep. Of fish men and fairy women, of swimming and swimming and never touching the bottom in our lake. He speaks of the legends of the natives on the mainland, and of the countries that lay beyond the ocean. Places Alarence has been, and Fisher only imagines. Sometimes I like his imaginings better, I think, than the real stories I have heard.

And when his voice is hoarse, The Lady in the Woods tells her own stories.

Some of them are so fantastic that I cannot believe they are not fiction. Fairy-tale drips like honey from each of her words, though she speaks as if it is her only truth. I wish I could capture her words fully like a fish in a net, but every time I press quill to paper, the words jumble in my mind, and I know I could not do her stories justice.

I worry for Da and for Phin. I worry for the island, though they have wronged me most foully. I worry too for Magda. She is not young, and she seems to grow older and more brittle by the day. She says it is because she needs the forest; the sweet sticky sap of the trees keeps her alive. She is the forest, and she cannot live behind iron and stone.

I no longer hear the sound of kindling being stacked to burn us witches to cinders. I do not hear the insults that used to come hurling through the bars of the high window. I hear nothing but the wailing of the wind and cries and sobs from my dreams. What silent storm rages over this island? What will become of us, these three souls who freeze under the stone, in this jail beneath the earth?

As I have written before, the cold has never caused me as much bother as it does other folk. It is the ice within that chills me.

21
HUGGER MUGGER
in a state of confusion or disarray

"I don't understand." Petra said simply, her voice a rasping whisper.

"Of course you do, my dear. Of course you do. A ghost. Thomas, dearest, is a ghost."

"But...but...how..." Petra could feel the tremors slithering up her shins, over her knees, ready to send her into a panic, a hysterical, sobbing...

And then Mrs. Garzing pressed her teacup to Petra's lips and the thick, gravelly sugar sludge slid down her throat. And oddly enough, she was calmer.

"Yes, Pebble. A ghost, of course. There's loads of them here, you know? Of course there are! Why wouldn't there be? An old place like this. A shame that you have only seen the one, now that I think of it. I can hardly walk from my bedroom to the door without bumping into someone. Anyway, what was I saying? Of course, the ghost. Thomas, yes."

Petra felt weirdly at ease. Like she'd slipped under

a warm blanket and Mrs. Garzing's strange words were snugly tucking her in. Harmonious. Pacific. Reposeful. Serene. Tranquil.

"Yes, my dear, you have been seeing a ghost. And I suspect you haunt yourself with many more phantoms of your past." Margaret shifted and took a dainty bite of cookie, offering the plate to a silent but watchful Dane.

Petra looked down. She was warm, and no longer felt a fit coming, but confusion swirled and her head was heavy. She leaned against the back of her chair and looked at Dane, focusing her eyes on him, willing him to speak, and yet, not wanting to hear what he would say. She had enough history that she carried around. Margaret was right; she had her own ghosts. Her father. Her life as a successful writer. Toby. Thomas.

Evan.

The panic rose like bile, and a jolt like electricity shocked her to her feet.

"Tell me." She said, her voice quiet but firm. "Tell me the things you think I don't know. All of them."

To her surprise, it was Dane who turned his body toward hers, standing up to meet her. The rain outside was still faintly drizzling, and he cast an eye toward the window before he answered her. "Would you like to walk outside a few minutes? I'm sure all this conversation is tiring Mrs. Garzing."

Petra glanced over at the old woman, who rolled her eyes in response, her mouth munching another cookie. Petra was struck again by the woman's appearance; it wasn't a face to get used to. Ancient, and yet childlike. All the same, she made a rolling motion with her hand that told Petra to agree with Dane's request.

He extended his fingers toward her, and lightly, she grasped them, not knowing what roads or what truths they would lead her on. He pulled her to the door, where they both bundled coats and boots on, before stepping out into the mist of a storm that had almost, but not quite, passed.

He walked toward the woods, and just before they entered he put his hand out in order to hold tightly to hers. She grasped his palm without a thought, and then afterward wondered if it were a familiar action. Had she done this before? Had they?

They walked for a few moments, raindrops falling on leaves and trickling through branches. When he cleared his throat to speak, she gathered herself inside her own mind to listen and listen only. No time for feelings and reactions, only truth.

"I was there. I know you already know from her story, but yes, I was there. I saw him as he was dying. I saw him as he died. I watched as his spirit left his body. But I couldn't do anything. I was underneath one of the car doors, you see. And even if I could have moved, I wouldn't have. It was shock. Do you understand? Perhaps you don't. But, I didn't move until the paramedics came and I didn't speak for a few months after. It was like…that moment had been so intensely loud, that I didn't need any more noise for some time."

Petra managed a quiet question, an involuntary squeeze of his hand accompanying it. "They both… Toby and Thomas…they both died at the scene?"

Dane shook his head, surprising Petra. "No, just

Toby. Thomas was in a coma for a few hours at the hospital. When they told his parents his brain had died, his mother requested that he be unplugged from life support." He looked straight at her in the darkness of the woods, "You were there, you know. You came. I don't know where you came from, but you found your way to Toby. You wouldn't let go of him. You didn't yell or scream, or cry, you just wouldn't let him go. I don't know what happened in the end, because they took me off to the hospital too. But, it...it made me feel better to see you. It made life...it made it ok to be alive. In that moment."

Petra nodded, taking all the information in. She felt calm, though she wasn't certain why. As though she had known all along, and hearing it spoken aloud healed something she hadn't known was ripped open.

Dane continued, looking away. "I don't know why it was only I that lived. I don't know why Toby and I switched seats. Not a scratch on me. Not a bruise. And Toby...so much. Blood. I didn't understand, I still don't. I'm sorry, Petra. I'm so sorry..."

A great sound like a sob came from his throat, though Petra could see him desperately trying to master his emotions.

"I'm glad you are alive." Petra said. Her voice was clear, but still quiet. Dane stopped, abruptly, and turned his body toward Petra's, his face incredulous. Confused. Befuddled. Inquisitive.

"Are you?" He asked, his voice almost a whisper.

"Yes." She answered. "I'm not glad that Toby is dead, but I'm very happy that the boy... the man that I...that you are still alive. I can't believe I didn't know you on sight."

Instead of a smile, Dane's face fell, and she could see he was holding back an intense emotion. Finally, after a few moments of gazing upward, he spoke. "When I came back from the hospital, I went out looking for you. I went to your house, I combed the woods, to all of our old haunts. But you weren't there. Every place I went was cold and dead, and I felt more alone than ever. It wasn't like you just weren't there at the moment, it was like…no one had ever been there. Ever."

"And then I found you at the lake's edge. You were humming and I was so excited to see you. Relieved. You had Toby's red book on your lap and your hair was knots and snarls, but when I talked to you, you didn't see me. You were mumbling words, rapidly, and humming. Too quickly for me to understand and too quietly to make sense of. You looked beyond me, through me, and just went on, dipping your toes and mumbling words, staring out into the blue of the lake. The next week, your father had taken you away. I came to your house, came in through a window; I couldn't believe you were gone now too. All that was left in your bedroom was a few blood birch apples and strange white stones. It looked like a bone collection in your room, and I was afraid to touch the apples lest my fingers make blood spatters across the flesh. I never saw you again, until two years ago."

Petra had involuntarily shuddered, and stroked the scar on her jaw. Dane was silent a moment, his face lost in the shadow of night. Petra's mind rewound like tape in a projector until she landed on the moment she was looking for, and then her mind pressed play.

Her recent book had been a success, *Monsters and Mystery Goblins of the Middle West*. She'd had a ball writing it, tracking down the names of the fiends and beasts of the tribes in the region. Stonechats and the Monster Bear of the Iroquois. The Mi-she-shek-kak of the Ojibwe, and the Windigo, the ice-cannibal. The names given to the monsters carrying as much fear and power as the demons themselves. But, Evan had published around the same time too. And where she had triumphed, he had failed. The writing was poor, his own research falling flat in academic circles. His sources, hazy, his assertions, vague. Was this when the relationship began to rot? Or had she been so buried in her writing and word sleuthing to notice it had always been putrid?

Angry words, long silences. Slamming doors and words unsaid. Strange numbers on his phone and voices in the background. The light that he had given off, that had shown so brightly before, she had come to realize had been her own light, which he had taken and shone on himself. And now that she was pulling it back to glow on her own happiness and achievements, she found only darkness for both of them. A darkness that had grown deeper and colder, freezing her out, and then he became violent.

She heard Dane clear his throat. The rain had stopped now, so that only the drip of tears on leaves, the steady rhythm of the drops falling from branch to branch to earth remained from the earlier storm.

"I read about you, of course. All those books published. And it was neat, because you seemed happy, and also, through all those words, it was like Toby's passions lived on too. I was always so excited to see your face on book jackets. You were a grown woman now, but the same little girl looked back at me out of that picture. The little girl that I knew as well as my own past self…" He cleared his throat again.

"And then your father moved back here for good, as it was so close to the hospital, and your mother had passed on, so there was nothing to keep him away. Although, I think he always wanted to return. I saw him around, tried to come by a few times, but he didn't like to see me, I don't think. But then, that night…he called me, told me I had to hurry. Because he knew. Knew that I had not forgotten about you. That I couldn't."

Petra looked at him, her eyes narrowed. Hurry for what? She had forgotten how dark the woods became, how far away and weak Traverston was in banishing that darkness. She couldn't make out his features, but she could sense him, the heat of him near her, and she kept her mind and the rhythm of her heartbeat trained on the melody of his voice. She didn't want to say any of the words herself; she wanted him to say them. They would feel less ugly coming from him, less and at the same time, more personal for him to speak them.

"I didn't know precisely what had happened, and I couldn't find anything online. Allegra was at my house, and so I had to drop her off with her mom before I could drive out. Julia, her mother, couldn't understand my fascination, my obsession with you. With a girl I hadn't seen since I was a child. She couldn't begin to understand. I didn't even understand, and I still don't, but…"

Petra couldn't hear anything else, except her story. She spoke, breaking whatever speech he was intended on into fragments that disappeared into the night. "Hospital? What hospital?" She knew, but she didn't know. She remembered, but she had forgotten. Had to forget. Don't remember. Even as a part of her begged him for the truth, something inside of her reached for words of comfort. Her words. Toby's words, Nerissa Swifte's words. Thole -to suffer, Mote -must, Craze -to shatter, Caddish -wicked. She exhaled. Words. Words were order and reason. They gave homes to feelings so that those feelings hurt less. Could be identified, filed, understood, dismissed. Her words, Toby's words.

"Yes, the hospital. Do you...recall?" His voice was gentle, and she did not need the moonlight to tell her his expression was pained.

"Tell me. I want you to." Her voice was still quiet, even to her own ears. She felt some part of her bundle up within her own skin, trying to hide away from the words he was about to speak, though she knew no matter where she hid herself, those words would still find her. The truth always managed to chase you down in the end.

He exhaled hard and sighing, prepared himself. "I don't know it all, honestly. And I don't think I'll ever want to. I know that your boyfriend, a fellow writer, had a history of mental issues. Minor run-ins with the law, lied in some of his academic applications and faked research. That was all on the news at any rate. And then he...he snapped. He hurt you. He cut you."

Dane's voice shuddered, but she wouldn't allow him to grieve her.

"He slit me from ear to chin. And then he turned the knife on himself. Slit his own throat and smiled while he did it." It made her sick to say it, but it also felt liberating, as though the words had been heavy stones on her chest, pushing on her lungs, never allowing her to breathe fully. And now she was gulping in the fresh air of the night like water at an oasis.

If Petra could have seen Dane, she would have seen his tears. She would have seen that he was remembering seeing her in that hospital bed, watching and willing her to live.

"He said I spent too much time in the past, that if he couldn't bring me into the present, then pain could." She smiled to herself in the darkness. "But he was wrong. He didn't know me at all. The past is my present. And I have always retreated into its depths and folds for comfort. The past had already happened. The wounds it inflicts are only the prodding of old scars. Dull achey pain."

She heard him laugh. "What?"

"I told you, I liked the past too, but it is because it forces the rawness of my feelings for it to the present. There is nothing dull or aching about the way I have waited for you. Have searched for you. There is nothing past about the way I love you, Petra."

"Don't. Please, don't. What are you saying? I'm damaged. Broken. Partially insane. I breathe in words and walk in a world that no longer exists and see ghosts of dead friends. I...don't belong here."

"You're wrong, Petra. You're so wrong. I love the past, even with the blood and the memories and the pain, because you are my past. This city, our time here is my present. And since I was a little boy stealing apple kisses in the orchard, you were my future. We've always known. You've always known."

Petra had turned away from his voice. It was a movie, a fairytale, a dream. She did love Dane. She did know that somewhere, some forgotten part of her always had. The girl, the woman, the version of herself that she missed, loved him.

But people don't fall in love when they're eight years old. Not for keeps. She wasn't that Petra anymore. That was a piece of her that had shattered and been swept up and thrown away. That piece was missing when they'd put her back together.

She was walking away from him, from Mrs. Garzing, following a memory of an idea of a trail, her eyes closed, trusting her feet and Toby to get her home.

22

AMBODEXTER
one able to play with either hand

The library was a mess. For the first time, she thought of it as 'the library' instead of 'her father's library'. Something in the last few hours had clicked in to place. The revelations that reminded her that this had been her home, that her history was here, buried beneath the secrets and her own carefully stitched veil of mystery. This was hers. This house was hers. This library, these books, these people in her life.

This life was hers.

As as elated as she felt, the lightening of her heart was short-lived.

Because, this life was hers.

The tragedy was hers. The pain was hers. The memories, sweet and stabbing, were both equally hers.

And the reminisces of Toby's hand pulling her into the forest on a cold morning, or all three boys running in between the rows of apple trees at the orchard, running, running, until your lungs ached and you were left breathless, but you ran anyway, for the thrill. These memories tugged the same as those of her scrambling into Toby's bed when her mother was screaming in the middle of the night, or the days when the police cars would pull in the drive, or the day that Toby didn't come home.

She remembered very little after that, like the bulb had burned out in the room she was standing in, leaving her in darkness. Even now, when the whole business had been laid bare to her, the Pandora's box of her own life, re-opened, she only had glints and flashes. A young Dane coming to the house, Dane calling her name outside the window. And then her father had packed up her room, and they left. She guessed her father hadn't even stayed for the trial. He'd grabbed Petra and run. Ran, ran, ran and never spoke of this life again. Willed Petra to forget, made himself forget.

Until he had run back. And Petra had torn the library apart to find the why of it. Why would he come back to a place filled with so many ghosts? That was the reason she continued to flip through pages and look under shelves. Some proof, some answer must exist—except she hadn't found it yet. The only thing she could think was that the island called to him, called him back. That the mystery and the truth and the past had been too tempting to leave behind.

It was certainly true for her, why not her father as well?

And Thomas… he had been so real. She had felt his presence as he walked beside her, heard the sound of his voice, had seen him. Flesh and bone leading her down the path to the graveyard, to his mother's house, to the answers she'd needed. But even as she convinced herself, his familiar features blurred in her mind. They were his as a boy, but also Toby's, and also the description of Nerissa's Alarence. A sandy-haired boy grown to manhood. He'd been close by, but never smothering. Kind, but not overly sweet. He was all of the men, and none of them, and a mixture of their ghosts perhaps. But try as she might, she could not remember anyone else ever having spoken to him, excepting herself.

And lying down amidst the careful chaos of the stacked books, which looked exposed and vulnerable away from the safety of their shelves, she settled back onto the oriental wool rug. Petra closed her eyes and remembered back, back and back before the accident. Before she and Toby were king and queen of Traverston, back to what she'd translated earlier that morning. Could it really have only been that morning? It seemed ages since she'd sat lazily with Jinks at the table, pointing out new words to the disinterested cat.

Her mind shuffled back, away from her own mess, and instead to the pressing plight of Nerissa Swifte.

She pulled a corner of a book out from underneath her back where it had been digging, and shook her head. Petra reminded herself that nothing concerning Nerissa Swifte was no longer pressing.

The past couldn't be—could it?

Diary Of Nerissa Swifte

Da is dead.

I cannot believe the words can come from my quill, but they have. Even as I write, in this moment, I find myself glancing back over the inked permanence of them, like a sailor's tattoo. I wish somehow they could be unwritten, but it would be wrong to do so. For dead he is, and he shall remain, and so shall the words I have written.

We are no longer in the gaol. I had thought before that if I were ever to be at freedom to write these words, that it would be done with a jubilant heart, in a spirit of victory. But, 'tis not so, for the only reason we are liberated is that there is no one to keep us within.

Phineas came, and in almost rude good health when taken with the tidings he brought. Sickness had blown around the island, preying on old and young, healthy and feeble alike. The gloating over the captures of the witches had turned to wails of suffering. One by one, the fires of the town had winked out, and the preparations to burn us evil witches and hang Fisher had been forgotten, rope left to rot and stacked wood stolen for the hearth of those that were ill. A very few that were able, these broken and lost families, escaped to Traver's Town, and all else are dead.

When Phineas did appear, I believe the sight of him alone was darker than any shadow I've seen, blacker than the most unforgiving night. I, with hair matted and covered in grime, left to freeze and die in gaol— I, who do not feel the fingers of cold as others do—I, whom tragedy cannot press itself into and linger as it does for others—I, Nerissa of Traversint, was chilled to see him. Chilled to the marrow of my bones. Frozen deep to the hollow place inside of me where the flame of my soul lives. For Phineas came to our cell door, keys and freedom in his hands—but Death, Death dogged his heels as though he had not done with our family. Phineas' eager eyes sought comfort in Fisher and myself. He looked desperately to Grandmother Oak as though she might fix the tear that was ripping through him. Death, my shadow, my companion among the sick, my confidant—Death could not meet my eyes.

And I knew without Phin's voice telling me so that Da was dead, and with him, some of the island's magic had died too.

I pressed my hand in Fisher's, he was now father and mother and brother to me. Phineas' trembling hand reached for mine, as he had when he was small, and uncertain and afraid of the dark trees when we explored the island together.

Our island.

It was Magda, the Lady of the Woods, who walked out last, trailing us in the tunnel back into the air of the night around us. She did not speak, nor did I expect her to. We had been so long together in the prison below the earth. I turned around once we reached the air of the night to say farewell. I wanted to thank her for confirming that I was a witch indeed, and though for reasons different than they thought, the island had cause to be awed by the powers within me.

But, I turned, and she was gone. Disappeared into the wind of the night, and for a moment, my breath caught and I wondered if she had ever been there at all.

My eye could only gaze backward for so long, it was the moment before me that beckoned. I drank the air like water, massive gulps of lake water on the breeze filling my lungs. I could almost feel the island itself flowing into my heart and from there to my fingertips and down to the nails of my toes. The ends of my eyelashes and the flesh behind my knees hummed with the magic of Traversint.

But, the rhythm of the vibration had changed. Da was no longer in the music. Without the beat of his heart, the melody was off. Phineas was speaking now, in a whisper, though I could see no reason why he should do so. The village was deserted, as though war had come and carried off the souls. There was no blood spilt, however. Only silence, which was worse to my ears than wailing and heart-rending screams of terror. Simple silence, that boomed and bellowed. A thousand questions trembled on my lips, and though I could see the words in my mind, I could not give them utterance. I squeezed both of my brothers' hands a little tighter, fighting a chaotic mixture of relief and grief that preyed upon me. Unable to find voice, I turned my attention to the whispers, like puffs of smoke, coming from Phineas' lips.

He was no longer my younger brother, that was clear. He had aged, become harder since Fisher and I had been taken, and his frantic gaze turned granite as he spoke of the misfortunes come to Traversint.

"…'twas the same sickness Nissa fought against, the same that she seemed to keep at bay. It was all but a memory, just a few spiderwebs of illness left hanging in a few of the houses. The whole island had regained strength, or seemed to. I did not know them, Fish. They became vampires, starving for witch's blood, delightedly rubbing their palms together, discussing her death. Each time Da's ear was caught by some such remark, it was as though a knife was plunged within him. He grew old before my eyes. I was not enough, Fish. I wasn't….I couldn't be enough for him. He needed the three of us, and I wasn't enough…"

His voice caught for a moment, and I watched as he pressed back his sorrow down into himself, hardening over the places that were soft. It broke me to see my brother, gentle and kind Phineas, become so hard and unfeeling.

"Annette began to show that she was with child, just a small swell…she glowed with health. And then…she died. They found her body, forgive me Fisher, they found her….her abdomen a black, swollen thing. It was not life she carried within her, but death. And when she was found, her mouth agape, as though she were surprised to realize that she had been carrying Death within her, as if she were carrying Death's own son…"

His voice trailed and I knew he was fighting to silence himself, ashamed of his words and the pain they gave Fisher. Annette was petty, and in her way, evil, but he had loved her fiercely. Fisher's face was a mask, and was I not his twin, his second self, I would have been deceived by his seemingly hard heart. No, I knew better. Fisher's heart was now scattered ashes, the only embers of which were kept alive by his love for Phin and I. It wasn't that he did not care, it was that he no longer could.

We found ourselves at the water's edge, and there I had my first moments apart, alone, since Fisher and Magda had been brought to the cell. They gave me privacy to bathe in the lake, to wash the grit and grime of the cell from my body and spirit. I rinsed out my dress, scrubbing it quickly against a rock, and let the waves bob and flow, bringing the moonlight back to my hair. I plaited it, and donned an old dress Phineas had brought me, and I realized it was my mother's, which hurt and comforted me in the same measure.

We were heading away from the lake now, Phineas was speaking again, and I tried to focus on his words as he led us back to Da's, though it wasn't Da's house any longer. It was just a memory. A dead thing of the past that looked warm in thoughts but was cold to the touch. That's what the past is. A mimic. A fake. A cold, slippery faded, dead image of what used to be.

Of what never will be again. The past is a lie we tell ourselves.

"….he wasn't himself after Nissa was taken, as you well know. Just sat in his stone chair, muttering the words of the old legends, his voice running over the words like water over stones in a stream, like a fluid spell. He sat there, mouthing these words as they drowned him deeper in despair."

"Aye" Fisher said, his voice low, "It was a sight that sent me into the rage at Annette. I could feel him floating away from us like…"

"…like a wave being carried to another shore. And you'd be right, brother. Though I wish, not for the first, that you were not always. For it grew worse. After you were arrested, he would not move, would not eat…would not go to the lake with me…"

"He wouldn't?" Fisher asked, his face becoming ever more etched with sorrow. "But, the water is our air…we cannot live without…"

Phineas nodded, and I realized that though I was a Swifte, that I was not connected to my brothers in this way. I loved Traversint, felt the earth mix with the lake water in my veins, but the lake didn't call to me like it did my brothers, like it had called Da.

"…it grew worse and worse still, it did. When you were taken, his face went white. And the years wrote themselves deeply onto his skin. Once in a while I would hear a howl, a forlorn keening thing. And when I would step into the room and see him in the great stone chair, I knew not if it was a sound a man could make. Even a man of the lake, a powerful fish-man like Da."

He cleared his throat, and his voice shuddered. I longed to take Phin in my arms as I had when he was a child. I remembered that faraway, long-ago boy who reached for his sister; he was gone, and now he was a man who did seek to protect *me*. It came upon me again the cruelties that lie in the past. The pain found in memory.

We knew the words he would speak next were of Da's death, and though we resisted them, there was nothing we could do to hold back the truth. He was dead, and we owed him the respect of listening to how he left this island. This world. Our lives.

The truth has a way of finding you, no matter where or how you hide. It always catches you up. Best to face it where it stands.

"Two mornings past, I woke up early, before the sun, as we do, for my morning swim. The ice of the lake called out to me, and you know, Fisher, the feeling of it, humming through you. I crept out of bed, part of me wanting to disturb Da's strange and haunting reverie, to force him to come along. But, as I stepped into the room, I saw that he was waiting for me. I knew not what changed his mind, but, oh, Nissa, I was full of hope. Fisher, he was himself, I swear it! He was quiet, but no more than usual, and he was humming an old melody as we approached the lake. But as we got closer, I knew something was amiss. He disrobed, but more slowly, carefully, and the tune he hummed grew melancholy. He walked along the sharp beach pebbles for some way, and he sat down on a rock for a moment, picking up the white stones, round like eggs, that sit just on the shore, washed smooth by the caress of the waves. He picked one up, tossed it into the water with a plunk, and turned to me and smiled. I will never forget the smile. So strange…and…final. Then he waded in. Slowly, so slowly, and when the water covered him crown to heel, I shivered as I watched from down the stretch of the beach, for in that moment, I realized he was gone. I knew that I could not swim fast enough, nor pull him to the shore to save him. He had made the choice, deliberately, and gone back to the waves we come from."

He paused a moment and went on. "And I also knew that now everything had changed." He spoke these last words as we arrived at the doorstep. My eyes sought out Fisher's, but he did not look at me; his eyes were darkness, his expression inscrutable. And I saw, in that moment, that my brother was changed as well.

We went in and ate some trout Phineas had brought from the lake, but we spoke little. Though we did not speak we were never far from one another. A hand held here, or our feet touching beneath the table, the contact we kept as necessary as breathing.

I am alone now, again, in the room of my childhood, but I am a child no more. We three, and Grandmother Oak, are all that is left of Traversint. Our island. The island of our ancestors, of our people that brought it into being. The island, a place between water and sky where two lovers could live together and make their home. But, it has fallen to ruin.

Do we stay? Rebuild? Is it our duty? Our destiny? I think it cannot be. I have seen my destiny, after all, and it lives in the eyes of Alarence Attwater.

But I cannot leave my brothers. It would be like leaving myself.

23

CAIRN:

stone mound set as a marker; tombstone

White stones like eggs. Petra wondered if they were the same as those in her father's study and that she'd placed on Toby's grave, and knew, somehow, that they must be.

She breathed out, and a little whimper escaped. Petra ran her mind over the grief counselor's words. Breathe. Survive. Find the light, find the light, find the light. Nerissa had described Phineas as **Narthenness,** which was a new word for Petra, but a thing she knew well. It was nothing, darkness, numbness, hollow. It was the thing in your soul that is left when the world has burned something inside of you away.

Reaching up to her neck, she traced her index and middle finger up and down the smooth scar. It bothered her, in a way, that it wasn't rough and scaly. It should have been. Shouldn't all monsters leave you a little bit of a monster too?

She let her mind go to Evan, a place she kept it from, normally. Usually she locked him up, or only used him as a way to remind herself of the person she had been. Before.

And, suddenly, with the past made clear to her, and her history laid bare, she felt she had to add this too. Her counselor would have been proud. She had spent months trying to get Petra to talk about it. Keeping the words inside only cut her more, she had said. But words were power; Petra knew that. If she let the words of what happened out, they might kill her. Words had that much power; she'd always known that.

Like her mother's words to Toby, to tell him to move to the backseat. Like the words in the thesaurus that healed Toby, that had somehow also kept her moving forward in life as well. Words were a spear; words were a poultice.

And now, she would release them, because the power they had was over her, and not in her.

She got up off the floor, and called Dane's number, her voice wooden. "Come over" was all she said, all she needed to say, before she heard a click and knew he was on his way.

He arrived, sooner than she expected, and if he was surprised by the state of the library, he did not say it. Nor did he try to touch her, or kiss her. Petra didn't notice. Her gaze was inward, backward. She laid back down in the middle of the floor, surrounded by the books, her father's books, her books, and listened for a minute to see if they would whisper their stories to her. But her own story was too loud, she could hear nothing over it.

Dane sat down on the floor too, and waited. She

remembered that about him. He could wait you out. It was a talent, and an unusual one when they were children. Most kids couldn't wait for their turn, were in a hurry to be picked, to try something, to be first,first, first. Dane could watch, and wait, and bide.

But she couldn't.

So, in the same voice that wasn't her voice, a voice from deep inside that was made of iron so that nothing could break it, she told her story.

She had told Evan that it was over. She didn't know how she'd worked up the courage to do it, with his recent bad moods, and failures. She felt bad for him, she had wanted to help him, but she couldn't, not anymore. He was hurting her, criticizing her work, her friends, the cities her agent arranged on her book tour. Her hair, her weight, her clothing, her voice… eventually nothing was off limits. He let her know what he thought of her, and she couldn't take it anymore. He had hit her, slapped her. And she wasn't the kind of woman who could stay after that. She couldn't forgive him.

People break up. Relationships don't work out, right? That's allowed, isn't it?

But it wasn't.

She had come home from a meeting with a publisher, and the whole apartment was dark. Narthenness, Petra said, a wry smile on her lips, though Dane couldn't know what it meant. Not yet anyway.

But it was dark, and the rooms felt strange, as though the familiar objects within had been replaced by new ones, or different ones, and they were no longer Petra's things at all.

And then she saw Evan. He was sitting in a chair in the living room. She remembered thinking it was unusual. It was a guest chair. The place company sat when they came over so that they wouldn't share the couch with Petra and Evan. But now Evan was sitting there. As though he were the guest, and not Evan at all.

That's when she should have run.

Because it wasn't Evan at all.

Was it?

He was sneering. People sneered in novels all the time and in old movies, period pieces, the villain sneers. She hadn't seen it in real life. Real people didn't sneer and mutter and say vile things. But he wasn't a real person. He wasn't a person, not that night.

He stood up, he yelled, but though his voice was loud, she couldn't understand what he was saying. He grabbed her by the shoulders, and shook her. At the time she was reminded of her mother, her mother had shaken her by the shoulders when she was very angry. But this wasn't scolding. It wasn't frustration. He was swearing, calling her names, it all garbled. He told her she couldn't live in the past. She had to forgive him, she spent too much time looking at her books and researching and not enough with him. She couldn't hear it all, it was too loud and too jumbled. But it came down to one thing, one message she could understand. She wouldn't be leaving. She was staying.

The knife was in his hand so quick, she still didn't know where he had been holding it. Was it in his sleeve? His pocket? Had he been holding it the whole time? Petra saw the light catch the metal, and she remembered she wasn't scared. Even then, she wasn't scared. It wasn't real. This couldn't be real. Things like this don't happen. Not to Petra.

But, things like this did happen to Petra. Had happened to Petra before, was happening to Petra right then.

He stabbed and stabbed and stabbed. It didn't feel like anything. Then it hurt, then it hurt more. He was smiling. Why was he smiling? Who was screaming? That couldn't be her voice. Who was screaming?

And then he stopped. He stopped, but the screaming didn't, and then it did. Evan, whom she had kissed and loved and supported. Evan, the man whose books she'd read and helped edit and had made coffee for and folded his laundry and danced at his sister's wedding. Evan, took his shiny knife and sliced her from ear to underneath her chin to the soft skin of her throat, and then slashed himself from ear to ear. And he smiled while he did it.

He was right, part of her would never leave. He would keep part of her with him, always, in that dark room. The dark room with her things, his things, their things in it. Objects she could never look at again without seeing blood. Evan's blood, mixing with her own.

But she hadn't died. Breathe, survive. She was on the floor, holding her neck together with her hands, there should be more pain, she kept thinking, but instead she focused on holding the skin together. The cut was thicker than she thought it would be. This skin shouldn't be cut, she kept thinking. How strange, it is supposed to be together. She could have laughed, but then her skin would come apart, and she had to hold it together.

She didn't know how, but she dialed 911 and then, nothing. She remembered nothing. Except waking up in the hospital. Her father had come. He didn't speak, he didn't even try to talk to her about it, and she remembered being so thankful. She didn't want to talk about it. So instead he told her about the books he'd been reading and a letter he'd had from a colleague. But the whole time, he'd held her hand, as though if he let it go she'd slip away.

The man she loved had tried to take her life by slashing her neck. He'd tried and he'd failed. And she was here, now, telling the story, because words had power.

Her mother had killed her brother and her friend, but Dane had survived that. Evan had tried to kill her, and she'd lived. They were survivors; Death had not come for them yet. Neither one of them should spend another moment feeling guilty that they had lived, or wondering why they had come through even though part of their souls had been slashed away.

Petra was finished speaking. All of the words were out, and like poison, she'd had to spit all of them off her tongue, though it cut her throat to do so. It was then that he silently stood up and walked over to where she lay, and laid next to her. Gingerly, slowly, as though approaching an injured cat, he reached his arm up, and over, and held her to him. She didn't know if he was holding her because he needed to, or because she needed him to. Perhaps, it was both.

24

CURGLAFF:

the shock one feels upon first being plunged into cold water

Sometimes, the past is the lie we've told ourselves over and over, until it becomes real and concrete, instead of an empty falsehood made of air.

This was what Petra had done. She hadn't forgotten, or become so scarred that her mind couldn't handle the truth. No, the mind is plastic. She simply bent and stretched the story of herself, of her past, of her brother and her mother, and repeated it in her mind until it was real.

The past isn't the past at all. It only exists when remembered in the present. And it can be remembered however one wants, and so Petra made it safe. Safer.

And as she lay there in his arms, she willed herself to heal. Petra wasn't so many shards of a teacup. But, instead a living, breathing, broken woman. Memories and pain and disappointments. Fragments of these things being forced at the joins with successes and late night kissing and too many drinks on a summer night. She wasn't looking for saving. She only was drowning sometimes—and she always had managed to swim her way back to safety. She was broken, damn it—but mending, maybe.

Slowly, the lovely splashed onto the ordinary onto the terrors. She didn't need love to do anything but float alongside as she sank and sputtered, ready with a hand or a slap when she splashed in her own misery too long.

She didn't need him for anything, nor anyone. But she *wanted* him, and that was the difference.

Turning to face him, she raised herself up on an elbow, and looking down into those lake blue eyes; she smiled and kissed him. As Petra. As the little girl and the confident woman and the broken woman, as the woman who had lost and found and lost and found. His lips were warm and finally, she knew, she was home.

Diary Of Nerissa Swifte

I am adrift.

It seems odd to even pick up my quill and write. As though in the writing more calamities know where to find and besiege me. But that is nonsense. Writing is healing. The stories we tell ourselves and keep alive, they keep the people we write about alive, in a way. That is what Da did always say about the legends, after all. That through them the past is kept alive.

But I did not ever think to relegate a piece of my soul to the past. Never. Never. Never.

We passed some days in the house, which shrank, as less of it was needed. A part of me had never believed Da when he said it grew and decreased with the needs of those who live inside it, but after a few mornings, I would find a room smaller from the last time I had stepped into it, and Da's room nowhere to be found at all. Instead, his things carefully stacked and folded in a chest. I found one for my own use as

314

well, a small thing, in which I put a few of my best garments, and the looking glass Alarence had given me, for I see not the moonlight woman I used to be in its reflection any longer. The being within frightens me. So the mirror, some stones I had found on the beach, and this diary I will keep within also. It is as though I had begun to collect my most precious things for leaving this place, though none of us had mentioned the possibility of doing so.

But now, it seems there is nothing left.

Fisher and Phineas set about burying the dead of the town. We have not a graveyard here, and instead it is a watery resting place that we send our fellows to. It is a long custom and a fitting one for island folk, but it seems somehow...troubling to see so many with rocks tied round their limbs, pulling them to the bottom of the lake. I had asked to be of assistance to my brothers, but they both shook their heads. I feel that my seeing the bodies would trouble them somehow more than they alone having to face them. And so I withdrew, I could do so little for either of them, I thought it best to acquiesce to their wishes.

For once, I had no cure. I know how to cure fevers and soothe pains, but not when the pain is in the soul and in the heart. They are too deep for even my magic to penetrate. And so we were like three drowned beings ourselves, dripping the waters of our misery every place we step, mouths desperate to breathe in the air of hope, eyes frantic for a different tomorrow.

But that tomorrow will never come for the three of us. Not now.

I was sure for some time that Alarence would come for me. But, he came not. I fretted and worried, wondering if he had been taken sick as well, but Phineas told me the pestilence did not travel to the mainland at all. But, this was because Traver's Town had been prohibited from trading or venturing to the island at all, the survivors from Traversint sneaking in, staying with relatives or sympathetic townspeople.

I wondered, is my lover there still? Does he wait for me to come to him? I cared more, before. I thought it was the balm to all of my sorrow. But that was before.

A few days ago, I awoke with a piercing pain that seemed to hollow out my body. I screamed and screamed, like a madwoman, and though Phineas ran to my bedside and held me fiercely, I could not stop. Fisher. Fisher. Fisher. He was not there, he would not have gone to the lake without Phineas.

I knew where you were, Fisher. I could feel the breeze, the earth beneath you, the first fingers of sun coming down to caress your face. Fisher.

We ran together; it was still as if a thousand knives plunged into my body, and I followed that pain, ran toward it, until I found Fisher, in a pool of blood, beneath the tree. Our tree. He had stuck a knife, an ordinary knife that we all have used to cut trout or perch a thousand times for our meal, into his abdomen. And he was gone. He had left me already. Glassy eyes like a fish at market, staring at nothing, seeing nothing, nothing. All of the fire within him, stomped out, stabbed out. The sun was the only warmth on him, and the rest of him grew colder by the moment. The blood still flowed, but trickling, like a weak forest stream and I wondered how late I was. If I had been here a few minutes sooner? Could I have stopped it? Or was he already a dead man? A dead man. I cannot bear to think of him so. He, that was life itself, vibrant and grinning and cocksure. My Fisher, my twin, you have taken part of my soul away to the next place, and it is right that you keep it with you, but you haven't left any of your own for me. How can I live with half a soul? How can I endure without you? We were connected, entwined, two hearts with one beat, one soul in two bodies, and now I am half dead, a wretch, not witch or human, but something halved.

We said nothing. Phineas and I. The blood—so dark and deep—pooled into the roots of the tree. We held hands and sat, looking at your body. We were as children again. Unsure and afraid, waiting for Da to come and tell us what to do. We spoke not at all, and moved not, only grasping one another's hand a little tighter when the pain grew too consuming. We sat all day. We did not even close your eyes, Fisher. We left them open, staring at a world they could no longer see. At a brother and sister that you left behind, a brother and sister who are broken without you. Any time the pain lessened, even for a moment, we made ourselves look to the knife that stuck out of your chest. You cannot put a knife there. It does not belong. It shouldn't be there, don't you know that? And with these images we stab ourselves back to bleeding and suffering. For if you are gone, what else is there?

In the morning, the next morning, we still had not moved. I did not know if I ever could. I could no longer feel my legs and I knew that if I remained so, then my body would eventually dwindle and sputter out too—maybe this was better, there wasn't much left to keep it going, with you gone.

But then, oh, then. Phineas squeezed my hand, and I did not want him to die too. I could not lose him too. Don't you understand? I do not want to live without you, Fisher, indeed, I will never really live again. But, Phineas, our baby brother, he cannot die because you and I are nothing without one another. He could go on. He could live. Live for both of us.

He squeezed my hand again, again and I opened my mouth, dry with disuse, and was going to tell him to leave me here. To go to Traver's Town. To Live. But I could not speak, still. For on the branches of the tree, our tree, had sprouted apples. Overnight. The strangest apples, as silvery white as moonlight.

Phineas stood up, shakily, letting go of my hand very carefully, and walked to the tree. He plucked a low-hanging fruit and ran his hands around the flesh of it, and it became blood red in his hands. It terrified me, I admit. I did not understand it. But, Phineas, he knew. He knew, Fisher. He said it was life, made from your life. It was your blood and your legend, held forever within the apples. Born from a tree that was forged with the love of three siblings. He found hope for us, Fisher.

You cannot die, because your memory lives within me, and within the waters of this place. And even if this island does sink into the lake, you will be there still, even if none of us is there to see you, we know you will be there, waiting.

The Word Collector ✧ A. Nolan

It is only time that separates us, brother. Only time, and I will be there, soon. Though not too soon, for I have a destiny to live, for both of us.

We are leaving this place. We will take nothing but a clipping of our tree, Fisher's tree, and ourselves. This diary I will tuck into the trunk, and drop into the lake.

We came to fetch Magda, telling her the tale of the island, saying it may sink into the waters when we leave it, but she says not to worry about her. She has endured on this island a long time, and if it sinks with her on it, then that is the will of the world. It is her duty to work within the gossamer weavings of the world, not against them.

Phineas hesitated; even with all that he has seen and endured as of late, he is still tender, beneath. It troubles him to think of an old woman suffering, scared, when he could have saved her. She only laughed, and touched his arm, and told him. She was old. So old. So very, very old.

We leave. We are leaving. I know, in my heart, that Alarence waits on the dock every day, I am sure of it, to see my face, to see that I am coming. He could not leave without me, because the little of my soul that is left is tied to his, and I would feel the pull if he had left. Even now I feel the tug of his yearning, of his love for me, and so I go. To him. To our future.

I have not filled the book, but that is because my story is not finished, even if it is not written within these pages. In that way, I am given hope. I have many more memories to recount. Much more of life to write.

So, little book, I will be looking in the sky.

I will be watching in the waves.

Fare thee well.

25

MONSTERFUL:
wonderful and extraordinary

When a decision is made, the mind immediately begins to set the pins in place and ducks in a row to arrange for the change to come. She wasn't certain when she had decided, for no question was ever asked or subject discussed, but the choice was made all the same.

Petra would keep the cottage in the woods, with its mis-matched plates and her father's books of lore and mysteries. The cottage where she had been a girl and a sister and a daughter and princess of the forest. And then a woman.

And Dane would keep the antique shop in town, Love's. It was good to keep pieces of the past, after all. The past was joy and pain and memories, and these were good things. People wanted pieces of these things for themselves. To make new memories with, or to sit and wonder about as the item sat on their coffee table or in their lap.

And maybe, one day, with her father's researches and those of his parents, there would be a small museum. Another place to store the proof of the island, to showcase the items that remained, that traced the lore and reality of a place that was part of their shared past. A place to bring that past into the minds of visitors, in hope they would take their own new memories of the island beneath the waves back home with them. And so, the Swiftes would live on.

First, there was a diary to publish, to make public, a world to invite into Nerissa's story. There were carefully collected words to accompany the book, not separately but as the first leaves of the story. A guide, an inside look into the brilliant and unique words Nerissa had used, had spoken, that had lived on her lips so many years ago. These things would be shared, the past would be cracked open and the future would be invited within.

The past had only the power you gave it, for good or ill, Petra thought. Petra and Dane were looking to the future. He wanted to move closer to Allegra, and Petra wanted this too. For no other reason than it was new and old at the same time. Dane was both past and future, and so he was her present, and being closer to the daughter he loved so fiercely felt like it was her place also. And so the arrangements were made and the cats were packed, yowling and spitting into crates. He did not ask her if she wanted to come, he simply assumed. She did not ask if she were welcome, she knew she was. They had been apart long enough; it was high time they spent their moments together. He had a gift for knowing where things belonged, where things and people should be. And Petra belonged by his side.

She did not ask him if it was forever, because it did not matter. They had now.

Now was everything.

Everything. All. The sum. The whole kit and caboodle. Altogether. Absolute. Entire.

EPILOGUE

Somehow she was even older than before. And yet, sometimes, some days, it seemed like it was only yesterday that she had espied the man in the water. Black haired, and body as sinuous as the waves itself. He swam like she flew. A fairy looked at a fish-man, and he had seen her too.

They had made this island together, and paid for it dearly. All of the people to care for, to watch out for, to tend to. But they had love, and so everything else mattered not.

She had given up youth and beauty, but she could not die. It is very difficult to kill a fairy, after all. But he, a man? A man who lives within the lake? He was mortal, he was human, though special. He grew old, he died, and she cast him adrift, to his grave in the lake. But she? She grew only older. Haunted and comforted by the memories of the life she had chosen.

Their children had the gifts of both of their parents, and after a while, as generations came and went, they forgot who she was. She became The Lady of the Woods. She was Grandmother Oak. She was Magda, Crazy Maggie, Margaret Garzing. The strange old woman, the elderly witch of the island.

When Nerissa and Phineas left, they came to her; they begged her to come along. And she was content. Her descendants, her darlings, they remembered her. And so sweet, they truly thought that she would be brought down with the island.

They did not suspect at all that it was she, the fairy, that would sink Traversint to the bottom of the lake.

And so, they left. They went away. Off to their destinies and their lives, away from the island she had made for herself and her beloved so long ago. So, so, long ago. It had been time for her then, after they left.

And so, when she stepped off the island in the dead of night, and her foot touched the shore of Traver's Town, she watched as Traversint dipped lower and lower, watched as the love they had made and grown was buried beneath the waves. The island was gone, but it wasn't, because it was a part of her.

The cemetery again. She always wound up here, though many of those that she had loved were not here. Instead they were in the lake, or their spirits moved on to the next place. Only a few bones, hard and white, buried beneath the earth, that was all that lingered in this place. She had spoken true when she told Petra that funerals were for the living, but cemeteries were for something else.

For Remembering. She walked to Thomas Marr's stone and wondered if his phantom had moved on. Now that his reason for lingering no longer remained. Which made her laugh. Who among us does not linger longer than we should? She certainly had.

She was old, so old. But love never died, did it? Even after she could not remember his face, or the sound of his voice, she loved him still. Loved him enough to look out over the lake every morning, to imagine the island beneath the blue, to see the lives and the past that had lived upon it. Their love had made that.

Margaret, the Lady of the Woods, Grandmother Oak, Magda the Beautiful as she was called before...she would live and linger forever, because love was never past to her. It was always glorious, living, breathing, and *now*.

Afterword

This novel is a complete work of fiction, (as though the fairies didn't tip you off). Its location is based loosely on that of Traverse City in Northern Michigan, but really it only exists in my imagination.

I have struggled with the past for my entire life. This book was a…cleansing for me. An opportunity to take a hard look at what dwelling in the past, and always looking backward will do to you. It stunts you and creates depression where it should not exist. But also, the past can be plumbed for answers about the present. Why does this hurt? Why am I broken here?

That being said, I always like a little magic, and I think there is always a little enchantment found in nature. I find that people who do not like fantasy, are generally people I like to avoid. You aren't looking hard enough if you don't see magic in the world.

I'd also like to quickly thank a few people for their eyes and ears on this project. My mother, Elizabeth, my first pair of eyes. Lauren, my agent and dearest friend, and Jill my newest editor—thank you all for helping make this book better than I could have alone.

Finally, it was important that Petra was strong and weak. She had to be both wax and iron. I like strong female characters and all, but I also like those that doubt themselves. That feel human. That feel like I do, and how the women I love feel. Sometimes it is when we lose part of ourselves that the other parts grow harder. But, I think it is important too, to be soft. There is room for both.

Houston, 2016

About The Author

ALEXANDRIA NOLAN was born and raised in Michigan's second motor city, Flint. She attended the University of Michigan, earning a Bachelor of Arts in English. After graduation from university in 2008, Alexandria moved to Texas to teach History, English and Writing in the public school system. In the spring of 2013, she left teaching to write full time.

She maintains a lifestyle blog, and writes for various print and web publications. Alexandria is the author of five other novels, including the *Starlight Symphonies* series. She loves to read, travel, and read about traveling. She resides in Houston, Texas with her husband and a menagerie of obnoxious pets.

alexandrianolan.com

www.ingramcontent.com/pod-product-compliance
Lightning Source LLC
Chambersburg PA
CBHW030415180626
46812CB00005B/2012